Last
Hurrah

M. E. Landress

DEDICATION

To my husband, Bob, with
Fond memories of our own
Mississippi houseboating days.

ACKNOWLEDGMENTS

Over the years there have been so many people who have contributed to the research, editing and all other aspects needed to make my scribblings into viable books it would take dozens of pages to name them all. The ones I really need to say thank you to are the dedicated fans who read my books and tell me how much they enjoyed the stories.

Prologue

Weather forecasters around the Tri-State area had all decreed that the coming weekend would be autumn's last glory days. A storm system was making its way southward from Canada bringing with it the chill of winter. The storm would hit Iowa just in time to close out the weekend. For now, the skies were a brilliant blue, the air crisp, and the temperature hovering in the low sixties. The pleasant conditions kept thoughts of winter at bay. It made folks want to get away from their ordinary lives one last time, before being trapped by winter snows and howling blizzards. It made them long for an escape from the mundaneness of their daily lives.

The glossy brochure from the houseboat rental company featuring a slice of tree-lined riverbank drenched in fall colors offered just that kind of escape. Eye-catching scenes of couples relaxing on the boat's deck, lifting wine glasses in a toast, filled the interior pages. Descriptive passages stated, "Fulfill your fantasies - *The Last Hurrah* - offering luxury accommodations, three staterooms with private baths, and a fully equipped gourmet kitchen. A front deck for fishing and a back deck for sunning. Eighty-four feet long and eighteen feet wide, powered by twin 250 HP Mercury engines, the Hurrah is the sleekest, most elegant boat afloat on the Mississippi River."

The brochure also listed three different vacation bundles. There was the basic package called the "Bring Your Own Tour" at just $250.00 per day, something called "The Adventure Cruise" that went for $500.00 a day, and the aptly named "Platinum Deluxe" available at a whopping $1,750.00 dollars a day. It included an extra three-man crew and a personal chef. "Luxury accommodations partnered with the serenity of nature" the brochure touted. "Escape from the hustle and bustle in style and comfort." The back page offered a colorful map of the river showing the boat's route plus a list of operating hours for the office with general contact information.

Holiday River Cruises

Far-A-Way Shores Marina

East Dubuque, IL

219-555-BOAT

Harold T. Penderschott, Owner

No one perusing the brochure ever seemed to notice the last few lines of fine print at the very bottom of the back page under the picture of the boat at dockage. It read, "This vessel is registered and operated as a floating hotel. No refunds without a 24-hour notice. The cost of fuel, propane, and water for the holding tanks is not included in the package prices. This vessel sails at capacity and can accommodate varied cruise packages in one trip."

Those overlooked lines would be the catalyst to a nightmare for the folks who rented *The Last Hurrah* that final weekend in September.

Chapter One

Janie Grayson staggered under the load of suitcases and grocery sacks she was toting down the boarding ramp at Far-Away-Shores Marina. Glancing back at her husband she noticed he wasn't doing much better. She still thought they should have opted for one of the pricier cruises instead of settling for the 'bring your own.' Jimmy, the voice of reason as always, had been quick to remind her that even the cheapest package was going to strain their budget. Just once she wished they could make plans without considering the stupid budget. Being poor sucked. However, if Jimmy knew about her little secret, they would not be taking the cruise at all. Janie smiled, rubbing her hand over her still flat belly.

Flipping her long honey colored hair over her shoulder she deposited her load on the deck, waiting for Jimmy to catch up. The narrow wooden boards beneath her feet snaked from the edge of the parking lot back around a thick stand of trees. The boat lay hidden from view by the colorful coat of autumn leaves clinging to the ancient oaks lining the riverbank. Janie didn't try to see the boat, she wanted Jimmy at her side for their first glimpse of the vessel.

Stepping around the thick stand of trees the couple stopped, mouths agape, staring in awe at the boat anchored at the end of the walkway. Slowly examining it from one end to the other, the enormity of its size barely registered in their stunned minds.

"Yikes!" Janie managed to squeak.

"Now that's a boat," Jimmy said slinging an arm around his wife's shoulders.

The Last Hurrah sat bobbing gently in the river's rippling current, sunlight gleaming off its snow-white exterior, dancing across its tinted windows. Deep blue swirls raced down its sides and around the stern. That same shade of deep blue colored the carpet in the sitting areas on the front and back decks. The rear deck boasted two bistro style table and chair sets, a gas barbecue grill, and three chaise lounges. The front deck had a section covered in skid free rubber just beyond the carpeted area. It held two top of the line fishing chairs. Gated segments in the side rails were fitted with drop down swim ladders. A second level that extended out over each end of the boat created small, shaded nooks for relaxing out of the hot sun. Above that level was a third one. This was the control center; half of it enclosed with huge, tinted windows, the other half an open deck area. A series of colorful yachting flags flew from atop a mast bristling with high tech electronics.

Janie turned and stared at her husband. "That can't be our boat."

"Man, oh man, I am so glad I took that Coast Guard boating course," Jimmy said. "I wouldn't want to look like some novice when I meet the owner. He might not let us take his boat out when he sees how young we are."

Scooping Janie up in his arms, her giddy laughter ringing out across the water, Jimmy carried his still almost new bride (they'd only been married a year) up a small ramp and through the entry gate at the front of the boat. Laughing softly Janie kissed him deeply almost making him lose his balance. He dumped her clumsily on the deck.

"Ouch!" Rubbing her backside, Janie winced up at her husband. "Is that what I get for kissing you?" Grasping Jimmy's outstretched hand for help in getting to her feet, Janie leaned into his broad chest. Titling her head back she caught his upper lip between her teeth, gently nipping, then boldly kissing him until he groaned.

"Woman, you better stop doing that in public or I'll be getting arrested for indecent exposure," Jimmy growled, sheepishly tugging his t-shirt down to cover the growing bulge in his jeans. He pushed her gently away, stepping back a few feet, swiveling his head to see if anyone was watching them from the shoreline.

Giving her husband a wicked grin, Janie purred, "Just wait until I get you alone in our cabin." Sauntering sassily back up to him, she leaned in and kissed him again. She never got tired of kissing him; he was the handsomest man she had ever known. She took a moment to let her eyes roam up and down his muscular form, taking in his tousled mop of chestnut brown hair, deep green eyes, and lopsided smile. Oh yeah, he was one good-looking man. Plus, he was as sweet as fresh honey with a heart filled with love for life, and her. She stood on her toes to nip teasingly at his left ear.

"You'd better stop that right now," Jimmy groaned, making no move to step away from her embrace.

"Make me," Janie laughed, slipping out of his arms racing off toward the back of the boat.

Acting like a couple of kids they whooped and chased each other around the deck, Jimmy threatening a tickle fest if he caught his swift-footed wife. Ever since the two had met in Junior High, Jimmy had been smitten. Those long legs, that stunningly beautiful face, and those deep blue eyes had captured his attention, but it was her gentleness and musical laughter that kept him enchanted. He never understood why she agreed to that first date, let alone all the ones that followed right up until he had proposed on bended knee the day after their high school graduation. *She could have had anyone, yet she chose me*, the thought had his heart swelling with pride. He watched as Janie jumped ship heading back down the dock towards their car.

"You better run faster than that woman," Jimmy yelled racing after her, leaping over their pile of belongings. His left foot caught on the handle of one of the suitcases sending him tumbling to his knees his backside waving in the air making him look like some strange ostrich with its head in the sand.

Chapter Two

Carter Williams eyed his still disgruntled wife, Lydia, from behind his designer shades. If her mood did not improve soon it was going to be a bitch of a weekend. When Lydia was in a snit, nothing but time could assuage her anger. He needed this weekend to be perfect. When ordering the deluxe cruise package aboard the houseboat he had offered the owner an extra $1,000 a day to include a supply of Lydia's favorite champagne, caviar, chocolates, and Lady Scarlet roses. He personally faxed a menu to the chef, being sure to include a list of Lydia's dislikes and allergies. Hell, he even agreed to her bringing along the nasty little walking rag mop of a dog she so adored. Personally, he thought TooFoo, a mixed breed rescued from the local animal shelter, was a nuisance who would be better off stuffed. The tiny animal looked as if an alien had crossbred a dog with a dust bunny. It also had a nasty disposition, which it was all too eager to vent on Carter. Lydia was the only one who could get near the beast without risking a nasty nip. She fawned over the ugly creature as if it were her child.

Carter had big plans for this weekend. No way was he going to change them because, if everything went right, his life was soon going to become a lot more enjoyable. *Widower has such a pleasant ring to it*, he softly smiled.

His smile quickly faded as he mulled over his reasons for booking the cruise. It wasn't as if he hated Lydia, he was just tired of her nagging, whining, condescending attitude about everything. Her father had always treated her like a princess, giving in to her every whim. Carter was expected to do the same. If the woman weren't as rich as Midas, he would never have agreed to marry her. She was so totally not his type. Thin to the point of emaciation, she insisted on dying her naturally mousy brown hair a brittle platinum blond. She wore deep blue contacts, which she thought gave her eyes an innocent appeal. Carter thought it made them look like huge glass marbles, bitter and cold. Lydia devoured fashion magazines like other women did chocolate; she had to have the latest style, whether it suited her age or not. She often ended up looking like some crypt keeper in teenage drag. Carter shuddered at the mental image, wishing she would come to her senses and dress appropriately for her age. At forty, with a little help from a gifted plastic surgeon, she looked no different than when they first married. Well, except for the ridiculous clothing she chose to wear. He swore every year her fashion choices got more ridiculous.

He, on the other hand, took great care to always present a professional appearance. He kept himself trim, but not too thin. His mahogany brown hair was styled to show off his best facial features, his patrician nose and slightly cleft chin. When he started getting a touch of grey at the temples, he left it, feeling it gave him a look of distinction. *I should be with someone younger and more attractive*, he thought, casting another glance at Lydia. Then he smiled, knowing that if things went as planned, that might just be a possibility.

Pulling their black Cadillac Escalade into the only shady spot in the cruise company's parking lot, Carter turned to his wife saying, "Lydia, darling, you are going to be delighted with this get-a-way. I promise you it will be relaxing and enjoyable."

Lydia Williams scooped up her little dog from the floorboard where it had been chewing on the toe of her expensive shoe. Climbing out of the car, she gave her husband one of her 'I am not amused' frowns. Since she hadn't been paying attention to what Carter was yammering on about, she didn't grace him with a reply, but tottered off towards the dock entrance on her spike heeled, leopard print mules. Carter stopped staring at her receding back long enough to grab up his laptop before following along behind her.

As the couple carefully shuffled their way down the swaying wooden ramp, they heard peels of laugher from up ahead.

"My Lord, Carter, I hope that's not the help," Lydia sniffed. "Of course, I'm sure they have trouble finding good people in such a depressing small town. Still, I won't tolerate that kind of behavior. My nerves are too overwrought for such rowdiness."

Carter rolled his eyes and shook his head; all he needed was for Lydia to be displeased with the quality of the help, or God forbid, the boat itself. She might demand that they go home at once, which would ruin all his plans.

"Now, Pumpkin," Carter soothed "I'm sure if it is the help, they are just excited about being on a cruise with you. They probably read that article in *Fashion Trends* about your summer soiree. It has made you a bit of a celebrity."

Giving her husband a condescending glance over the top of her designer sunglasses, Lydia replied, "I thought you were still miffed about the cost of my little soiree. Imagine you now singing my praises for throwing the affair. Really, Carter, you are so shallow. I assume this tawdry little weekend is your idea of an apology. Well, is it?" Lydia gave her husband a wintry smile, cold enough to freeze most men in their tracks. Carter merely returned her ingratiating smirk with one of his stiff smiles, which always made her skin crawl. Inwardly she steeled her emotions, ready to do battle at the slightest affront by the buffoon she had married. *Really,* she thought, *I should have listened to Father and waited for a banker or a corporate lawyer.*

Carter let Lydia's thorny dig about this being a tawdry weekend slide off his back, gritting his teeth to keep from snarling something witty and rude back at her. Carter scanned the dock ahead for signs of the crew; he had no intention of carting Lydia's mound of luggage on board himself. He spotted two young people running about the back of the boat in a most unprofessional manner. Raising his hand to hail them, so they could transfer the luggage onboard, Carter heard a horrible screeching behind him in the direction of the parking area. Whirling around he glared across the tarmac, afraid some fool had gotten too close to his precious Escalade. He stared in horror at the metallic monster careening recklessly towards them.

Chapter Three

Isis Winters and Bosco Blue crossed their fingers and prayed that their old van would make it to the cruise office before it died completely. The aged Chevy had been spitting and sputtering for the last five miles. No matter, not even a breakdown could put a damper on the day. Isis and Bosco were so excited about their upcoming adventure neither of them had slept a wink the night before. Up at dawn, they had shared a quick shower, swept their long graying locks back into neat waist length braids and rushed through their chores, eager to be on their way.

"Hold on, Babe, we're almost there," Bosco grunted, man-handling the bucking beast of a vehicle around the corner of the building.

"This is so exciting," Isis chirped. "Another thing we can check off our bucket list." She began rummaging in the console beside her, pulling out plastic canisters of 35 mm film. She had brought along two dozen, to record all that they saw along their journey down river. She wanted to capture every glorious moment of the trip. Though digital was now all the rage, Isis felt a kinship with the old-fashioned medium of real film, chemical baths and controlling every aspect of the images she captured.

Bosco, on the other hand loved new gadgets. He'd borrowed a video camera from one of his buddies at the art co-op to catch the action. He was hoping there would be enough footage to piece together a brief documentary or at least a travel video. The couple had been saving up for this trip for over five years. The thought of cruising and exploring the mighty Mississippi River had been a life-long dream. Even this short trip could prove to be something special.

Stomping down on the van's almost nonexistent brakes, Bosco managed to lurch into a parking slot. The brakes squealed in protest, metal rubbing against metal, but they held. He narrowly missed side-swiping a monstrous SUV, which had him heaving a sigh of relief, he didn't need any more points on his license. Hopping out the couple began to unload the mountain of gear stowed in the back. Fishing poles, tackle boxes, scuba gear and a guitar case piled up on the pavement. Isis added an easel, camera case, box of painting supplies and two yoga mats. Bosco hauled out three duffle bags, two gym bags, and one battered red suitcase. Slamming the van door shut, he loaded up his arms with as much stuff as he could carry and headed down the dock. Isis was right behind him, dragging two of the duffle bags. Up ahead they could see a well-dressed couple climbing onto the boat and a younger looking couple already on board.

"Looks like there are some more folks here," Bosco called over his shoulder. "Wonder if they just got back from a cruise. Maybe we'll have to wait for them to refuel the boat and clean it up before we can head out."

As Bosco and Isis got closer, they realized the two couples on the boat had begun arguing. The older man in the business suit was shaking his finger in the face of the dark-haired younger man.

The older woman, obviously the businessman's wife, was hissing loudly at the fresh-faced young blond girl.

"Hey, folks, is there some kind of problem here?" Bosco yelled as he stepped up to the side of the boat.

"There most certainly is," the man in the suit roared back. "These teenagers are on our boat. Get them off at once."

Isis and Bosco looked at each other mystified. Why would this man think they could evict someone from the boat? And why were these people even on the boat?

"Did we get the wrong dock?" Bosco muttered, leaning around his wife, scanning the name painted on the side of the vessel. Yup, it was *The Last Hurrah* all right, the boat they had reserved for the next three days. Bosco turned to give his wife a dumbfounded look, shrugging his narrow shoulders. "It's our boat."

"Just what is going on here?" Isis inquired stepping up onto the deck. Both couples, red faced from yelling, stood with their arms stiffly held at their sides. *Such bad karma to start the day with,* Isis sighed. "Surely we can discuss the situation amicably and resolve any problems.'

"I am Carter Williams the Third and I rented this vessel for the next three days. These ruffians are saying the boat is theirs this weekend," Carter shouted. "I have a receipt. Now throw them off my boat!"

"Hell, no!" the younger man yelled back. "Me and my wife Janie rented this boat for the weekend. We have a receipt right here. So, you tell them to get the hell off."

Bosco looked at Isis, scratching his head. "Folks, we aren't going to be throwing anybody off."

"I am paying for your services, and you will do as I say!" Carter snarled. "Get them off right now or I'll see that you get fired from your jobs...today!"

Bosco burst out laughing. "Looks like we got us a real pickle here folks. Isis and I aren't the hired help. We rented this boat for the weekend, too."

That statement only got the other two couples yelling again. Just when Bosco thought the other men might come to blows a voice called out cheerily from the other end of the dock.

"See you folks all got here on time."

A tiny little man in a pinstriped suit and pale pink shirt was ambling slowly towards them, his long, thin, white hair blowing out across his cheeks. He took his time getting down the dock and onto the boat. Ignoring all the angry voices, he held out his hand.

"Let me introduce myself. I'm the owner of this fine vessel, Harold T. Penderschott, at your service."

Bosco and Isis stepped up to shake his hand, but the others just glared at the man. When the couples tried to engage him in their squabble, Penderschott moved off through a door leading to the interior of the boat. He left them no choice but to follow.

Ensconcing himself in one of the rich chocolate brown leather chairs in the living room, Penderschott gestured for everyone to take a seat. Lydia claimed the other single chair, Carter perching on the arm beside her. That left the sofa for the other two couples to share. Once everyone sat down Penderschott pulled several sheets of paper from his jacket pocket. Clearing his throat, he began reading off the information for the packages that each of the couples had ordered. After listing each package's amenities, he stopped to ask if the information he had read was correct. The couples nodded their agreement. Then he popped a pair of steel framed glasses on his upturned nose and ran his finger down to the very bottom of the last page of each contract. Nodding his head he smiled, loudly reading the last few lines his voice raised slightly to emphasize his words.

"This vessel is registered and operated as a floating hotel. No refunds without a 24-hour notice. The cost of fuel, propane, and water for the holding tanks is not included in the package prices. This vessel sails at capacity."

"What the hell does that mean?" Carter roared.

"Oh, my, I think there might be a bit of a problem," Isis sighed, reaching over to take her husband's hand.

"Are you telling us we have to share the boat?" wailed Janie. She gave the Williams a horrified look before turning to stare at her husband. "Jimmy!" she cried, "Say something."

"You never told us about that clause in the contract," Jimmy grumbled. "We thought we had the boat to ourselves."

"Contracts are perfectly clear," said Penderschott. "This is a floating hotel, and it sails at capacity. That means with six people on board."

Lydia gave her husband a wicked jab to the ribs. "Do something about this, Carter, right now."

Carter stood, puffing out his chest, deepening the frown already etched on his face. "Sir, I have an entire firm of attorneys who will sue you for every dollar you possess if our weekend is ruined. My wife and I booked this vessel under the assumption we would be alone. Now throw these interlopers off our boat."

Carter's rude words got everyone yelling again. Each couple claimed to have exclusive right to the boat. Each insisted that the other two couples should be the ones ousted. Penderschott just sat there looking smug. When the others finally quieted down a bit, he once again read the last lines of the contract. This time putting special emphasis on the point of no refund without a 24-hour notice. He told them they were free to leave, but that there would be no refund. Before Carter Williams could open his mouth to shout about his firm of lawyers, Penderschott pointed out that he also had a whole cadre of them on his payroll. Gathering up the papers, he carefully folded them before stuffing them back in his pocket. Standing, he headed out the door. Before he stepped off onto the dock, he turned back to the group telling them he would wait in the parking area for twenty minutes if any of them wanted to leave. He added that otherwise the boat would set sail as planned. Then he simply walked away.

Everyone was too stunned for a moment to move or comment. The Graysons were the first to speak up, saying they were staying. Janie said they hadn't had a honeymoon after they got married, so this was it. Isis and Bosco said they had saved for five years for this weekend and weren't about to leave. They added that they had no problem sharing the boat if everyone tried to get along. All eyes turned as Lydia Williams got shakily to her feet tottering on her spike heeled shoes the small creature in her arms yapping loudly. She glared at each of them, before turning and heading for the door, screaming back over her shoulder for Carter to take her home. Carter, however, had other plans. This was too important a weekend to be ruined by a few squatters. He figured that if he were unpleasant enough, they'd all stay holed up in their cabins for the entire trip. He assumed it wouldn't take long to dissuade them from using any of the ship's amenities as he was an expert at making things unpleasant for those around him.

Chapter Four

"Lydia, darling, we need this weekend together," Carter Williams crooned, racing to catch up with his angry wife. She'd begun marching unsteadily on her stiletto encased feet towards the front deck. "This is a large boat, and we will just avoid those people. It's only for the weekend."

Turning to face her husband, Lydia gave him a glacial stare. "Just what is so damn important about spending the weekend floating on this muddy river?" she snapped. "I would have preferred a trip to New York... or at least Aspen."

"But Sweetums, we only have the three days," Carter whined. "You know I have that convention coming up. It will keep me away from you for weeks. I just want to have some time alone, that's all."

Lydia continued to stare at Carter her face scrunching up like a shriveling grape in the scorching summer sun.

The other passengers, stepping out on the deck to gather their belongings, felt awkward watching the couple argue, afraid they would get caught eavesdropping on such a private conversation. Jimmy nudged his wife, leaning in to whisper in her ear, "She looks like she's gonna blow a gasket. Let's make ourselves scarce." Grasping his wife's arm, he began steering her towards the back of the boat.

"I'm with them on that one," Bosco snorted. "Let's beat our feet in retreat, Isis."

The four trooped off hauling their belongings inside leaving the battling couple behind - the husband still trying to woo his wife into staying. They could hear him whining, her screeching, and their little dog yapping. Everyone was thinking, "*Oh, Lord, it's going to be a long weekend if those folks continue the trip.*"

Being gregarious by nature, Isis struck up a conversation with the Grayson's asking all the usual 'get to know you' kind of questions. She learned that Janie was studying to be a nurse and that Jimmy worked as a diesel mechanic. She also learned that the couple didn't have any kids yet, had no pets, and loved to play video games. Isis told them how she and Bosco had lived in a commune for ten years. Last year though they had struck out on their own. Now they were renting a small farm where they raised goats and llamas. It was only five miles from their old commune, but it gave them a sense of independence. While the women continued chatting the two men shared the task of carting stuff from the parking lot hefting it up onto the back deck so they could drag it inside the boat. They had to step around Carter Williams and his wife who were still in a heated argument. The couple giving them angry glares every time they walked past.

On the last trip to their vehicles Bosco and Jimmy ran into five large men unloading a catering van along with four guys sitting in a small tan colored compact car. The caterers began wheeling dollies filled with crates and boxes towards the boat. The men from the car stepped out, pulled suitcases from the trunk, and followed the others down the dock. It was obvious from their apparel that the men were boat crew.

"I thought we were supposed to pilot the boat ourselves," Bosco remarked.

"Yeah, that's what old man Penderschott told me, too," Jimmy grumbled, "he said a crew only came with the deluxe package. What package did you take?"

"We got the adventure one. We plan on doing a bit of kayaking, hiking and stuff like that."

"Our money is pretty tight right now so all we could afford was the basic package. You know, the 'bring your own stuff' one," Jimmy sighed. "Does your package come with catered food?"

"Not sure about the catered part, but it did say the kitchen would be stocked with basics enough to create three meals a day," Bosco said.

When Jimmy and Bosco arrived back at the boat with the last load of gear the three women were arguing again. This time it was over the sleeping arrangements.

"We paid the most for this horrid little trip, therefore, we should have the second-floor suite," Lydia bristled.

"No way are you deciding everything on this trip," Janie snapped back.

"Surely there's a way to compromise and make everyone happy," Isis admonished. "There is no need for this continual disharmony."

"I cannot deal with this any longer," Lydia screeched stepping over to yell out the open door, "Carter, get your ass back in here and tell these people we are staying in the suite!"

When Carter didn't immediately appear, Lydia stomped her left foot and burst into tears. Her wailing set off the little dog who began running in circles at her feet, yapping like someone had stepped on one of its tiny feet.

Just then the caterers appeared with empty dollies heading back out the door. "Everything's stored away folks, you all have a good trip," they mumbled not waiting for a reply, they raced for the exit. It was obvious they were trying to avoid getting caught up in the verbal battle between the women.

As insults and demands continued to fly around the group one of the men from the car walked into the room closely followed by Carter Williams. The new guy sported a snappy white uniform with lots of gold braid. A shiny brass nametag proclaimed him to be Captain Mike.

"What seems to be the problem here, folks?" the man asked. When everyone tried to talk at once, he held up his hand.

"One at a time, one at a time, please."

"Since I paid for the deluxe cruise package you work for me," Carter snapped. "Tell these people to take the bedrooms on this level."

Captain Mike frowned. "I am the licensed captain for this cruise and as such, I oversee this vessel and work for the owner, Mr. Penderschott. Therefore, you will all do as I instruct, or this boat will not move from its moorings." Pulling a small notebook and pencil from his left breast pocket he ripped out three pages. He then wrote a letter on each page, A-B-C. Folding them, he tossed them into a swirled sapphire glass bowl siting on the coffee table.

"Each couple will draw a slip of paper. The letters correspond to one of the cabins. Whatever letter you get is the cabin you sleep in." Lifting the bowl, he offered it to Janie.

"Oh, no, no, no, no, we will be the first to draw," snapped Carter, reaching around Janie, snatching a slip from the bowl. "We have cabin C."

Bosco and Isis let the Graysons go next. Janie and Jimmy waited for Isis and Bosco to draw their slip before looking to see what letter they had gotten. The Graysons had picked B while Bosco and Isis had gotten A.

Captain Mike laid out one of the company brochures, gesturing for the group to come take a closer look. On the center page was a diagram of the ship. Cabins B and C were on level one. Cabin A was located on the second level. Of course, Lydia began squawking to Carter that they paid more so they should have the private second floor suite. Isis and Bosco offered to give up the suite, just for the sake of getting the weekend off on a friendlier note. However, the Graysons chimed in that everyone had agreed to the anonymous method of cabin assignment and therefore should stick to it. The couples began talking at once filling the room with angry words. Captain Mike had to once more step in and exert his authority. He said if the two couples wanted to trade it was up to them. Though Bosco's face wore a frown he handed over the slip of paper with the letter A to Carter Williams, who snatched it out of Bosco's hand with a satisfied smirk. With the room trade a done deal, everyone separated and went off to stow their belongings.

Chapter Five

Opening the door to their room Isis and Bosco couldn't help grinning - it was beautiful. A queen size bed on one wall and tall oak cabinets with tons of storage space on another. Mirrored panels in the cabinet doors made the room seem even larger. Rich brocade drapes graced the sides of a large picture window with a fantastic view of the flowing river outside.

Isis couldn't resist jumping on the bed. The mattress was firm but springy, just the way she liked it. Bosco grabbed her mid-jump pulling her into a bear hug. They fell back on the bed laughing with delight.

"Now this is what I call high class," Bosco chuckled. "Can't imagine why anyone would complain about getting this room."

"That couple sure are uptight," Isis sighed. "Did you see those shoes she was wearing?"

"Could she get any skinnier?" Bosco snorted. "Looked like one of them starving models you see in fashion magazines all bony arms and legs wearing weird clothing. Being that skinny at her age I wonder if she's sick or something." Bosco bit his tongue as soon as those words left his mouth. He hoped Isis wouldn't pick up on the fact that he had been losing weight for several months now. It would be at least another week before the test results were in, and he didn't want to worry her over nothing...if that was all it proved to be.

Shaking her head at his naiveté Isis told Bosco, "Being ultra-thin is stylish. So are those spike heel shoes, the too tight Capri pants and the midriff top.

"But she's a grown woman. Hell, she has to be at least fifty," Bosco grumped. "Why would she want to look like some teenager?"

"Well, it might have something to do with being married to a much younger, pompous ass," Isis chuckled.

Puffing out his chest and lowering his voice to a throaty growl Bosco whined, "I am Carter Williams the Third and my shit never stinks. It comes out gold-plated."

Isis fell back on the bed roaring with laughter. "You have got him down to a T," she whooped. "Let me try doing her. Carter! Carter, you worm, kiss my feet and smile while you're doing it."

Bosco had to hold onto his sides to keep them from aching he was laughing so hard. "Man, we have got to stop this, or we'll slip up and do it right in front of them."

Wiping at the tears streaming down her cheeks, Isis barely managed to nod before she began laughing again. "Oh, we are so bad, Bosco. It's not like us, well at least not like me, to instantly have such a strong dislike for someone. It's bad karma to talk about them like we've been doing. We must give them a chance. Maybe some good karma will rub off us onto them this weekend." When Bosco rolled his eyes at her letting out a snort of disbelief, Isis gave him an eye roll of her own. Sometimes her husband wasn't as generous with his opinions as he could be.

"Come on let's go find a place to stash our fishing gear," Bosco said. "Then we'll come back here and find a place to stash our stash. Maybe we should have a toke or two before we face that obnoxious couple again." Pulling Isis to her feet, Bosco linked arms, steering her out of the room.

Chapter Six

When Janie and Jimmy Grayson opened the door to their room, they had much the same reaction as Bosco and Isis. Their accommodations were a mirror image of the other bedroom except for the color scheme – pale greens with canary yellow accents.

"Jimmy, this is the most gorgeous bedroom I have ever seen," Janie sighed. "I'd like to have a room like this in our home someday."

Walking up behind his wife Jimmy slid his arms around her slender waist. "Babe, I promise some day we will." He nuzzled her neck, pulling her tight against his muscled chest.

"Ummm, you'd better stop that," Janie groaned. She turned and stood on her tiptoes, pulling Jimmy's head down for a lingering kiss.

"Don't kiss me like that if you don't expect something else to happen," he managed to gasp. "Woman, you know your kisses drive me crazy."

Poking him in the side, Janie tickled his rib cage. She felt his grip on her loosen and used it to her advantage ducking out of his embrace. "Later Macho Man," she admonished. "There are too many people roaming around right now."

Jimmy made an unsuccessful grab at her as she moved away and began opening drawers. He sure hoped the presence of so many people on the boat wasn't going to make her self-conscious. He had been looking forward to some hot hound dog sex this weekend. For the last couple of weeks Janie hadn't been her usual exuberant self when it came to being intimate.

"What did you think of our shipmates?" Janie asked trying to distract her husband.

A scowl slid across Jimmy's face. "I was about ready to punch that Carter dude's lights out. What an asshole."

Janie laughed. "I felt like doing the same thing to his wife."

"That other couple seemed pretty cool though. Kind of like old hippies," Jimmy said. "Think they brought any weed with them?"

"They are old hippies," Janie said. "They were trying so hard to instill good karma. I'd love to see their farm." Glossing over her husband's comment about smoking anything illicit that might harm the baby she hadn't told him about, she wondered if now was a good time to speak up about her little secret. She rested her hand gently on still flat stomach.

"When I was helping them haul their gear on board, I saw they had a battered old guitar case. Maybe we can do one of those campfire sing-along things," Jimmy said. "Oh, and Bosco told me they're going kayaking. He asked if we wanted to come along."

"That sounds like fun," Janie said. "Isis told me they do yoga every morning - in the nude. She invited us to join them."

"No way," Jimmy yelped. "I don't need to see two gray haired old farts in their birthday suits."

"I think Isis has beautiful hair, all that silvery gray with those two white streaks in front," Janie sighed. "I will be thrilled if I look that good when I get her age."

"How old do you think they are? They have to be like eighty or something if they were around in the sixties."

Shaking her head Janie laughed. "No, she told me they are both sixty-three."

"I kind of liked his tie-dyed shirt, very retro," Jimmy grinned. "And her leather headband was cool."

"What about those other two," Janie sighed. "She had on a ton of jewelry, and I bet not one of those diamonds was under a carat."

"Didn't notice," Jimmy muttered. "Did you see he was wearing a suit and loafers with no socks? And what the hell was that animal they brought with them? A long-haired rat?"

Janie shook her head. "I think it's a dog. Poor little thing looked so pathetic. I wonder where it's supposed to poop once we get out on the river. Do you think they'll just hold it over the rail and let it go?"

Jimmy busted out laughing. "Now, I'd pay to see that

show. Her in them stilt heels, leaning over the rail with that dog hanging from her fingertips, blowing turds into the wind."

"Oh, you are so bad," Janie giggled. "You won't think it's so funny if you're swimming down below them."

"That is too gross to even contemplate," Jimmy groaned. "We'd better go put our grub away before all the ice in the cooler melts."   Grabbing her hand, he dragged her off towards the kitchen.

Chapter Seven

Once Carter had managed to convince Lydia to stay for the weekend, he heaved a sigh of relief. Now, he just had to keep her in a good mood until his plan fell into place. Having other people on board might not be such a bad idea. Especially since that old couple looked like sixties radicals. They more than likely both had criminal records and smoked drugs. Yes sir, having them on board might just work to his advantage. They might keep Lydia on edge, which meant she'd need a few extra afternoon cocktails to ease her tension. Since drinking only made her more waspish than usual, she'd be even nastier to their shipmates. Carter figured by the second day Lydia would be so soused, carrying out his plan to off her would be as easy as popping peas from a pod. After instructing the crew to bring their luggage from the Escalade, Carter followed his wife up the spiral staircase to their second-floor suite.

Lydia stood in the doorway of their room surveying the quarters they were to share for the next three days. At home they each had their own suite of rooms, which was how she preferred things. How could Carter have been such an idiot to rent rooms on a hotel boat? Lydia shuddered in horror at the thought of spending time with the other passengers. Really, hippies and a pair of teenagers? What was the man thinking? Plopping TooFoo down on the end of the king size bed Lydia continued inspecting the room. *Humph. Well at least it looks clean*, she muttered to herself. Though she would have preferred separate sleeping and lounging areas, she had to admit the room was adequate. Hearing a small cough, she turned to see Carter gazing at her in his usual hangdog fashion, waiting to see if she approved. The man had no backbone, no backbone at all!

"It's a rather nice room, don't you think?" Carter asked. "The blue and white color scheme is relaxing."

Lydia gave him a pained look. "I suppose it will have to do," she sniffed. "It certainly isn't up to Five Star standards." She drifted out the open French doors, flinging herself into one of the chaise lounges on their private deck. The still yapping TooFoo followed, scurrying underneath her chair, curling up in a hairy ball.

Carter watched his wife for a moment, her petulant behavior rubbing his nerves raw. How could she not like the suite? He turned to take in the full measure of the room. Lavish bed linens, an oriental rug over thick blue carpet, a fireplace, a whole wall of closets and a private deck complete with a large Jacuzzi. What was there to complain about? Oh, but leave it to his darling wife to find the accommodations lacking. Unless they booked space in one of the trendy hotels her gruesome friends frequented, Lydia was not satisfied. She and her debutante sisters were thick as thieves. If one of them went to an overpriced spa in Arizona, then they all had to go. Though they professed to be the best of friends, Carter had quickly learned that the underlying link they shared was a competitive streak a mile wide.

Shuddering over the thought of spending the next three days cooped up with his whining wife, Carter quickly found the well-stocked bar. The mini fridge held two chilled bottles of champagne, both Lydia's favorite brand. Hoping to appease her, Carter popped one open and poured two crystal glasses half full. Plucking up an orange from the fruit basket sitting on the counter he added a dash of freshly squeezed juice to each champagne flute garnishing the rims with fresh orange slices.

"Darling, I have a treat for you," he crooned, swaggering his way out on the back deck. "Are we a might thirsty?"

Lydia glanced at him over her sunglasses, frowning. "I suppose that's some kind of twist top beverage," she sniffed.

"No dearest, I had them stock only your favorite things for this voyage," Carter replied. His lips smiled but behind his dark glasses his eyes blazed with loathing.

Taking one of the champagne flutes from Carter's outstretched hand, Lydia took a sip. It was tolerable. "Carter, I cannot believe you wanted to continue this trip with those people," she admonished. "Really, they're positively trailer trash."

"But **we** are paying for the crew," Carter reminded her. "Money talks, darling, I plan on paying the help a generous bonus to see that those lowlifes stay far, far away from us."

"Did you smell that hippy woman?" Lydia continued her rant. "What was that foul odor?"

"Um, I believe it's a type of perfume," Carter said. "I heard her tell that young girl it was patchouli oil."

"What did that young man say he did for a living?"

"Diesel mechanic," Carter answered.

"Really? For a moment I thought they might all be jobless riffraff," Lydia grumbled. "So scruffy looking. Unshaved faces, socks with sandals, khaki," she shuddered. "Unless they are off this boat before we sail, I will not be leaving our room until we return to the dock."

"Yes dear, I understand perfectly," Carter oozed. "Don't worry your exquisite little head about a thing. I will see to it that you are not inconvenienced for even a second." He sipped his drink, watching as his wife's scruffy mongrel crawled out from under her chair to lift a leg and pee off the side onto the deck below. Carter frowned. *Oh yes, enjoy the cruise you little rat dog, as soon as your mistress is gone, so are you.*

Moments later, Carter heard Captain Mike calling "Lift anchor." The boat moved swiftly out of its backwater mooring, headed for the river's main channel. Their adventure had begun.

Chapter Eight

The Graysons met up with Isis and Bosco on the front deck to watch the scenery slide past. It was spectacular. The trees lining both banks were displaying autumn's full range of colors from dull gold to brilliant yellow and deep russet. A stand of maples made themselves known with fiery reds and flaming oranges. The river lived up to its nickname of 'The Big Muddy' the water looking thick as maple syrup, the surface dotted with fallen leaves and glints of sunlight. The two couples settled into comfortable deck chairs a cooler of drinks between them. Content with the soothing sounds of nature no one spoke for close to an hour.

"Hey, Isis, think you could whip up a sandwich or two?" Bosco asked, his stomach loudly rumbling.

"Sure, Babe. Janie, Jimmy would you like one?"

"Nah, that's okay, we brought our own food. We're on the cheap cruise," Jimmy muttered his face flushed with embarrassment.

"Nonsense, we're sharing the boat so we might as well pool our resources," Isis told him. "Want to help me whip up some grub for the men folk, Janie?"

"Okay," Janie smiled back. "I have to warn you, though; I'm not very accomplished when it comes to domestic stuff."

"My old lady is a whiz at that shit," Bosco bragged, grabbing Isis around the hips as she walked past. "She can make a feast from a handful of beans, a road killed squirrel and an onion."

"You don't really have any roadkill in that cooler, do you?" Jimmy asked, looking a bit green around the gills. "If I stare across the water for too long, I'm getting a bit queasy."

Roaring with laughter, Isis herded Janie towards the kitchen. Bosco slapped Jimmy on the back and told him he had just the thing to cure his seasickness, making a toking gesture with his thumb and finger.

Though smoking pot wasn't something Jimmy engaged in on a regular basis, he wasn't averse to accepting a hit when it was offered. He and Janie both felt the recreational use of marijuana was no more hazardous to their health than a couple of beers or a bottle of wine. Besides, he didn't want to seem like some wimp in front of Bosco.

*****

"Do you believe the size of this boat?" Janie marveled as

she followed Isis to the kitchen. "It's bigger and nicer than our apartment."

Passing through the living room the women gawked at the marble trimmed fireplace. They ran their hands over the lush leather furniture. They shuffled their feet through the thick carpet. Everything matched to perfection, from the crystal vases of fresh cut flowers to the throw pillows on the sofa. Subdued lighting reflected off the highly polished pale oak tables. Abstract sculptures in brass, dark wood, and gray marble graced both the mantel and several tables. One corner of the main room boasted an entertainment center complete with a flat screen TV, DVD player and an assortment of the latest movies. The dining room table was large enough to seat ten. The chairs tucked around it had thick damask covers in an icy shade of blue.

The kitchen was just as incredible. It boasted top of the line, full sized appliances in sparkling stainless steel. The countertops were charcoal colored granite, topped by glass-fronted cabinets. The floor, tiled in tumbled marble pavers, was a softer shade of gray. A breakfast bar separated the kitchen work area from the dining room.

When Isis and Janie walked into the kitchen, they saw a man standing behind the work counter in full chef's regalia. He was already making use of the six-burner stove and most of the counter space. He glanced up when they walked in, a scowl on his pudgy face. "What do you want?" he barked in a thick French accented voice, sounding like some great bear. "The food is not ready. I have just started my preparations."

"Um, we weren't expecting anyone to be cooking for us," Janie replied giving him her most winsome smile. "We brought our own food."

"Are you not Mrs. Williams?" the man demanded.

"No, we're Isis and Janie."

"I do not cook for you then. Only for the Williams," he snapped. He turned his back, grumbling under his breath as he stirred something on the stove.

Isis mumbled to Janie, "Got his shorts in a bunch, don't he?" Janie clamped a hand over her mouth to stop an explosion of giggles.

The women moved to the far end of the room, clearing counter space to start their own meal preparations. They pulled out loaves of bread, bags of chips and jars of condiments from the brown paper sacks sitting on the floor in the corner. They chatted as they worked both eager to learn about the other's life.

"I have some Tahitian Chicken Salad already made, so let's use it for our sandwich filling," Isis said, moving over to the fridge to retrieve the covered plastic bowl she had tucked in there earlier.

"What do you think you are doing?" the chef bellowed at her.

"Whoa, chill out I'm just getting some of our food," Isis told him.

Glaring and stomping his way towards her, the man snarled, "There is only my food in the refrigerator, and you are not to touch it."

"Well, I beg to differ, I distinctly remember putting our

supplies away and I put several items in that fridge," Isis huffed back at him.

"Those wretched plastic covered abominations have been removed," the man haughtily told her.

"Just what did you do with those abominations?" Isis demanded.

"Tossed them in the garbage bin on the dock where they obviously belonged," he snorted. Turning his back on them, he resumed chopping vegetables at the center island. The women's sputtered gasps fell on deaf ears as he completely ignored them.

"I'm getting Jimmy and Bosco," Janie said, heading for the front deck. Isis trailed in her wake shaking her head in disbelief. *We should have just let those snobs have the boat,* she thought.

Both men sat in stunned silence when Janie informed them of the chef's behavior. Then their chests puffed up with manly pride and they headed for the kitchen. Isis told Janie she didn't like the look in Bosco's eyes, that maybe they should go find Captain Mike.

"Yo, Chef Dude!" Jimmy yelled as he stomped up to the counter where the man was working. "Just where the hell do you get off throwing out our stuff?"

"Yeah, that was so not cool," Bosco chimed in, ambling up behind Jimmy.

"Go away, I am trying to create," the man angrily snapped back.

"You're gonna pay us back for that food," Jimmy snarled,

slamming his fists down on the countertop.

The chef waved the large knife he was holding right in Jimmy's face. "I told you to be gone!" he roared.

That just provoked Jimmy into making his own crude response. Leaning across the work surface Jimmy stiff-armed everything onto the floor. Carrots and onions rolled everywhere. The glass cutting board made a loud thunk as it hit the marble tiles, splitting in half. The chef wailed in outrage charging around the island towards Jimmy, still brandishing his large knife. Just then the women showed up with Captain Mike. Janie's terrified scream stopping the men in their tracks.

"What the hell is going on here?" Captain Mike demanded.

All three men began yelling at once. The chef kept waving his knife. Janie burst into tears, and Isis began chanting. Then to top off the chaos, Carter Williams came roaring into the room screeching that his wife was trying to rest. He demanded to know what the reason was for all the noise. Everyone kept trying to talk at once the air ripe with their jumbled words.

Finally, the chef got everyone's attention when he threw his knife into the stainless-steel sink. It skittered around the edge before settling to the bottom. "I cannot work like this!" he wailed. "I quit! Take me back to the dock now!"

"You aren't going anywhere!" Carter Williams shouted. "I paid for your services for the next three days, I expect you to hold to our agreement."

"Oh, let the pompous ass swim back to shore," Jimmy snorted.

"Karma, people, karma," Isis interjected. "We all need to calm down."

"Everyone get a grip," Captain Mike yelled. "I suggest you all grab a chair and wait for me to sort this out."

"FINE," the lot of them chorused, moving uneasily away from each other.

Having separated the warring parties, Captain Mike listened to each person's complaints. He sympathized with Isis and Bosco over the loss of their food. He assured Janie and Jimmy that the chef wasn't going to chop anyone up in their sleep. He tried his best to sooth the chef's ruffled feathers. Nothing worked. Even Carter Williams' offers of a hefty bonus to the chef, and compensation to the other couples didn't ease the situation.

"Fine, you folks leave me no choice," Captain Mike sighed. Pointing to the chef he said, "Pack your gear, we will be returning you to shore." Turning to face the others he informed them that if they chose to stick with the cruise all of them would share the food on board and the cooking chores. Before anyone could comment he spun on his heel and headed out the door. He had to notify the crew that one of them would be using the dinghy to take the furious chef back to the dock.

While the chef stormed off to gather his belongings, Isis and Janie began cleaning up the mess in the kitchen. Bosco and Jimmy went back to chilling out on the front deck. Carter Williams slowly made his way towards the second floor, taking his time getting there. He was not looking forward to telling Lydia about this latest disastrous change to the weekend. *Although,* he mused, I *might be able to use it to my advantage.*

Lydia hadn't heard the argument below, nor her husband's stealthy return to their cabin. Overwhelmed by the sheer horror of a weekend spent with 'hillbillies' as she had taken to calling their sailing mates, she had downed several valium. Now she lay stretched out prone in the middle of the king-sized bed, oblivious to everything. Little TooFoo had whined for a bit trying to get her attention, wondering why he wasn't being petted. Unable to rouse his mistress, he eventually stretched out beside her and fell asleep.

Carter heaved a sigh of relief when he found Lydia snoozing, now he wouldn't have to face her wrath until she woke later in the day. It would be too late by then to turn the boat around to take her back to shore. Things were still working out, just not as he'd planned, but then maybe that would prove to be for the better. Carter smiled down at his sleeping wife. "Rest up, darling, it's going to be a long three days." Chuckling to himself, Carter snagged a bottle of scotch and a glass of ice and headed for the outer deck to enjoy the view.

Chapter Nine

As the huge vessel made a cumbersome turn around a sharp bend in the river, Janie and Isis were putting the finishing touch on lunch. One yell to the men, informing them the food was ready, and they came thundering into the kitchen.

"What's for eats?" Bosco asked. Sniffing the air like an old hound dog.

"Roast beef sandwiches with tomato, butter lettuce and sweet onion slices," Isis told him. "There's also creamy cauliflower cheese soup and Rocky Road cake for dessert."

"You whipped all that up already?" Jimmy gasped.

"That chef person had most of the ingredients cut up and ready to go, I just had to finish things up," Isis replied. "Come on, let's dig in."

The meal, set up buffet style along the countertops, included jars of condiments, salt & pepper, bowls, plates, and utensils on one side of the stove, the soup on top, and the sandwiches and dessert on the other side. There was even a crystal vase filled with Lady Scarlet roses and a sprig of Baby's Breath.

"Man, we are never gonna eat all this, Babe," Bosco smiled at his wife, as he piled a plate three sandwiches high.

"I thought it might be nice to invite the crew and that other couple to join us," Isis smiled back at him.

"Damn, let us get a few bites in first before you call those two snobs down," Jimmy grumbled around a mouthful of roast beef. Bosco and Janie both nodded in agreement.

Isis shook her head in resignation. "Fine, we'll call the crew up first." Moving over to the stairway that led to the lower level, she hollered down the stairs.

It didn't take long for the First Mate and Cabin Boy to show up. They mumbled thank you before piling their plates full, disappearing back below deck. Once Captain Mike sauntered in and filled his plate, Isis called up to the second floor that lunch was ready.

"My God, Carter, what is that cow bellowing about now?" Lydia groaned. She was never in a pleasant mood after waking from one of her drug-induced slumbers. TooFoo began yapping as soon as he heard the nasal tone in her voice.

"I think the Chef has our lunch ready, dear," Carter murmured. "Shall I just go fix you a tray?"

"I suppose I must try to eat something," Lydia sniffed. "Just a bite or two, with some bottled water. Don't forget the lime slices." Rising from the bed, she staggered across the room plopping down on one of the chaise lounges, dramatically covering her eyes with one rail thin arm.

Carter obediently trooped down to the galley. Without a word to the others, he hunted down a serving tray, piling it with food for himself and Lydia. Snatching up the rose bouquet he turned and glared, "These were ordered special for my wife, do not use them again." Not waiting for a response, he stomped off, staggering a bit under the weight of his over laden tray.

"Good Lord, that man is such a horse's ass!" Isis snapped. "I'd love to slap that arrogant smirk right off his face." Realizing how mean-spirited her comment sounded, Isis shook her head in disgust. "I have never met anyone who brought out such demons in my personality."

Her comments brought a round of laughter from the others. Since she had been the calming influence ever since their journey had started, hearing her spit out an angry tirade was a real shock. *Guess everyone has their limits,* Jimmy Grayson thought.

Chapter Ten

Upstairs, Carter laid out the food he had fetched on one of the coffee tables, before calling Lydia to join him. She dragged herself to the sofa, collapsing on it in a heap.

"I don't know why I feel so exhausted." Lydia closed her eyes, laying her head against the back of the sofa. "I don't think this river air is good for my sinuses. Why did you ever think I would enjoy this?"

Carter gritted his teeth trying to ignore his wife's biting complaints. Sometimes he thought there was nothing in the world that would ever make the woman happy. Well, except for her odious rat dog. The fact that she loved the tiny creature so much only made Carter's contempt for it even stronger.

Lydia kept up a running litany of complaints, never taking notice of the fact that no one was listening to her tirade. TooFoo was out on the deck wandering from corner to corner, christening everything with a thin stream of urine. Seated on the opposite end of the sofa, Carter ignored her, busying himself with the preparation of her plate. He knew exactly how she liked everything and hoped presenting her with the delicious looking meal would put an end to her whining for at least an hour or two. Her voice got so petulant when she was on one of her rants, it made Carter want to throttle her until she turned blue.

"I'll have your lunch ready in just a moment, Dearest," he crooned, adding two slices of lime to a glass of crushed ice filled with imported spring water. While Lydia began sipping the water, Carter cut the crusts off one of the sandwiches, then cut it into triangles. In the center of a small saucer, he placed a bite-sized square of the luscious looking chocolate cake. He handed her a steaming mug of the delicious smelling soup topped with a small crumble of saltine crackers. Only when his wife began eating her soup did Carter begin to prepare his own plate. Once his food was ready, he took another saucer and diced up half a sandwich for TooFoo. Calling the dog in from the deck, he put the plate down on the rug, earning a nasty nip for his efforts. To add insult to injury, Lydia laughed at him crooning to the ragged little dog, "Oh, is my TooFee Woofie hungry? Did he think daddy's fingers were sausages? Oh, you are such a silly puppy wuppy."

Carter cringed, biting his cheek to keep from snarling at her or kicking the mutt.

The three ate in absolute silence each lost in their own thoughts.

Carter was surprised when Lydia asked for more of the soup. She even demanded a second tiny square of the cake. She rarely ate more than a nibble. *Her larger appetite is a good sign,* Carter thought, attacking his own food with renewed gusto. He had barely finished his last bite when Lydia suddenly swept to her feet.

"I wish to sun for a while," she haughtily sniffed. "Find my lotion and hat, Carter," she ordered, before sweeping off towards the bathroom to change into her bathing suit.

Carter sighed laying down his half-finished sandwich, shaking his head, before getting up to do her bidding.

After dutifully rubbing Lydia's back with her imported Swiss SPF 50 rose scented sun block, Carter gulped the last of his sandwich before gathering up their dishes to take down below.

*****

"Snob alert," Janie mumbled when she saw Carter Williams creep into the kitchen. He shoved the tray in his hand onto the counter, quickly fleeing back the way he had come.

"I guess we peons will be doing the clean-up chores," Isis remarked. "At least he could have said thank you for the meal," she added with a frown. As soon as the bad-tempered words were out of her mouth, she wanted to take them back. Ever since they had come on board this silly boat bad karma seemed to be winning out at every turn. She wasn't usually so quick to complain about anything, or anyone.

Bosco, whistling a poor rendition of Bad Moon Rising, grinned at his wife before turning to ask Jimmy, "How about we do some fishing this afternoon? Captain Mike said there's a real good spot coming up along a wing dam. We brought plenty of extra gear if you two want to join us."

Jimmy and Janie thought it was a great idea. "Maybe we'll catch a big enough mess to have them for supper," Jimmy said.

Janie rolled her eyes. Her hubby was already thinking of

supper! He always seemed to be hungry. Glancing down at her own still flat belly she wondered what things she might begin craving once the little person inside started making itself known. She bit her lip trying to decide if now would be a good time to take Jimmy aside and tell him he was going to be a father.

"Do you know how to cook fresh fish?" Jimmy turned to ask Isis. He knew Janie wouldn't have a clue, and the only fish he had ever cooked came in little frozen sticks.

Before Isis could answer Bosco spoke up saying, "My woman could cook a whale if you caught one." Slapping a blushing Isis on the backside, he headed for the front deck. "Come on, let's get to fishing."

"Um, I thought maybe you menfolk could lend a hand cleaning up this lunch mess."

Bosco slid to a halt giving his wife a sheepish grin. "Yeah, I guess since you cooked, we could help with the cleanup. Dibs on washing the dishes!" Bosco hated doling dishes but thought drying them was the worst chore since you then had to put them all away.

The afternoon passed at a leisurely pace for all those on board *The Last Hurrah*. The crew went about their chores like ghosts, invisible to the guests on board. The Williams lay sleeping in the sun on their private deck. Little TooFoo amused himself by peeing in every corner of the bedroom. Captain Mike decided to take a short nap while the boat was at anchor at the wing dam. Jimmy, Janie, Bosco, and Isis wiled away the hours pulling in a bountiful catch of perch and blue gill. Everyone appreciated the afternoon for its solitude and late autumn warmth.

As the sun began to dip beyond the western edge of the sky, Bosco announced they'd hooked enough fish. Promising to teach Jimmy how to slice a perfect fllet, the two men ambled off to the aft cleaning station. The women headed for the kitchen to whip up a few accompaniments for the fish. Captain Mike began moving the big boat down river to a sheltered inlet for the night. The Williams had moved indoors but were still napping. TooFoo was busy chewing the edge off one of the pristine white towels hanging in the bathroom.

Chapter Eleven

By six o'clock the first floor of the boat was filled with delicious aromas. The tantalizing smells drew Bosco and Jimmy inside to the living room where they slouched in twin recliners watching a football game on the big screen TV. The crew kept finding excuses to wander up from below, hoping for a dinner invitation. TooFoo yapped and snorted at the top of the stairs as if he too wanted to put in his order for dinner. No one heard a word from either of his masters, but there was a faint sound of running water from their shower.

"It's soup!" Isis sang out from the galley, clanging a large pot lid with the backside of a wooden spoon.

One of the crew popped their head in asking if there was anything wrong. Isis laughed at the man's obvious attempt to secure a plate of food. She courteously invited them to grab a bite. For the next few minutes, the only sound was the clanging of dishes and scraping of serving spoons.

Once again set out buffet style, steaming platters offered a colorful array from which to choose. There was baked perch almandine or pan-fried blue gill, a choice of crispy French fries or steaming rice pilaf, fresh peas in dill butter, a spinach salad garnished with blueberries and walnut halves with a tangy blueberry vinaigrette dressing. There were hushpuppies, corn fritters and flaky buttermilk biscuits. Huge strawberries, blanketed in a coating of dark chocolate, rested in a crystal bowl on a bed of ice.

The crew took a moment to chat with the guests, thanking the ladies for the meal. Captain Mike even brought an addition to the feast - a bottle of aged brandy. Isis agreed that it would make a superb accompaniment to the dessert.

"I wonder if Carter and Lydia are planning on eating any time soon," Isis commented. Her gaze roamed up the staircase, coming to rest on the drooling face of the couple's little dog.

"Who cares, they won't appreciate it anyhow," Bosco muttered. "You don't have to always try to be nice to everyone, Babe. Some people just don't deserve it."

"Bosco Blue that is just bad karma talking," Isis admonished. "Maybe if we are nice, it will rub off, and they will be nicer, too." Bosco just rolled his eyes and grunted.

"Well, we appreciate the grub," Jimmy mumbled through a mouthful of fish. "This is the best fish I've ever eaten."

"Yes, Isis, thank you so much for cooking for all of us," Janie chimed in.

"Well, goodness girl, you helped," Isis smiled back.

"Right, I fetched stuff and sampled.

"Sampling is real important work," Isis smiled, "I wouldn't want to poison anyone."

A loud gasp from the bottom of the second-floor stairway startled everyone. Heads whipping around, they stared at Carter Williams standing midway down the stairs, a look of shock on his face.

"Is there something wrong?" Bosco asked.

"Ah, well, no, um... I just..." Carter's words stammered to a halt. When he realized they were all staring at him he snapped, "No one called us to dine."

"There's plenty of grub, come on down and dig in," Bosco snorted. "You didn't expect us to cart it upstairs, did you?"

Carter scowled, "I don't think my wife is feeling up to coming down. Just fix a tray and I'll take it to her."

"And what if I wish to dine downstairs tonight? Am I not allowed that choice?" Lydia's simpering voice floated out of their bedroom, drifting down the stairs.

Turning round, Carter began apologizing to his haughty wife. Though everyone else was seated around the breakfast nook in the kitchen, Lydia sashayed her way into the main dining room. Trailing behind her, Carter rushed to pull out her chair. Then he fussed with lighting the pale blue candles in the crystal holders that graced the center of the table.

"Sit down, Carter, so they can serve our meal," Lydia snapped. Pointing at Janie she barked out orders. "You, girl, bring us our first course." Pointing in Bosco and Jimmy's direction she admonished, "One of you take TooFoo his meal. Well, don't just sit there...hop to it, people, we're waiting."

When no one jumped up to do her bidding, Lydia turned to Carter and began whining, her venomous onslaught encompassing everyone in the room. She called Isis and Bosco reprobates. She considered Jimmy and Janie white trash. She called her husband a useless excuse for a man. She even snapped at TooFoo for barking. All because no one had jumped up to wait on her hand and foot like her servants did at home.

"Please, just serve us some food," Carter pleaded. "When Pumpkin's blood sugar gets low it makes her a bit testy." He knew that if he jumped up to serve the meal, Lydia would just get angrier.

Always the peacemaker, Isis opted for the path of least resistance. Better to take a minute serving them food than listen to more of that dreadful woman's venomous comments. Quickly filling two bowls with salad, Isis took them to the table. Then she brought over the cruet of dressing, glasses of water and a basket of assorted crackers. The others just sat there glaring at Carter and Lydia. Silence reigned while the Williams gobbled up their first course.

Moments later, tapping her water goblet, Lydia screeched, "Where is our main entrée? Did you not see that we were finished with the first course? Really, such slovenly service, it is intolerable."

Though Bosco and Jimmy growled about not serving the bitchy woman any more food, Isis once again took the diplomatic route. She dished up generous portions of the two fish dishes adding generous portions of rice pilaf, the peas and a side dish of lemon wedges. Sliding a plate in front of Lydia, then Carter, she smiled and bid them "Bon Appetite."

"Fish?" Lydia gasped. "Is this river fish?" She shoved the plate across the tabletop. "How disgusting! But then, you people wouldn't know any better, would you?"

Carter stared at his wife. *My God, she is such a shrew,* he thought. "Just try a bite dear, it really is quite tasty," he said, trying to appease her growing temper. All he needed was for these people to see her throw one of her infamous tantrums. The last time she'd had one, they were asked to leave the five-star restaurant they were dining in; it had been quite embarrassing. When Lydia got on her high horse her words could be quite scathing.

Glaring at her husband, Lydia stood and picked up her plate. Stomping across the room to the kitchen she flung it into the sink. The delicate China shattered. Food flew up onto the countertop, spattering over the stove. Part of it even pelted Janie in the back of the head.

"We paid for gourmet food to be served to us on this abomination of a trip," Lydia screamed. "And you low life hillbillies lost me my chef. Now, one of you women get off your lazy ass and make me a presentable meal!"

Before the others could recover from Lydia's malicious onslaught, Isis pushed back her chair and stood. She bowed to Lydia. Then she scooped up a handful of rice pilaf and flung it in Lydia's face. For a moment no one said a word. Then it was total pandemonium. Lydia slapped Isis across the face. Isis slapped her back. Jimmy and Bosco fell on the floor roaring with laughter. Janie just sat staring in shocked disbelief. Carter ran outside screaming for Captain Mike.

"You bitch," Lydia roared. "I will sue you for everything you own."

"Oh, go back upstairs before someone decides to throw you off the boat," Isis yelled back.

"Are you threatening me?" screamed Lydia. "Carter! Carter! Do something! Where the hell are you?"

"Maybe he jumped overboard to escape from you," Bosco chimed in.

Rubbing at her still stinging cheek Lydia screeched, "You assaulted me, you white trash bitch! I'll have you arrested for this! Arrested! Do you hear me?"

"Assault? You call that an assault?" growled Isis. Then she hauled off and smacked Lydia on the side of her head.

Staggering backwards, wailing, still threatening legal action, Lydia dashed for the stairs to the upper level. Turning around she sputtered, "I'll get you for this! You will regret ever having heard the name Mrs. Carter Williams the Third!"

Flipping her the bird with both hands Isis retorted, "Threaten me one more time you evil hag and it will be the last thing you ever do."

"Ladies, what is the problem here?" Captain Mike demanded, hurrying into the room, Carter following closely on his heels, wringing his hands and whining.

Lydia burst into tears, admonishing Carter to "deal with this mess." Wrapping her long, thin arms around her shaking body, she fled into their suite slamming the door behind her.

Once Lydia was out of sight, Isis tried to calm herself before telling Captain Mike about the woman's deplorable behavior and her own uncharitable response. Hearing the story again set Bosco and Jimmy off into more fits of laughter. Janie bravely spoke up saying that Isis had been justified in her reaction. Carter just kept sputtering that someone was going to get sued.

Captain Mike shook his head. Realizing he would have to separate the two groups, he took Carter's arm and escorted him up to the door of the couple's suite. He murmured soothingly that he would rectify the situation, trying to placate Carter's wounded ego.

By the time he returned to the first floor the others had cleared away all signs of the altercation. Isis apologized profusely, saying she "didn't know what had gotten into her." The rest of the group still insisted that Lydia only got what she deserved. Captain Mike reminded them that the cruise was only three days long. He suggested they try to be a bit more tolerant of Lydia and Carter. Though Bosco said he thought it totally unfair to lay the burden of accommodating the Williams couple on them, everyone else agreed to try.

The rest of the evening passed far more pleasantly. Bosco pulled out his guitar, Isis her harmonica, and a rousing evening of old campfire style tunes ended the day. No one heard a peep out of Carter or Lydia, even their little dog was silent. It was as if the earlier altercation had never happened.

Sometime after midnight, when the lower deck grew silent, Carter snuck down to the kitchen. Though not especially handy when it came to cooking, he managed to scrape together a snack from several bowls of leftovers in the fridge. Lydia had been bad-tempered all evening snorting and ranting about everything and everyone. Carte had quickly gotten a headache. He figured if maybe he fed Lydia she might go to sleep and give him a few moments of peace.

Chapter Twelve

The next morning brought a brisk wind out of the north and a smattering of gray clouds. It kept everyone confined to the inside of the boat looking for ways to amuse themselves. A supply of board games, jigsaw puzzles, and the latest magazines kept them entertained. By the time lunch was over the wind had died down and a weak sun shone between the thinning clouds. Bosco and Isis convinced Jimmy and Janie to go kayaking. After a safety briefing, the crew hauled out four bright yellow kayaks from the bowels of the ship. They helped launch the small boats, reminding the group to use the police whistles if they had a problem. Captain Mike yelled down from the bridge for them to be back by four.

*****

"Have they gone?" Lydia snapped at Carter. She had been hoping their fellow passengers wouldn't linger on the boat the entire day, she was sick of being cooped up in her cabin.

"Yes, dear, and it looks as if they won't be back for some time. Would you like to take a walk around the lower deck?"

"Well, I certainly don't want to stay confined in this tiny room the entire cruise," Lydia snapped back at him. Scooping up TooFoo she headed for the stairs. "Really, Carter, I don't know what you could have been thinking when you booked this trip. Didn't you do any research? Didn't you ask our friends where to get deluxe accommodations? You never think, Carter, you never think of me at all." As Lydia disappeared her verbal haranguing continued to drift back up the stairs.

Oh, but I did think of you dear, Carter chuckled to himself. *This trip is turning out perfectly. Even better than I had planned.* Smiling coldly, he followed his wife below deck, nodding and agreeing with everything she said.

Just as Carter and Lydia moved onto the front deck, the First Mate popped his head out to tell them that the boat would be moving. He suggested they take a seat inside out of the draft until the maneuver had been completed. When asked why they were moving the crew member told them that the captain wanted to get the boat anchored out of the wind. He said the others wanted to barbecue steaks for supper and it was too windy to do it where they were currently anchored.

Lydia glared at Carter. "Again, we must succumb to the needs of those lowlifes. If I must smell the odor of charcoal scorched meat, I will be violently ill." Thrusting TooFoo into Carter's arms, telling him that the little creature needed to "make doody," she swept regally back to their quarters.

Walking up and down the back deck with Lydia's yapping

mongrel nipping at his heels, Carter brooded. He didn't know how much more of life with Lydia he could endure. If it weren't for the fact that he enjoyed the leisurely lifestyle her money afforded them, he would have divorced her long ago. She was a truly repugnant excuse for a human being. However, her money had been tied up in an irrevocable trust by her even more reprehensible father. If Carter walked out of the marriage, he wouldn't get a dime. That was why he was taking steps to change the situation as soon as possible. By the end of the trip, he planned on being a much happier, much wealthier, grieving widower. He knew he was going to face some tough obstacles ahead to make his dream come true. He hoped he was up to the task. An extra sharp nip on the ankle from TooFoo brought him out of his reverie. The mutt ran ahead of Carter, stopping to squat over a pair of sneakers lying on the floor. The little beast farted loudly before dropping a smelly load right inside the left shoe. Carter chuckled, "That should be a pleasant surprise for someone" he laughed scooping up the little dog before heading back inside.

Chapter Thirteen

The kayakers had been drifting along one of the river's back sloughs for over an hour. In no hurry, taking their time, enjoying the wildlife and scenery. They spotted several raccoons racing down the shoreline as if playing a rousing game of tag. Deer popped out of the woods to sip delicately from the small pools trapped in the rocks along the river's edge. The woods themselves offered an ever-changing panorama of color, from the yellows and oranges of towering hardwoods to the deep blue greens of thick branched pines. They passed a small creek that tumbled out into the river, bringing a floating carpet of leaves quickly carried off by the rushing current.

"Look at that log full of turtles," Bosco yelled back at the others strung out behind him.

"Slow up so I can get some pictures," Isis called back.

"They are so cute."

Bosco back paddled for a bit, until Isis was done snapping off at least half a dozen shots of the turtles. Figuring the Graysons needed a rest, Bosco gestured towards a large island in the middle of the river. Nodding in understanding, everyone turned and began paddling towards its shoreline. Beaching the kayaks, they picnicked on sack lunches of thick ham sandwiches, chocolate brownies and crunchy kettle fried potato chips. Quickly devouring the food, the group decided to explore the island before heading back.

A little over three acres in size, covered in pines, wild grape vines and blackberry bushes the island was alive with wildlife. Tiny brown birds darted in and out of the trees, peeping loudly. They were too small and quick for anyone to identify them by name. In the center of the island was a small pool of fresh water, left by a passing storm. The soft earth around its perimeter was etched with paw prints.

"What kind of animal do you think made these?" Janie asked, poking a stick at the prints.

"Looks like raccoon and squirrel," Bosco grunted.

"How would they have gotten out here on this island?" Jimmy asked. "Didn't think they could swim this far."

"They come across in the winter when the river freezes," Isis chimed in, shading her eyes, gazing across at the far shore.

"Yeah, sometimes you even see deer out here," Bosco added.

"Oh look," Isis called out waving a hand towards a stand of

oaks, "A whole patch of mushrooms. They'll be great simmered in butter with our steaks for supper." She dashed forward the others trialing behind.

"Are you sure those aren't poisonous?" Janie asked, looking doubtfully at the mound of odd-looking things growing at the base of the trees.

"Isis knows her fungus," Bosco proudly said. "She grew them at the commune, sold them to local markets and stuff."

Janie ran back to get their empty lunch sacks from the kayaks, while the others began picking mushrooms from the patch. By the time they finished, they could hear a large vessel coming from the north side of the island. Through the trees they could make out the name painted on the side of the boat – it was the *Last Hurrah*. It appeared to be anchoring just offshore. Which made the trip back a whole lot easier, for which Jimmy and Janie heaved a sigh of relief. They hadn't ever kayaked before, and their arms were a bit sore. Plus, the wind had gotten up again making it more difficult to maneuver the small boats. Instead of paddling around the island the couples picked up the boats and portaged them around to the Hurrah.

*****

While the women started preparing their part of the supper the guys moved out to the back deck grilling area. When Bosco told Jimmy he hadn't ever used a gas grill before, Jimmy was stunned, he thought everyone used gas now days. He assured Bosco that he had tons of experience and would be able to grill their thick T-bones to perfection. He fired up the grill adding some mesquite chips in the wire racks under the grill plates. Jimmy had been surprised how many steaks the Chef guy had carted on board since he was only supposed to be cooking for the Williams. No sense in letting them go to waste.

"How you want your steaks done?" he yelled over his shoulder as he piled a platter full of the thick steaks.

Bosco shouted, "I like mine still mooing."

"Well done for me," Isis called out. "I like knowing my meat is really, truly dead when I eat it."

Janie frowned at Isis. "I'm surprised you and Bosco eat meat. Isn't it bad karma or something?"

Isis turned a deep red, mortified by the question. "Well, I tried to be a vegetarian, but three weeks into it I was sneaking off to town for Burger Boys with the works. I'm embarrassed to admit, I just couldn't kick the meat habit. I must have been a carnivore in a past life somewhere."

"Babe, you do so many other good things for the planet, I think the gods will overlook you eating a piece of meat now and then," Bosco teased.

"Should we cook some for the snobs?" Jimmy asked, tossing the first of the steaks on the sizzling hot grill.

Bosco shrugged, leaving the decision up to Jimmy. If it were up to him, they could starve. A moment later he was bellowing, "What the freaking hell?" leaping around the deck as if someone were chasing him with a big stick. He had just stuck his feet in the sneakers he had left lying on the back deck. "They let that mutant dog of theirs shit in my shoe," he wailed, flaying the air with another string of colorful curses. Jimmy couldn't help it, he busted out laughing. The look on Bosco's face was priceless.

"Man, that blows," Bosco growled. "We ought to barbecue that mutt." Then he got a better idea. Yanking off the shoe, hobbling on one leg, he leaned out over the railing as far as he could without falling off the boat, and tossed the shoe up on the second level deck. "I hope one of them steps on it or that useless excuse for a dog eats it." This statement only got Jimmy laughing even harder. He wished he could see old Carter the Third's face when he discovered the shit filled shoe sitting on his deck.

It wasn't long before Bosco and Jimmy strutted into the kitchen with a heaping platter of sizzling steaks. Once again, they had prepared enough for themselves, the crew, and even the snobs. To go with the perfectly grilled steaks Isis had prepared oven roast herbed potato wedges and garlic bread. The mushrooms they'd gathered earlier had been cooked in a butter rich sauce seasoned with minced fresh onion and snippets of parsley. The vegetable choices were pan-fried cauliflower with a sprinkling of grated cheddar cheese or dilled carrots. For dessert, Janie had helped bake blond brownies topped with boiled caramel icing. Isis told her that she'd done a wonderful job, even though the dough had been spread too thin on one side of the pan, making the brownies a bit lopsided.

As a gesture of peace and to restore her karma, Isis made up a large silver serving tray for Carter and Lydia. She included both a rare and a well-done steak, small servings of all the other dishes, plus two large squares of the caramel topped brownies. Then she toted it up the stairs. Setting it outside the Williams' door, she called out loudly that supper was served. Beating a hasty retreat, so she wouldn't have to deal with any of their unwarranted whining, she hoped the meal would appease the couple's tempers.

After the kitchen was cleaned up the group retired to the front deck for another songfest. Captain Mike joined them for a nightcap. He brought along another bottle of aged brandy for them to share. He even offered up his rendition of an old sea shanty.

By ten o'clock the passengers were getting concerned with the decreasing quality of the weather. The wind was now blowing steady at about ten miles an hour, with occasional stronger gusts. Distant rumbles of thunder echoed across the water. Captain Mike assured them that there wasn't anything to be concerned about as *The Last Hurrah* had been pulled around the backside of the island, anchoring it out of the ever-increasing wind. The boat's nose had been run aground on the sand to decrease any rocking motion. He guaranteed them that it was the best spot for the night, since it appeared the storm might be headed their way. He told them the First Mate would be on duty the entire night, so there was no need for concern. He never mentioned the flash flood and high wind warnings they'd received from the local Coast Guard station. He figured there was no sense scaring them if it wasn't necessary. Besides, trying to navigate the river in the dark was hard enough, let alone in the face of a raging storm. Returning to the marina was out of the question. They would be safer right where they were anchored.

By midnight a light steady rain had begun falling. Nobody but the First Mate noticed; the others had all retired to their cabins and were sound asleep. Well, everyone but Carter Williams. He'd waited until he was sure no one was still roaming the decks below before venturing down. He plopped the tray of empty supper dishes on the kitchen counter. Then he snuck to the front of the boat. Noticing the First Mate was awake up on the main bridge, he called softly up to him. "My wife's dog needs to relieve himself. Would it be okay if I went ashore for a bit?"

"Don't matter to me," the crew member snorted. "You do know it's raining, right?"

Carter rolled his eyes at the man's patronizing words but kept his comments to himself. Accepting the man's offer of a flashlight, Carter promised to be back as quick as possible. He scurried back to their suite to grab TooFoo before heading off the boat and into the cold drizzling rain.

Just as the First Mate began to worry that something had happened to the rich dude and his little dog that would require him to go hunt them down, Carter appeared on the deck. He waved up to the bridge before disappearing inside. *Rich people are idiots* the First Mate muttered to himself. Relieved that Carter was safely back on board the boat, he settled back with the latest sports magazine he'd snagged from the living room to help the night pass more quickly.

Making a stop in the kitchen for a quick bedtime snack, Carter scarfed down several pieces of leftover steak. Those interlopers sure did know how to prepare some decent food. Using one of the pristine white kitchen towels, he dried off TooFoo, who was shivering so hard his teeth were chattering. When the tiny dog began whining, he shoved a piece of steak in its mouth. "We don't want to wake up mommy now, do we?" he hoarsely whispered. Tucking the dog under his arm, he slithered back up the stairs to their cabin.

Chapter Fourteen

Earsplitting peals of thunder woke everyone on the *Hurrah* around three a. m. Within moments an almost continuous barrage of lightning filled the sky. Fierce winds howled around the boat like a deranged beast. Rain fell in drenching sheets. Though the boat was securely anchored it was bucking on its tethers like a wild bronco. The crew raced around checking for wind driven leaks in the windows or along the bottom of the doors. Bosco and Jimmy helped secure items on the deck. Isis huddled with a terrified Janie, trying to comfort her. Even Carter popped down and asked if there was anything he could do to help. No one wondered why Lydia didn't show up to complain.

The storm raged on into the early morning hours. Isis tried to make coffee but gave up after spilling the pot three times in a row. All they could do was huddle together and wait it out. Bosco told tales from his Berkley college days trying to lighten the mood. He had to yell to be heard over the violent storm. Jimmy did his infamous robot dance which got a laugh from Isis.

Just when the storm seemed to ease up a bit, they heard a horrendous crashing sound. The boat swayed violently. Then the lights failed. Screams rang out, followed by loud cursing. The emergency generator kicked in popping on the safety lights, their eerie glow barely keeping the shadows at bay. The sound of running water could be heard from the level below. The huge vessel groaned loudly before dipping to one side. Two of the large statues ringing the room toppled over on the floor.

"Are we sinking?" Janie cried with a terrified shudder, reaching out to grab Jimmy by the arm. The others merely shrugged, no one able to surmise what had happened.

Before their worry could turn to panic, Captain Mike strode into the room, rain cascading off the dark green slicker he wore. "We have a problem in the lower level. You men need to come with me. Isis, you ladies stay here. Everyone get a life vest from the closet next to the front entry."

The men headed below towards the sound of the rushing water. Isis moved Janie to the back of the main room, tossing her one of the bright yellow life vests. Then she hurried to the staircase to check on the Williams couple. At the top of the stairs, she banged loudly on their cabin door. "Carter? Lydia? Are you two all right?" There was no answer. Isis pounded harder. Still no answer. Twisting the knob, she discovered the door was locked. She pounded for several more minutes trying to rouse the couple, until her hand began to throb. Then she raced back down the stairs calling out for Bosco.

"Babe, you alright?" Bosco asked as he popped back into the room, moving quickly to pull his wife into a hug.

"I can't get an answer from Carter or Lydia and their door is locked."

"I'll get a key from one of the crew," Bosco said. "Don't worry, I'm sure they're both fine."

It seemed to take forever for Bosco to get back with one of the crew members. Isis joined them as they climbed the stairs, calling out once more to Carter and Lydia. When no one answered the calls or the crewman's loud bangs on the door, all of them got a bit worried. The crew member used his passkey and flung the door open.

The suite was in total disarray. The branch of a huge tree protruded through the side of the boat above the bed where the stained-glass panel had been. The air reeked of spilled perfume and lotions from the open bathroom door. Broken glass, clothing and pillows were strewn across the room. Rain blew through the broken window soaking the carpet. On the floor next to the bed was a heap of linens with TooFoo lying on top. The dog was shivering violently making a low keening noise. Isis rushed over to gather the tiny animal into her arms.

"Oh, my Lord!" she gasped, pointing at the floor. "I see someone's hand under there."

Bosco and the crew member rushed to her side. Ducking under the thick tree branch, Bosco spotted the hand. It was barely visible beneath a mound of covers. They all scrambled to remove the linens and debris. In a moment, Lydia's ashen face appeared. Then they uncovered Carter's head, resting on Lydia's chest. When they raised his head, he moaned loudly. Clearing away more of the tangled bedding, Bosco put an arm around the man's waist tugging him to his feet. A trickle of blood from a narrow gash on Carter's forehead coursed its way down the man's face. They moved him gently to the doorway, before heading back to get Lydia. Isis hovered over the moaning man trying to assess his injuries.

Bosco stepped back over beside Isis shaking his head. "We'd better get him down below. There's nothing we can do for his wife."

"My God, you d-d-don't mean…" Isis stammered.

"Afraid so, Babe," Bosco sadly nodded.

They maneuvered the still barely conscious Carter down the stairs, gently laying him on one of the sofas. Isis pulled a powder blue cashmere throw across his chest before going to hunt down a first aid kit. The crew member went to tell the Captain about Lydia. The task of telling Janie fell to Isis, since Jimmy was still below with the rest of the crew.

The sudden roar of a chain saw startled them all, rending a small scream from the still terrified Janie. It was followed by the sound of gushing water and the hum of a small engine. Minutes later the boat began to right itself.

Captain Mike sauntered into the room, followed by a sodden First Mate and an equally wet Jimmy. He nodded to Bosco, who followed them up the stairway to the second level suite. The women huddled below with the still silent Carter. When the men returned, their solemn faces spoke volumes.

"Has he come to at all yet?" Captain Mike asked, nodding at Carter.

"He moans once in a while, but that's all," Isis replied.

"What's happened Captain?"

"The flooding and high winds toppled a large old oak tree into the water. The swift current carried it down river ramming it into the side of the boat. We had to cut it up to move it off the prow. It left a big gash in the fiberglass along the side that will need to be repaired. We've managed to do a temporary patch for now. Plus, we need to pump out the water that rushed into the hull. It's a real mess down below. The tree was so large one of the upper branches punched out the window in the second-floor suite."

"And Lydia?" Isis softly asked. "What happened to her?"

"We're not sure at this point," Captain Mike said. "All we know is she's dead."

Clean-up duties were assigned to the shocked passengers. Captain Mike knew that keeping busy would pull their minds away from the night's horrors. Power had been restored, thanks to the backup generator making it safer to move around on the boat.

Isis went to make coffee and throw a meal together. Janie got assigned to stay with the still unconscious Carter. She patted his hand, talking to him softly, hoping he would respond. He just lay his face a pasty shade of gray. Bosco went back down below to help the crew with the mop up chores. Poor little TooFoo huddled on the end of the sofa by Carter's feet, whimpering pitifully.

Chapter Fifteen

As dawn broke across the river the rain slowed to a misty drizzle. The worst of the storm had passed, though the river remained swollen from the storm's run-off. Everyone on *The Last Hurrah* was still working to clean up the damage done by the rampaging river. Several large black garbage bags sat on the back deck filled with debris. Floors and carpets were mopped up with a shop vac. Pillows, linens, and throw rugs lay in heaps below deck, waiting for their turn in one of the dryers. Isis was kept busy making coffee and sandwiches for the ravenous men folk. Janie just continued to sit with the unconscious Carter.

Dragging himself into the kitchen Captain Mike dropped into a chair. "Coffee, please," he groaned. "I'm so tired I can't think anymore."

Pouring him a steaming mug Isis took a moment to rub his shoulders. "How are the repairs coming?" she asked.

"Well, we've managed to temporarily seal the hole where

that tree rammed us. We'll need someone to bring us some better repair materials before we can attempt the trip back to our dockage."

"How long will that take?" Isis asked. "Will we passengers stay with the *Hurrah*, or go back on the supply boat?"

"Depends on who brings the stuff and what size boat they have. Old Man Penderschott is tight with a buck. I figure he'll come himself in his skiff. Don't think you'd want to go back with him in that old derelict of a boat."

"Should we send Carter back? He still hasn't come round yet," Isis sighed. "And what about, Lydia? We can't just leave her lying up there."

"As soon as Penderschott radios me back, I'll let everyone know what our options are. Until then there's not much I can do for either of them," Captain Mike sighed with frustration. "Damned rotten situation for everyone. Sure ruined the weekend for you folks."

Isis managed to smile despite the circumstances. "Well, Bosco and I did sign up for the adventure cruise. And I gotta tell ya, Captain, this has been one hell of an adventure."

When Captain Mike stood up to return to the repair work below deck Isis gave him a fierce hug. Surprised at first, he stiffened, then relaxed and hugged her back. *What a wonderful person* he thought, *she's always thinking of everyone else.*

The morning rapidly sped past with everyone busy getting *The Last Hurrah* back in shape, while listening with one ear for the ship-to-shore radio to buzz. When the call finally came all work ceased, crew and guests alike waiting anxiously for information on their situation.

Calling everyone into the main living area, Captain Mike told them the news. "Looks like it will take another day for Penderschott to get the supplies we need. The stuff is supposed to be in sometime tomorrow afternoon. If it's too late in the day by the time the delivery is made, then he won't be starting down river until the morning after that."

"Couldn't the Coast Guard haul us back?" Jimmy asked.

"We aren't the only vessel damaged by the storm," Captain Mike replied. "They got two barges upriver run aground, five smaller boats torn from their moorings adrift, and several log jams at the lock and dam. We're small potatoes compared to those troubles."

"What about Carter?" Isis asked, her voice filled with concern. "He still isn't awake."

"His vital signs all seem stable. I think it's just a matter of time," Captain Mike replied.

"And L-L-Lydia?" Janie stammered. "What about Lydia?"

"We'll mover her below deck to the walk-in freezer," Captain Mike replied. "It's all I can do at this point."

Though everyone was less than thrilled with the news, things could have been worse. At least the storm was over, there was plenty of food, and the boat was no longer in danger of sinking.

"Men, if you would come with me, we'll move Mrs. Williams below," Captain Mike softly said. "Isis, if you could come along and see that she is properly clothed before the men see her, I'd really appreciate it."

The group trudged off to carry out the sad task leaving Janie alone with Carter and TooFoo. The little dog had been strangely quiet ever since Isis had pulled him from the chaos of the upper cabin. Sometime during the night, he had dragged four small pillows under the coffee table, making himself a nest. He cowered in the middle of it only coming out to drink a bit of water. As for Carter, he occasionally moaned, twitched or tossed from side to side. He had not opened his eyes or spoken a word. Janie checked his pulse, as Isis had taught her, and then went to get herself a cup of coffee.

Opening his eyes just a slit, Carter glanced around to see if anyone was nearby. He spotted Lydia's dog under the coffee table staring at him with its beady little eyes. He heard sounds from the direction of the kitchen and cautiously lifted his head. Probing the large bandage covering most of his forehead he winced as a spear of pain shot through his skull. He closed his eyes for a moment to stave off the nausea that had his stomach rolling in a knot. Opening his eyes to narrow slits, he could see that young girl, Janie, in the kitchen but she didn't see him. Then he heard heavy footsteps from overhead. *Perfect timing,* he thought, sitting up, shaking his head, and moaning loudly.

Janie heard the movement in the living room and turned to see her patient sitting up. Before she could get back to Carter's side, Jimmy appeared in the stairwell, part of a sheet-covered bundle cradled in his arms. His back was to the room, so he didn't see Lydia's husband watching him with calculating eyes.

"OH! MY GOD!" Carter suddenly screamed.

Jimmy almost dropped his end of the bundle, stumbling backward, pulling the others on the stairwell down and into the room. They all turned to stare at Carter, unsure what to do. Both Janie and Isis made a beeline towards the sofa, dropping on each side of Carter, patting him on the back.

Carter burst into tears, trying to struggle to his feet. "Oh, my darling Lydia," he wailed. "No, she can't be dead, she can't be!" He staggered to his feet only to fall to the floor sobbing and shaking with grief.

Captain Mike strode forward motioning for the women to leave him alone with Carter. He scooped the trembling man upright depositing him back on the sofa. The others quietly moved off toward the lower deck with their stiff and silent bundle.

"Mr. Williams, I am terribly sorry for your loss," Captain Mike said. "I know it may seem harsh to ask you questions right now, but there are some things I need to know about your wife's accident."

"A-A-Accident?" Carter stammered.

"Yes, Mr. Williams, her accident," Captain Mike reaffirmed, hoping to head off the inevitable lawsuit someone like Carter Williams was sure to file. "The storm caused flash flooding, which dropped a large tree into the water. The current brought it down river at a rapid pace, ramming it into the side of the boat. The upper branches punched a hole into your cabin. Your wife must have been struck by the branch causing a fatal head injury."

Carter looked at the man in stunned disbelief. *Oh, this is just too perfect,* he thought. "So, you're saying this was just an unavoidable act of God?" Carter managed to sob. "That no one is responsible for my darling Lydia's demise?"

"I know things like this seem impossible, Mr. Williams, but accidents happen," Captain Mike soothed. "I've been in touch with Mr. Penderschott, he asked me to convey his condolences. He also said to tell you he will help you with whatever legal necessities arise."

"Legal what…" Carter muttered, lowering his head, moaning softly. "I don't understand, you said it was an accident. Why would there be any legal problems?"

"Yes, I did say it was an accident," Caption Mike replied. "However, there will be an investigation by the Coast Guard into the incident. They will want to be sure that everything reasonable was done to protect this vessel and its passengers."

"Oh, well, yes, I understand," Carter huffed. "But I can assure them that both you and your crew provided exemplary service to my wife and me. Isn't that enough?"

"Don't worry about it, Mr. Williams, it's just routine procedure," Captain Mike assured Carter. "We'll try to keep their intrusion to a minimum. I know this must be exceedingly difficult for you, losing your wife in such a horrible manner.

"I think I'd like to be alone," Carter sighed. "I can't possibly go back into that cabin. Where will I be staying now? I'd like to lie down."

"Isis said they would bunk out here and you can have their cabin," Captain Mike told him. "She went off to move their things and get the room ready for you. You just lie here and rest for now."

Carter shook his head in dismay, sighing deeply. He flung himself back on the sofa, turning to bury his face in the pillows. His shoulders shaking with sobs. Captain Mike patted him awkwardly on the back, unsure how to comfort the man. "I have to go below and see about a few things. Will you be okay on your own until Isis gets back?"

"Just go," Carter sobbed. "I want to be alone now." He curled up in a tight ball, listening to the sound of the captain's retreating footsteps.

Thinking *I almost blew it*, Carter managed to get his laughter under control. Luckily, that idiot of a Captain had thought he was shaking with sorrow. He would have to keep up the tearful whining, so everyone would feel sorry for him and not ask too many questions. It was going to be hard, though, pretending he was sad about his shrew of a wife's death.

Chapter Sixteen

Taking full advantage of his situation, Carter had the women running in circles the rest of the afternoon trying to appease him. He loved every minute of it. After taking a long nap, he returned to the main living area, plopping down on the sofa with an audible groan. Then the real torture of his boating companions began. He was hot. He was cold. He was thirsty. He needed his hand held. The litany of needs just went on and on.

"So help me if he whines one more time about his damn head hurting, I'll smack him there again," Janie grumbled. "He is a royal pain in the ass."

"Honey, we need to try and be patient with him, he did just lose his wife," Isis murmured. "Some people become totally helpless when they have to look death in the face."

"Please Isis, you know he was like that before this happened," Janie admonished. "He's probably glad she's gone."

"Janie! What a terrible thing to say," Isis gasped.

"Oh, come on, she was nothing but a rotten bitch," Janie snapped. "You even lost your temper with her."

"Yes, and I have regretted it ever since. Bad karma is best appeased by doing something good for the person, or at least turning the other cheek."

Both women cringed as they heard Carter calling out from his throne on the sofa. He needed more hand holding, pillow plumping and another glass of water with lime slices. The women did a quick rock-paper-scissor to see who had to attend him this time. Janie groaned out loud when she lost. Isis gave her a reassuring hug, before pointing her towards the living room.

By sundown everyone was tired and on edge. The evening meal was a simple one of hearty vegetable soup and ham sandwiches, with chocolate sundaes for dessert. Conversation was at a minimum. Once the meal was over everyone scattered off to their separate quarters. Doors slammed shut, and *The Last Hurrah* echoed with an eerie silence.

Isis waited until the others had left before rearranging the living room to make a more comfortable sleeping space for her and Bosco. She dragged an ornate shoji screen from one of the corners using it to block the view from the kitchen.

"Bosco, did you ever see a dead body when you worked at that clinic in Berkley?" she asked, shaking out a set of floral sheets for the sofa.

"Kind of a morbid question to ask right before bed, Babe."

"Well, it's just that Lydia didn't look like I thought she would," Isis commented, her brow creased in a deep frown.

"She looked dead enough to me when we moved her," Bosco shuddered. "She already

smelled a bit putrid, too. Good thing Captain Mike had us stash her in that freezer."

"I know she looked dead, but she didn't look like she was injured. You know. . .no cuts, bruises or anything like that."

"What are you getting at?" Bosco hesitantly asked.

"I mean, she didn't appear to have any injuries from that tree that crashed through the side of the boat. She just looked grayish green and smelled like vomit. I think we need to look at her body again."

"What do you mean we need to look at her again?" Bosco spluttered. "Once was enough for me. Besides what do you care how she died?"

"It just seems odd to me, that's all. I have this hinky feeling. You know what that means, Honeybear."

Bosco groaned. He did know what that meant. Isis thought she was having one of her premonitions. She had gotten this wild idea a few years back that she was psychic. Whenever she got one of her 'premonitions' there was no stopping her from following up on the supposed vision. One time, when they were living in California, she had made him visit every John Miller in the Los Angeles phone book. She'd supposedly seen the death of a man with that name in a dream. They didn't know anyone by that name, but that didn't matter. Three days and dozens of slammed doors later they came to the home of a John Miller who had just died in a car accident. Isis had bemoaned their late arrival, saying if they had started at the bottom of the list, instead of the top, they could have saved the man. No matter how hard Bosco had tried to convince her otherwise, Isis thought the man's death was her fault. She'd been depressed for weeks over the whole thing. Telling her to "buck up and get over it" had only earned Bosco a few nights on the sofa. This time was no different. He would have to look at the dead woman or never hear the end of Isis saying, "I told you so."

Hunting up two flashlights, a bundle of dried sage for cleansing Lydia's spirit, and a notebook, the couple headed below. The lower level of the huge boat housed lockers, storage cabinets, crew quarters, and a large freezer. There was no lock on the freezer's outer door, so Bosco swung it open. Stepping through he drew Isis in beside him. There on one of the metal shelving racks, next to the drums of ice cream, was the sheet-draped form of Lydia Williams.

Isis lit her sage bundle waving it in a slow circle over the body. She softly chanted, asking the spirits of the nether world to greet Lydia with love and compassion. When she finished, she gave Bosco a nod. Stepping forward he carefully tugged the sheet back from around the body.

"See," Isis hissed at him. "No lumps on her head, no dried blood anywhere not even any bruises."

Bosco leaned closer scanning the woman's face carefully for any telltale marks. Then he slowly tugged the cover lower continuing to look for any signs of trauma. There was nothing. No bruises. No scratches. No cuts. No broken bones. Absolutely nothing to show she had been battered by the storm. He did, however, notice her ashen color and the lingering smell of vomit

"Man, you're right, Babe," Bosco muttered. "There's no sign of injury at all."

"What are you two doing in here?" a gruff voice snapped from behind them.

Isis nearly jumped out of her skin. "My God don't ever do that again," she shrieked, spinning around to slap Captain Mike on the arm.

"Well," he asked again "What are you doing down here?"

Bosco quickly told him about Isis' premonition and their subsequent examination of the body. The couple's obvious distress made Captain Mike feel he needed to check Lydia's condition himself, if for no other reason than to lay Isis' fears to rest. Initially planning to just make a quick scan of the body once he got a closer look, he grew puzzled. There really didn't appear to be any reason that Lydia should have died. Carefully covering the body back up he motioned for the others to exit the freezer. Once outside the room he walked to a supply shelf, plucking a padlock and key out of a small white plastic bin. He walked back and secured the door to the freezer dropping the key in his chest pocket.

"I think we need to see that the body isn't disturbed anymore," he told Isis and Bosco. "And I need to have another talk with Carter Williams, excuse me."

Back in the living room, Bosco pulled a shivering Isis into his arms. His wife was so sensitive to emotional disturbances in the universe. It was one of the things that had drawn him to her, her limitless capacity for empathy. Sometimes though, it would leave her vulnerable and clingy, nothing like her usual save the world independent self. This was one of those times. All Bosco could do was hold her until she finally stopped shivering and fell into a fitful sleep.

Sometime during the night Isis woke to the sound of pitiful whimpering. It was TooFoo, still huddled under the coffee table in his nest of pillows.

"Poor baby," Isis softly crooned as she reached out to lift the tiny dog up beside her. He licked her hand before settling down in the crook of her arm.

Chapter Seventeen

Everyone slept in the next morning exhausted from the storm clean-up chores and the emotional turmoil. Isis seemed preoccupied all through breakfast. She even burnt the toast. When Janie asked her if anything was wrong, Isis had given her a puzzled frown. However, when it came time for someone to take Carter his food everyone was surprised when Isis volunteered to perform the onerous task.

"Coming in," Isis announced before flinging open the door to cabin B. "Brought you some breakfast," she added, letting her eyes sweep over the room.

Carter was awake, propped up in bed cell phone in hand. "Just leave it on the table by the window," he huffed at her. He waited for her to leave so he could continue his conversation, but she stopped at the foot of the bed, giving him an odd look. "What?" Carter snapped impatiently.

"I'd like to talk to you about Lydia. I'm getting some bad

vibes about what happened to her."

"Good, God, woman, I'm in mourning!" Carter gasped. "How can you be so insensitive? Get out! Just get out!"

Isis looked at him, shrugged, and left the room. *He doesn't look very mournful to me* she thought.

Once the annoying hippy woman left Carter continued his conversation. He was on the line with Lydia's attorney, discussing her demise. The man was being a real pain in the ass. He kept telling Carter that he could not just take Carter's word that Lydia was dead. Without proof that his client was no longer among the living, he was unable to divulge the contents of her will. Though Carter roared, blubbered, and threatened, the attorney stuck to his guns. Carter made one last sarcastic remark before hanging up on the man. What the hell, they'd be back at the Marina soon enough, and he would deal with the insufferable buffoon then. Smiling, Carter dug into the breakfast tray Isis had brought him with gusto.

Chapter Eighteen

As the day wore on, Isis became increasingly convinced that something about Lydia's death was very, very wrong. She replayed that night in her mind, dissecting every detail. There was one glaring fact that kept coming up - Lydia had no visible signs of injury. Even though she talked to everyone on board, except Carter, about her concerns no one seemed to take them seriously. That's what made her sneak into Carter's room while he was napping out on the sundeck. She took his cell phone out to the kitchen, hitting the button that called up a record of his calls. The last two he had made were to law offices. *Now why would he be contacting two legal firms*, she mused. *If anything happened to Bosco, I'd be calling family and friends*. Punching "0" to get an operator, Isis asked them to connect her with the Jo Davies County Sheriff's Office. When a pleasant-sounding young man asked how he could help her today, Isis almost hung up. She shouldn't be butting into someone else's business. But what about poor Lydia? Shrugging back her shoulders, she committed to forging ahead with butting into Carter's affairs. Lowering her voice to a throaty whisper she said, "There's been a murder on the *Last Hurrah* houseboat, out on the river just south of

Dubuque." She snapped the phone shut. Slipping back into Carter's room, she tucked it inside his jacket pocket, careful to arrange the clothes on the chair in the same neat lines as she'd found them.

At lunchtime everyone noticed that Isis was in a much calmer mood. She was humming along to a tune on the radio, flipping thick burgers on the indoor grill. There were plates of sliced tomato, onion, cheese, crisp bacon strips, lettuce leaves and avocado wedges. A serving platter held freshly baked oatmeal raisin cookies. She had even brewed up a pitcher of iced tea, southern style, with lots of sugar.

"Glad to see you feeling chipper again," Bosco smiled, giving his wife a hug.

"Oh, things are looking up," Isis replied. "Come on everyone dig in before it gets cold. Janie, would you go knock on Carter's door, I think he went back in there a few minutes ago."

Before Janie could get out of her chair, Carter made his appearance. He was clad in a pair of too large pajamas, a pale blue Afghan draped over his shoulders. His eyes were red rimmed, his complexion pasty, but he seemed to be navigating okay, and even managed a brief smile.

"I thought maybe a bit of food might do me some good," he softly intoned. "My head isn't hurting so badly now, and I think I'm actually hungry."

The others made room for him at the table offering up words of encouragement. Janie took his burger order, dished it up, and placed it front of him. Conversation was stilted at first, but gradually everyone just ignored Carter. They talked about the boat repairs and what they were going to do once they were home again.

"I just can't do this," Carter suddenly wailed. He shoved his half-eaten plate back, stood and stumbled back to his room.

"Humph," Isis snorted at Carter's retreating back. "As if he really cared about his wife."

"Babe don't be like that," Bosco sighed. "Just because he handles his grief different than we're used to doesn't mean he isn't devastated."

"He hasn't even asked to see her," Isis snapped.

"I wouldn't want to see her if she was my wife," Jimmy spoke up.

Janie punched his arm "And why not?"

"You know, all that gross stuff that happens to a dead body," Jimmy shuddered.

"Jimmy Grayson, you are such a horse's ass," Janie said, again punching him on the arm. "I'd want to look at you."

"Yes, a loving spouse would want to look," Isis murmured, casting a glance down the hall at the closed door of Carter's room. *I did the right thing*, she thought, *calling the sheriff's department*.

The talk around the table drifted back to everyone's plans after the end of the trip. Isis was once again oddly quiet. When Bosco asked if she was okay, she frowned at him saying, "Right as rain." Shrugging, he gave up on trying to pry out what she was worried about; she'd tell him when she was ready. For a fleeting second, he wondered if she suspected anything about his lack of appetite and weight loss being more than a simple seasonal fluke. He wasn't ready to tell her about the tests he'd had done since he still did not know the results.

*****

The day wore on with little for anyone to do but wait to be rescued. Jimmy and Bosco sat out on the back deck talking about manly things like trucks and hunting. The women played dominos on the front deck. The crew went about their usual chores. And Carter...he snuck out to the kitchen on his hands and knees, shaking like a leaf the whole time, worried that someone would spot him. He planned to feign confusion from his head injury if anyone saw him acting so strangely. His little pretense at lunch might have gotten him a bit of sympathy, but now his stomach was growling with hunger. He snatched up fruit, bread and cheese, and a handful of cookies before slinking back to his room.

As the group sat down to eat supper that night, Captain Mike popped his head in the back door to let them know he'd heard from Penderschott. The repair materials would be there first thing in the morning. If all went well, they could be under way later that day. His news brought a round of rousing cheers.

The noise must have woken Carter as he showed up in the kitchen asking if he could get a bite to eat. When no one jumped up to wait on him he filled a plate himself, carting it back to his cabin. *Scummy lowlifes can't even help a distraught widower,* he thought, *I'd rather eat alone then sit with them.*

Everyone turned in early that night, after packing up their belongings, since tomorrow would be their last day aboard the *Hurrah*. Captain Mike made the rounds asking if anyone had questions or needed help with anything. His last stop was at Carter Williams' room. Knocking, but not waiting for a reply, he flung the door open striding boldly into the room.

"Do you need help packing up your things for tomorrow?"

"Well, I don't see how I can pack anything," Carter whined. "You won't let me back in my old cabin. I guess Penderschott will see to it and have the items sent on to me."

Captain Mike frowned. "You do understand why you can't go back in that room, don't you?" Carter merely glared back at him. Captain Mike let out a frustrated sigh before continuing, "While I'm here there are a few things I'd like to ask you about the night of the storm."

"Must I go over it all again?" Carter whined. "It's all so horrid."

"Well, I might be able to smooth things over later with the Coast Guard if you answer a few questions now."

"Fine, if you think it's necessary," sniffed Carter. "But I am very tired, and my head still aches, so be brief, sir."

"You got quite a blow to the head that night. You suffered a number of small bruises and scrapes," Caption Mike said looking Carter up and down with a critical eye. "Kind of strange then that your wife appears not to have suffered even a scratch. You know why that is?"

"No, Captain, I don't," snapped Carter. "One minute I was asleep, the next I was thrown about, bashed in the head and unconscious."

"Did anything else unusual happen?"

"What do you mean unusual? The fact that my wife and I had to share this vessel with those lowlife bums? The fact that your incompetence left us beached in the middle of a ferocious storm. Hmmm? Just what would you consider to be unusual about this whole God forsaken trip?"

"Anything that wasn't normal behavior for your wife is what I meant," Captain Mike calmly explained. "Was she moody, depressed, nervous, drunk…anything like that?"

Carter barely managed to control the smile that wanted to take over his face. "Hmm…she did complain of not feeling well earlier in the evening, but that had nothing to do with the storm. She ate too much of that rich food. Lord knows what kind of spices or herbs that hippie woman used."

"We all ate the same food and no one else got sick," Captain Mike countered.

"My wife had a very delicate constitution the least little thing could upset it," Carter snapped back. "She complained for over an hour of having heartburn. Then she downed two valium, along with several Mimosas, and finally managed to fall asleep."

"What about you? Did you get an upset tummy?" Caption Mike sarcastically asked.

"No, I did not," Carter gasped shocked by the other man's tone. "Really, Captain, I don't appreciate your sarcasm. I don't like it at all. I hope your investigation does show something wrong. I hope it proves that you and the owner of this tub were neglectful of passenger safety. I can hardly wait to report the results to my attorney."

Captain Mike shook his head in exasperation. "I'm not implying anything, Mr. Williams; however, your wife's lack of injuries seems a bit odd is all. You get a good night's sleep, sir. We'll be back at the dock tomorrow afternoon, and we'll get everything sorted out then."

Once the Captain left, Carter began mentally rehearsing his new story, the one that was close enough to the truth to sound believable. Lydia had become ill from something she ate. He'd cry just a bit of course, then pretend his memory was just coming back to full clarity. The blow to his head and the stress having made him forget most the events of that evening. Yes, he'd be ready for those Coast Guard clowns. They were no match for his skill as a liar. Hell, he'd managed to fool his shrew of a wife into believing he loved her for fifteen years, how hard could it be to fool total strangers? Carter went to bed with a smile on his face.

Chapter Nineteen

Bosco and Isis conked heads when they jerked awake the next morning curled up in each other's arms on the narrow sofa. A loud voice outside the cabin window was bellowing "Ahoy." They heard the crew yell back, then felt a dull thud against the side of the boat. Realizing it had to be Mr. Penderschott with the repair supplies they rushed to dress and get out on deck.

The bump to the side of the boat was from a dirty white skiff now tied up beside the *Hurrah.* Two muscled young men were handing supplies up to the crew. Mr. Penderschott stood swaying at the helm of the smaller vessel directing the operation. He waved to Isis and Bosco, calling out a cheery good morning. They waved back, Isis calling out an offer of hot coffee. Penderschott declined saying he had business to deal with and must get back to shore. The crew took possession of the last of the supplies as the young men in the boat caught the lines tossed at them, and the skiff headed back upriver.

Despite all the noise, Jimmy and Janie didn't pop their heads out of cabin A until they smelled bacon frying. Joining the others in the dining room they scarfed down heaping plates of waffles, bacon, and scrambled eggs. As soon as the meal was over all the men moved below deck to help with the repairs. Except Carter Williams, of course; he never even cracked his door to ask for a breakfast tray. Bosco suggested that it was probably because he was afraid of being asked to lift a finger to help with the work.

By lunchtime the repairs to the damaged boat had been completed. Captain Mike had maneuvered the vessel back into the main channel and was rapidly making way upriver. He had her running full out, anxious to get back home and shed of all the troubles from the ill-fated cruise. The guests were just as eager to get back. Their gear sat piled inside the front door ready to off-load. Isis and Janie had cleaned the kitchen area and helped the crew strip the bedding in all the rooms. Jimmy and Bosco had accepted Captain Mike's invitation to ride back on the main bridge. The two men sat glued to the wide windows watching the shoreline speed past. Carter kept to himself, still perfecting his role as the grieving husband. When told there was nothing more for them to help with, Isis and Janie took seats on the back deck, talking about the storm. Little TooFoo finally came out from under the coffee table where he'd been hiding. He seemed to sense that something was happening and ran out on the back deck yapping excitedly.

The sky was just beginning to darken when they reached the cut that led to the boat's dockage. As the big vessel swung into the slough, they could see that the Marina up ahead was brightly lit. A small Coast Guard boat sat tied up next to the *Hurrah's* slip. Half a dozen cars filled the small parking lot, two of them sporting law enforcement lights and logos. A crowd of people waited at the door of the marina office for the boat to come to anchor.

"Wow, the cops are here," commented Jimmy. "Guess Mr. Penderschott must have called them about the accident."

"No, Jimmy, I called them," Isis calmly said.

"Babe! You called the fuzz?" Bosco gasped in horror. "Man, that is bad karma. Real bad."

"Well, someone had to show concern over poor Lydia's death," Isis said. "Her husband sure doesn't seem too broken up by it. And Mr. Penderschott is hoping it will all just disappear, so he doesn't have to worry about being sued. No one is thinking about Lydia."

"I understand you feel sad for the woman, Babe, but the fuzz?" Bosco groaned, shaking his head in dismay. "You know those law-and-order types bring bad vibes. They'll only make things worse than they already are."

"Trust me on this one, Bosco, we need them here. I think there is something really wrong about that woman's death. I've been having dreams," Isis said. Bosco rolled his eyes. "Don't give me that look," Isis snapped. "You know the whole thing stinks to high heaven."

Though allowed to unload their belongings from the boat, everyone was told not leave the parking area. Penderschott, Captain Mike, two Coast Guard officers, and the County Sheriff all boarded the boat, headed down to the crew deck. Carter complained bitterly about them disturbing his wife's remains. He got on his cell phone, screaming at his lawyer. Evidently there was nothing he could do to prevent them poking at his wife's corpse, so he stalked over to his Escalade, ensconcing himself inside. The others gathered around Bosco's van talking in hushed whispers. TooFoo, whom Carter had left to fend for himself, was busy sniffing around the parking lot, occasionally yipping with interest at something he smelled. Over an hour passed before the men came back from the belly of the boat. They did not have Lydia's body with them.

The Sheriff called out "Could you folks all gather over here for a moment?"

Jimmy went over and knocked on the window of the Escalade motioning for Carter to come out. The rest of the group moved over to the dock area to hear what the Sheriff had to say. Carter looked ashen and visibly shaken as he approached. He slid in beside Janie, hoping she would offer him a gesture of comfort, which he planned to use in making an extravagant scene. Everyone was muttering their voices growing louder with worry and apprehension.

Loudly whistling to draw their attention the sheriff called out, "Let me introduce myself, I'm Sheriff King, with the Jo Davies County Sheriff's office. After a preliminary examination of the deceased, we have decided the death warrants further investigation. You will all need to remain here until we can take your statements. After that, the body will be transported to the County Morgue. Until an autopsy had been completed no one is to leave the area."

"What the hell do you mean no one is to leave the area?" Carter bellowed. "I am taking my wife's body home - today."

"No, sir, you are not," replied Sheriff King. "Mr. Penderschott here has kindly offered to put all of you up in the marina cottages at his expense. So, you will be staying here until I tell you it's okay for you to leave."

"I AM CALLING MY ATTORNEY," Carter screeched, whipping out his cell phone. "What is your name again, I need to tell my attorney so he can spell it right when he files the lawsuit."

Sheriff King just shook his head in disgust, spitting out a stream of tobacco on the ground next to Carter's left shoe. Carter squeaked and leaped backwards. King really hated dealing with these rich snobby types; they just rubbed him the wrong way. "Mr. Penderschott will assign you a cottage. Once you're settled in, Deputy Harris will be by to take an initial statement," King flatly stated, ignoring Carter's continued protests. Then he stepped off towards the main Marina office to confer with the Coast Guard people.

"Gather round folks, I'll get you set up with a room key," Penderschott called out to the group. As they stepped forward, he gave each of them a large brass ring with two keys and a numbered brass tag. He also handed them a packet of brochures from some of the local restaurants and businesses. "Afraid you're on your own for meals, folks. The cottages do have mini kitchens with utensils and such, so feel free to use um," he added. Not waiting to see if there were any questions, he turned and dashed back toward his office.

The group silently gathered their belongings before heading off to look at the accommodations. As Isis and Bosco walked away TooFoo scampered after them, dancing around their feet, yipping with delight.

"Carter, did you want to take TooFoo with you?" Isis called out.

Turning to give her a condescending look, Carter huffed, "I don't care what you do with that cur. Keep him if you like him so much. If it's left up to me the useless thing will be put down."

Gasping in shock, Isis stooped to gather the tiny dog into her arms. She murmured softly in its lopsided ear, telling it that no one was ever going to hurt him. She cooed lovingly at him all the way to their cottage. Bosco walked behind her shaking his head, knowing they would be keeping the butt ugly critter until it died of old age.

Cottage One, assigned to the Graysons, displayed a small hand-painted plaque over its entrance stating, "Welcome to Rose Cottage." When Janie opened the door, she gasped with pleasure. The room was large, airy, and decorated with real antiques. The bed was ivory colored wrought iron with a wedding ring quilt in shades of pink. A small table with two chairs sat beneath a double window that looked out onto the backwater slough. The tiny kitchen was spotless. To the left of it was the bathroom, just as small, and just as cute. It had a claw foot tub, rose embroidered fluffy white towels, and a big rose shaped rug on the glossy white tiled floor. All the curtains were filmy white lace with large silk roses used as tiebacks. There were even rose shaped soaps in a milk glass dish by the bathroom sink.

Isis and Bosco's cottage, named Daffodil, had much the same décor as the Grayson's, except in rich buttery yellow tones. Isis flung the windows open, letting in the earthy scented air rich with the smells drifting off the river. When she put TooFoo down, he ran in a circle for a moment then raced over to leap up on the bed, snuggling down in between the pillows for a nap.

Carter flung open the door to his cottage, the Scotsman, and stormed inside. *Oh my God* he thought, *could this day get any worse*. The red, black, and tan plaid color scheme made him want to vomit. Moreover, if that oaf of an owner thought he was going to cook or clean the dump he was in for a rude awakening. Yanking his cell phone out of his breast pocket, Carter called his home. Those worthless servants that Lydia insisted on having had probably been loafing the whole weekend, time to make them earn their keep. He snapped out orders for the house cleaner and cook to come to the marina motel at once. If he had to stay in this dump at least he was going to have someone to cook and clean for him.

Chapter Twenty

"Honeybear, we need to go ask that nice Mr. Penderschott where the nearest market is located. We're going to need some supplies for us and for TooFoo," Isis called over her shoulder as she began poking through the cabin's sparsely stocked cupboards. At the sound of clinking cans TooFoo lifted his head and began whining.

"Babe, I can't believe you want to keep that mutt," Bosco sighed. "It doesn't even like me. You know it pooped in my shoe?"

Giving her husband one of her patented sad soul looks, Isis told him, "The poor little thing needs us. I had a dream about TooFoo, and in it we were all together and happier than we'd ever been before in our lives. I think he's going to be good luck. And he wouldn't have pooped in your shoe if you hadn't left it lying on the deck."

Grumping about "always taking in strays," Bosco went to ask Penderschott where he could find a market. If Isis wanted to keep that stupid dog, there was no stopping her. Besides, his wife knew that he would do anything to make her happy. And he needed her to be happy right now, especially if he was going to have to impart his medical test results. He still hadn't gotten up the nerve to tell her so, when the doctor's office called with the results, he knew she would blow her top that he hadn't confided in her before he had the tests.

When Bosco tried to start their van for the trip to town, it sputtered and died. Cursing under his breath he turned and turned the key in the ignition, stomping on the gas, but all he got for his efforts was a headache. Just when he thought he would have to walk the ten miles to the store, Jimmy and Janie popped out of their cottage.

"Hey, you guys going to town?" Jimmy yelled.

"If I can get this old heap to crank," Bosco yelled back.

Isis popped out of their cottage, tiny TooFoo tucked under her arm. "How bad is it this time?" she groaned watching Bosco climb out and pop the hood.

"Don't know," Bosco sighed, a puzzled frown creasing his brow. "You know I ain't mechanically inclined. Sounds like the...the...the thingamajig that makes it start ain't working."

Loping over beside Bosco, Jimmy stuck his head under the hood. After about ten minutes of poking and prodding he declared the van a goner. It would need major work before it would be road worthy again. Janie suggested they all go in their jeep, to which Isis readily agreed. Bosco gave the van one last kick in the tires before climbing in the back seat of Jimmy's vehicle. No one bothered to ask Carter if he needed anything. When Isis suggested they stop by his cottage, Janie huffed that he was rich and could afford to pay someone to deliver him his meals. Since she wasn't in charge of the transportation, Isis could only shrug and climb in the back seat beside her husband.

As the Grayson's jeep roared out of the parking area, Sheriff King popped his head out the office door. *Damn,* he thought, *I wonder where they're going, I told them to stay put.* He noticed Carter Williams looking out his door. At least one of them had listened to what he'd said about not leaving. Stepping back inside Sheriff King told Deputy Harris to go question the guy before he slipped off, too. Then he went back inside to look at the registration paperwork Penderschott had kept on each couple.

Following his boss's orders, Deputy Harris ambled over to Scotsman Cottage. "Mr. Williams, I need to ask you some questions," he said, as he stepped up to where Carter stood in his doorway frowning down the road. He motioned for Carter to go back inside, and then followed him into the room. Closing the door, Harris sauntered over to the kitchen table dropping into a chair, pulling out a notebook, motioning for Carter to take a seat. He asked Carter to go over the events the night of the storm. Taking careful notes, he only stopped Carter's monologue when he needed clarification of a statement. It seemed like Carter needed to vent, as he rambled on and on, stopping occasionally to dab at his red-rimmed eyes.

Back from their shopping trip, Isis invited Jimmy and Janie to come over for supper. She planned on making vegetable lasagna with garlic bread. While she laid out what she would need for cooking, Bosco busied himself setting up a feeding area for TooFoo. Isis had insisted on getting the tiny dog two bowls, a feeding mat, a big rawhide bone, and a tiny beanbag bed. She'd also picked out a sweater, two collars and a natural boar's bristle hairbrush. *Yup, she's hooked on the little rodent*, Bosco softly sighed. It was one of the things he loved about her though, her big heart when it came to animals, children, or the less fortunate.

Deputy Harris, who had been lounging outside the Grayson's cottage waiting for them to return, did not look happy. He was annoyed by the fact that they had left the marina when the sheriff had specifically told them to stick around. He was a bit gruff when he ordered them to take a seat inside, so he could question them about the ill-fated boat trip. Though neither of them had anything to hide, Jimmy and Janie both felt a bit intimidated. They stumbled and stammered their way through the telling of what they remembered from the night of the storm and its aftermath.

Stopping outside Isis and Bosco's cottage, Deputy Harris noticed the smell of garlic wafting out the screen door. Despite the chilly air, the couple had blocked the front door open to allow a breeze inside the cozy cottage. As he loudly knocked on the wood frame, Deputy Harris could hear a small dog yapping inside. The man called Bosco strode over to open the screen door. "Guess it's our turn to be interrogated," he growled when he saw Harris standing on the stoop.

"Just a matter of routine questioning, sir."

"Bosco Blue, you let that man come inside," Isis yelled from the kitchen. She slid a pan of garlic bread into the oven next to a bubbling casserole of lasagna. "You weren't born in a barn, show some manners."

Bosco stepped away from the door, bowing deeply at the waist, sarcastically saying, "Do come inside, sir, we wouldn't want to seem rude or like we had anything to hide."

The deputy gave Bosco a frown, moving around him to take a seat at the kitchen table. "In your own words, tell me what happened aboard the boat the night of the storm," the deputy instructed.

"What do you mean, "in our own words," who else's words would we use? Are you implying that we're liars?" Bosco snapped, figuring he'd get the upper hand in the situation if he presented an aggressive stance.

"Honeybear, he is just doing his job," Isis scolded. "We have nothing to hide, just talk to the man."

So, Bosco began telling their version of the story, with Isis occasionally chiming in to add her point of view. Halfway through she took over telling the deputy of her concerns about Lydia's lack of apparent injuries. Bosco visibly cringed when she told Harris about her premonitions that something was hinky with Lydia's death. The deputy just quietly took notes, nodding every now and then at something she said. When they had told him everything they knew, and everything Isis thought she knew, they clammed up and waited for the deputy to speak.

"That's all you remember?"

"Yeah, you got a problem with it?" Bosco snapped. Isis gave him a swift kick under the table to remind him of his manners.

"No, no problem, just trying to be thorough."   Harris closed his notebook, tucking it into his chest pocket. He thanked them for their time and left.

Ten minutes later, Jimmy and Janie popped over for supper. The two couples stayed up talking most of the night about the strange situation they were all involved in. After the young couple finally went back to their cottage, Bosco took TooFoo for a before bedtime walk. When he got back, Isis was already in bed, tossing, turning, and mumbling in her sleep.

No one had thought to check on Carter since they had arrived back at the marina. Nor did they extend an offer to him to join them for supper. Carter was in a foul mood as the staff had not shown up yet. Once he realized he was on his own, Carter rang the front office, demanding that Penderschott provide him with a meal. Penderschott politely reminded Carter to look at the brochures he had received, pick a place, and order his own damn food. Penderschott was in no mood for dealing with the arrogant man. He about had his belly full of the whole group, even though the others were not presenting him with any demands. He never once thought that the entire situation could have been avoided if he had been less greedy about renting out his houseboat.

Angered by Penderschott's response, but too hungry to argue, Carter ordered food from a place called The Big Pitt Barbeque House that offered free delivery.

The smoked pork, BBQ beans, fries and coleslaw were barely tolerable by his standards and left Carter with a mild case of heartburn. Popping two of Lydia's valium he had managed to rescue from the mess in their suite on the boat, he collapsed on the bed thinking, *I don't know how much more of this I can take.* He wasn't used to dealing with such low-class people and surroundings. At home, their headman Doyle, or one of the other servants, dealt with the unpleasantness of daily chores. Lying in bed, grumbling a litany of complaints under his breath, Carter bemoaned his fate until the valium kicked in and he drifted off into a troubled sleep.

Chapter Twenty-One

The next morning started off cool with a scattering of gray clouds in a dusky sky, clearing by mid-morning to a brilliant autumnal blue. With nothing to do but wait for the Sheriff's office to release them the passengers of the ill-fated trip wandered around the marina. They discovered a shack that sold worms and grubs for fishing. The guys bought an assortment then spent the afternoon fishing from the bank of the slough. TooFoo took great pleasure in rolling in the dirt, grunting, and making happy dog noises. Covered in a dusty film he plunked down beside Bosco for a nap, his tiny feet twitching with dreams of chasing cats. The women went back to Isis's cabin so she could teach Janie to bake bread. Penderschott popped his head out of the office once or twice, but never came out to talk to them. No one saw Carter all morning and no one cared.

Carter's day started badly. His household staff still hadn't arrived at the motel, so he didn't know what to do about getting some breakfast. He wondered if he should whine to the hippy woman, but then decided that was beneath him. The rest of the morning was filled with screaming matches over the phone with Lydia's law firm. By noon he had a headache and was in a truly foul mood. When the house cleaner and cook finally showed up at two, he lit into them. By the time he was done chastising them the cook had quit and the house cleaner was in tears. Carter roared at the girl that if she wanted to keep her job, she had better go get him some food - immediately.

Sheriff King showed up at the marina around four. He had Penderschott call everyone to the marina office. He waited until they were all settled before saying, "The coroner has completed the initial autopsy of Lydia Williams. We have a tentative cause of death."

"Well, hallelujah," Carter sarcastically snorted. "Now maybe we can get the hell out of this backwater dump."

The Sheriff eyed Carter with disdain. *That man is a real piece of work* he thought. Pulling silver-rimmed glasses from his shirt pocket, King opened the folder and began to read. After rattling off some basics like the name of the coroner and vital statistics about Lydia, he got to the cause of death. "The coroner suspects the presence of an organic poison in the victim's system. Cause of death is therefore ruled suspicious and further investigation is warranted." He snapped the folder shut, waiting to see how those assembled would respond.

After hearing what the Sheriff said, no one spoke, they were all too stunned. Poisoned? Lydia had been poisoned? They gazed around the room at each other in disbelief.

Suddenly, Carter leapt to his feet. "Are you trying to say

that someone murdered my wife?"

"No, sir, we haven't made any conclusions here. Could have been accidental. Could have been environmental. Until we investigate further though, we must err on the side of caution," Sheriff King responded.

Isis began softly crying, her hand clutching at Bosco's. "I knew it. I just knew something was wrong."

"Got any idea what kind of poison?" Bosco asked.

"Well, right now all the corner knows is that it looks organic in nature," Sheriff King said. "We'll need to talk to each of you again."

"She did it!" Carter suddenly screamed leaping to his feet, pointing a shaking finger at Isis. "She made us mushrooms on the boat. Wild ones she found in the woods. Lydia got sick right after supper. Right after she ate some of them with her steak."

"You shut the hell up you lying bastard," Bosco shouted, jumping to his feet and making a move towards Carter.

"Keep him away from me Sheriff," Carter bellowed, dancing backwards to duck behind Mr. Penderschott. "They're hippies; they lived in a commune and went to Berkley. They probably have criminal records."

"You take that back you sack of shit!" Bosco yelled.

The room erupted with shouts and threats.

Sheriff King's voice thundered above the ruckus. "ALL OF YOU SIT DOWN AND SHUT UP!" Once everyone complied, he had each group escorted back to their quarters. He posted one of his men outside the cottages to be sure no one decided to leave until he had questioned them again. Stepping over to his patrol car he pulled out a red binder that had been sitting on the front seat. Opening it he attached the first of many forms needed to create an official 'murder book' which would be used throughout the investigation. At the top of the first form, under name of deceased, he wrote - Lydia Collette Jackson Williams.

When Sheriff King went to question Carter Williams, he had Deputy Harris run a search for outstanding warrants or criminal records on the Grayson's, Bosco Blue, and his wife Isis Winters. Maybe one of them had something in their background that would affect the case.

Chapter Twenty-two

"Babe, do you think you could fit out this window?" Bosco called from the bathroom.

"Why on earth would I want to climb out the window?" Isis had a good idea why Bosco was asking but didn't want to believe he could be that dense.

"They're gonna run our rap sheets. They're gonna know about us being radicals," Bosco loudly hissed. "You think we could make it to Canada by midnight if we left now?"

Isis shook her head in exasperation. Bosco was a wonderful man, but he could be such an idiot sometimes. Sure, they had been part of the peace movement and gone to their share of rallies but that was over thirty years ago. She pulled her husband away from the window, calmly telling him they had nothing to worry about; they were innocent of any wrongdoing. Bosco managed to calm himself a bit, but swore he was going to "take the fifth" if he didn't like the questions Sheriff King asked. Isis told him to get a grip that no one cared anymore about what happened in the sixties. Bosco took a seat at the kitchen table, shaking his head, muttering under his breath about "fascists and freedom." Upset by the human's stressed-out behavior, TooFoo nervously bit Bosco on the ankle, temporarily taking Bosco's mind off their worries.

Bosco and Isis weren't the only ones worried about what Sheriff King would ask them. When King knocked on Carter Williams' door, Carter was prepared to act the part of grieving widower. He had rubbed at his eyes until they were red rimmed and watering. He had consumed several mugs of extra strong coffee, so his hands shook, and his voice stuttered from the caffeine jolt. He certainly presented the picture of a grieving husband. He hoped it would help keep the questioning to a minimum.

"Oh, Sheriff, it's you," Carter rasped, opening the door to usher the man inside. "This is all so upsetting, just so upsetting. My poor, poor Lydia…gone…so hard to believe." He snuffled into a large linen handkerchief, his eyes watering, his voice cracking.

"I'll try to be as brief as possible, Mr. Williams, but there are questions I need answered," Sheriff King said, settling into one of the kitchen chairs. He flipped to a clean page in his notebook. "First of all, how well did you know the other folks on this cruise?"

"Why, not at all," Carter said in surprise. He had expected the initial questions to be about his marriage not about the other passengers. Carter nervously explained the circumstances of the boat sharing fiasco. "We had no choice but to allow them to stay onboard. If I had only known how the cruise would end…" Carter squeezed his eyes shut letting a single tear slide down his cheek.

Sheriff King ignored Carter's tears. "The crew told me that Isis Winters and your wife had a really loud fight the day before the storm. They said the woman threatened your wife. Is that true?"

"Yes, that's right, they had a bit of a spat. It wasn't anything to kill a person over though. Just an example of the kind of crass behavior one would expect from those kinds of people."

"What did you mean by your earlier comment that Ms. Winters had poisoned your wife? Do you have any proof to back up that statement?"

"Proof? Well, no, Sheriff. But she did pick wild mushrooms out on some island they kayaked to and then cooked them up for supper," Carter replied with a shudder of distaste. "That night Lydia became quite ill. Since my wife had a delicate constitution, I figured she was just reacting to the rich meal. We'd hired a chef to prepare our food you know, but that hippie woman ran him off."

"I wonder why none of the others got ill from the mushrooms," Sheriff King countered.

"I'm not sure. However, they all ate in the kitchen, while my wife and I dined separately. That woman made up trays for us and delivered them to our door. We never asked her to wait on us, she volunteered."

"Do you know if there were any leftovers from the meal?"

"How would I know something like that?" Carter indignantly sniffed. "You'd have to ask the crew or those hillbillies. We paid for the top-of-the-line cruise; it didn't include performing menial chores."

"Oh, we'll be talking to everyone who was on board, you can count on that," Sheriff King grimly smiled. "Now, let's talk about your marriage and your late wife's will, shall we?"

Chapter Twenty-three

Deputy Harris caught up with Sheriff King just before he went to talk with Isis and Bosco. He had found out several interesting things concerning the couple. They both had records for public disturbance, plus one minor drug arrest for him and one dismissed charge of practicing medicine without a license for her. That last charge got Sheriff King's attention. He told Harris to go back and dig a bit deeper and find out the full details. Pulling out his cell phone he called the deputy he had left guarding the boat. King instructed him to search the boat for any sign of the steak dinner that was served that fateful might. He especially wanted to know if there was any of the mushrooms left that Isis Winters had harvested earlier in the day.

Knocking on the door of Daffodil Cottage, Sheriff King mentally ran through the questions he would be asking. He didn't want to tip his hand too early about the mushroom thing. He would need more proof than the bereaved husband's word. He gave the door another sharp rap.

"It's open, come on in," Isis called out. Turning to glare at Bosco, she reminded him to be civil. "The man is just doing his job," she hissed.

Sheriff King casually strolled into the cottage as if he were an old friend come to visit. "Ms. Winters, Mr. Blue, I just have a few questions," he smiled as he extended his hand to Bosco, who ignored it. Sitting down at the kitchen table, King took his time laying out his files, notebook, and pen. He had found over the years that a void of silence begged to be filled. It often got people rattled and rambling trying to fill up that empty space. This time, however, no one jumped in to break the silence.

"I understand you were responsible for the meals cooked on board the boat?" King began his questioning, pen poised over an empty page in his notebook.

"Well, I wasn't officially the cook, but I did prepare most of the meals," Isis answered, not elaborating on her reply. She didn't want to give the man fuel for further deliberation on her potential guilt.

"What do you mean asking her that?" Bosco growled. "It's not like she got paid for it, she wasn't hired to do it. She did it out of the goodness of her heart when that snotty chef dude up and quit."

"Yes, the Captain told me about the chef quitting," King said pretending to jot a note but just scribbling a bit of nonsense. "Did you gather those mushrooms yourself?" he suddenly snapped at Isis, trying to keep the couple off guard.

"Yes, I did," Isis calmly replied, once again keeping her reply to the fewest words possible.

"How did you know they were safe to eat?"

"Hell, we all ate the damn mushrooms!" Bosco snarled. "Nobody got sick but that rich bitch." Bosco felt Isis give him a swift kick under the table and clamped his mouth shut.

Sheriff King gave the couple a hard look meant to put the fear of God into them. Then he again employed a moment of silence, trying to get them to slip up. Scowling, he waited for one of them to speak. He soon discovered he had met his match with this couple. They just sat there staring back, silent as stones along a riverbank. After five minutes passed without even a yawn from either of the suspects, Sheriff King had to admit defeat and get on with the questioning. "What kind of mushrooms did you pick?" he asked.

"They're called Black Trumpet. They have a very distinctive appearance, color, and flavor. It's virtually impossible to mistake them for anything else."

"And you know this because..." Sheriff King prompted.

"I have a degree in Botany from Berkley. Twenty years of field experience. And I raised and sold mushrooms as a business for six years," Isis smugly replied.

"You tell um, Babe!" Bosco growled, raising his fist in a power salute.

Sheriff King took time to jot a note before asking his next question. "What was the fight about?"

Isis closed her eyes, shaking her head in regret. She had known that moment of bad karmic behavior would come back to haunt her. "Mrs. Williams had an extremely negative aura, I let it bring out the worst in me. She pushed my buttons and I pushed right back."

"She was an arrogant bitch," Bosco chimed in not bothering to use any diplomacy in choosing his words. "She got what she deserved."

"And just what did she deserve?" Sheriff King asked, arching his brows inquisitively.

"Whoa, hold on a second, that came out wrong," Bosco grumbled. "You're trying to railroad us with double talk – well, it ain't gonna work."

Resting a restraining hand on her husband's arm, Isis interjected, "Really, Sheriff King, it was nothing."

Taking a minute to doodle around on his notepad, King jumped to another subject. "I'd like to ask you about something that came up when we ran your names through our computer."

"Oh, yeah, here it comes. Well, oinker, we ain't got nothing more to say. We take the fifth!" Bosco shouted. He leaped to his feet, knocking over his chair. Striding across the room, he yanked opened the door gesturing for the sheriff to leave.

"Honey, he's just doing his job," Isis sighed. She turned back to face the sheriff. "I assume you're talking about the charge of practicing medicine without a license?"

At the sheriff's nod Isis told him all about the incident. It had happened back in 1968 at the Lasting Sunshine Free People's Commune. One of the young women living there had gone into labor with her first child. It came on so quickly that nothing could be done except to deliver the baby right there on the living room floor. Isis had taken it upon herself to act as midwife. The child had been delivered with no complications. However, the mother had needed an episiotomy, which Isis had performed, stitching up the incision afterward with sterilized bright red embroidery thread. Four days later when the young mother felt up to going to the local clinic for a check-up the doctor there had been horrified by Isis's handiwork. Isis knew using the bright red thread wasn't the smartest move, but the young mother had asked her to "pretty things up down there." The clinic physician, however, found it appalling and turned Isis in to local authorities. The charges eventually got dropped as the young mother refused to cooperate with any investigation.

Isis finished the story by saying, "So you see, Sheriff King, it wasn't anything criminal or diabolical, just a bit of a misunderstanding."

Stepping back over to the table Bosco snorted, "Why would we want to kill that Williams woman anyhow? It's not like we had anything to gain from her dying. Besides, killing someone would give us bad karma for years to come," he added with a shudder.

Another half hour of questioning the reluctant couple elicited nothing significant. Sheriff King warned them not to leave town until he cleared them. As he left Daffodil Cottage his phone rang. It was the coroner asking him to drop in as soon as possible.

When King arrived at the county morgue, he learned that the poison which killed Lydia Williams did indeed come from a mushroom. A particularly nasty one called a Death Cap. They grew wild in the area but would be readily identifiable to a trained botanist. The coroner said normally it would take five to seven days for the toxin to kill an adult. When King asked why it had worked so fast on Lydia Williams, the coroner explained that the mushrooms were only the tip of the iceberg. The toxicology screen had also shown that Mrs. Williams had ingested a large quantity of alcohol, plus several valium. Both would have contributed to her death. In addition to those factors, he also said that Lydia had been severely underweight and slightly anemic. All these issues meant she had been more susceptible to the toxin in the mushrooms. He surmised that someone had only meant to make Lydia ill, but the unknown health and substance abuse factors had instead led to her death.

The mitigating factors didn't matter to Sheriff King, dead was dead. Whether accidental or intentional it looked as if Isis Winters was the reason for Lydia Williams' demise, after all, she was the only one onboard who'd had both a residual anger towards Lydia, and the knowledge to find and use those poisonous mushrooms.

The deputy poking around on board *The Hurrah* had come up with some of the mushroom dish in the boat's refrigerator. After taking photos, he'd bagged it up to send off to the lab. He also found several prescription bottles in the Williams' cabin, along with two empty champagne bottles and pieces of a broken vodka bottle. The prescriptions were for valium and penicillin. Both had been refilled just two days before the cruise. Counting out the pills in the containers showed that only the normal doses were missing. He also found two broken plates under the pile of sodden bedding. One was shattered into pieces so small there was no way to tell what had been served on it. However, the other one had only cracked evenly in half. The deputy noted some dried pieces of what appeared to be mushrooms still clinging to the surface. He'd carefully placed everything into evidence bags and toted them back to the lab.

Chapter Twenty-four

The next morning found Sheriff King hunched over his desk comparing statements taken from the crew and guests who had been onboard The Last Hurrah for the cruise. He rechecked the file sent over from the coroner. He reviewed all the interviews he had conducted. He poured over the reports about what was found when his deputy searched the boat. In the end there was only one conclusion to be reached. Sighing in resignation, Sheriff King yelled for Deputy Harris.

*****

"Look who's back," Isis smiled as she opened the door of Daffodil Cottage to find Sheriff King and Deputy Harris standing on the stoop. "You're just in time for some fresh baked cinnamon coffee cake and a cup of freshly brewed coffee," she added. Their solemn faces had her stepping back a puzzled frown sweeping across her face. "Is something wrong?"

"Ma'am, I need you to turn around and place your hands behind your back," Deputy Harris intoned, pulling a pair of handcuffs from his belt, reaching out to grasp Isis by her left arm.

As the visibly stunned Isis began to follow his request, Bosco came storming out of the bathroom. "Get your hands off my wife, pig!" he roared, taking a swing at the deputy.

Since Harris and King were younger and faster, both Isis and Bosco were soon cuffed and being stuffed into the waiting squad car.

Jimmy and Janie came charging out of their cottage yelling for the deputy to stop what he was doing. Janie was in tears, sobbing loudly as she clung to her husband's arm.

Carter Williams stood on his front stoop wringing his hands, crying, and calling out, "I told you so, I told you! Oh, my poor, poor Lydia. You rotten people… you horrible…you…you…" He stuttered to a halt, loudly hiccupping, his nose running unchecked down across his thin lips.

When the squad car door slammed shut behind her, Isis called out to Janie and Jimmy, "Take care of TooFoo for me!"

As the car carrying Isis and Bosco disappeared, Jimmy rounded on Carter. "You lying bastard," he screamed, taking a step towards where Carter stood huddled in his doorway. If Janie hadn't begun sobbing again, Jimmy might have done something he'd regret, ending up in the cell next to Bosco and Isis. Instead, he flipped Carter the bird, slung an arm around his still sobbing wife, and went next door to get TooFoo.

As soon as Jimmy walked away, Carter scooted out of his cottage, racing to catch Sheriff King before he could get away. "Does this mean I can leave here?" he anxiously asked.

"Yes, Mr. Williams, you can go home. If I have any further questions, I will call you. Someone will be in touch about making arrangements for your wife's body."

Carter managed to choke out a sob, thanking the Sheriff for his quick work. Back inside Scotsman Cottage he ordered the staff cleaning his room to go home and get the house ready for his return. Then he called Lydia's attorney to tell him about the arrest. He warned the man that he would tolerate no further delays regarding his late wife's will. If he wasn't apprised of where he stood immediately, he would be calling in his own attorney. Carter hung up feeling vastly relieved. He was finally going to get what he deserved.

The Graysons stood outside Isis and Bosco's cottage, staring down the road until there was nothing left to see but a trail of dust.

"This is a nightmare!" wailed Janie. "You know they didn't do it."

Jimmy knew his wife was right, at least he thought she was. He couldn't imagine Isis deliberately doing something to hurt another living soul. And if the mushrooms had been poisonous ones, why hadn't they all gotten sick? Still, there was the whole cat fight thing that had happened between Isis and Mrs. Williams. Shaking his head in bewilderment Jimmy asked his sobbing wife

"If Isis didn't do it, then who did?"

"What do you mean if she didn't do it?" Janie wailed louder. "You know she didn't, Jimmy. She is the nicest person I have ever met. She wouldn't hurt a fly. She's all like Zen or something."

"But she did yell at Lydia and hit her upside the head."

"She was provoked, and you know it," Janie snapped. Wiping the tears off her cheeks she added. "I'm calling Daddy. He'll know just what to do." Scooping up Toofoo, who'd been sniffing around her shoes, Janie headed back inside their cottage.

Since Janie's father was an accountant, Jimmy doubted the man could be much help. But Jimmy knew who might - the members of that Sunshine Commune that Isis and Bosco had belonged to for all those years. Leaving Janie crying to her father on the phone, Jimmy went off to check out Bosco's van before the police called in a tow truck to haul it off. Hopefully, there would be something in the van to point him towards the commune and some help for their newfound friends.

Chapter Twenty-five

Deputy Harris had a splitting headache by the time he got Bosco and Isis delivered to the jail. Bosco had alternated between chanting anti-war slogans and shouting "Attica" the entire drive. When told to shut up, he only yelled louder, tossing in comments about freedom of speech, democracy, and communism. It was the longest twelve miles the deputy had ever driven.

The fun didn't stop there. Trying to extricate the still screaming Bosco from the squad car took four men and a shot of mace. This got Isis in an uproar. She refused to walk inside the jail, dropping to the ground chanting, her hands folded in prayer. The aggravated deputies just scooped her up, legs still in the lotus position, and toted her inside. They deposited her on the floor next to the intake desk her legs still folded up like a pretzel. Bosco had to be hog-tied and dragged inside. Though the mace had his eyes streaming and snot dripping from his nose it didn't stop his tirade. Neither Bosco nor Isis would cooperate with the intake process. Sheriff King was not happy when he showed up and found them lying on the floor in the intake room. He had them hauled off to separate cells without completing the paperwork, figuring a little time in the tank might calm them both down.

*****

The rest of the night was not restful for any of those involved with the demise of Lydia Williams. Bosco yelled from his cell until after three, only stopping then because he was too hoarse to continue. Isis remained in the lotus pose, chanting until her legs began to cramp from sitting in one position for so long. This had her climbing onto the cell's cot, resorting to singing old folk songs until even Bosco begged her to stop. She didn't exactly have the voice of an angel when it came to carrying a tune.

Jimmy and Janie stayed up until four plotting how to help their friends. Jimmy's ideas, which bordered on the illegal, only got Janie crying again. She was afraid they would both end up in jail right beside Bosco and Isis.

Carter Williams spent the night greedily figuring out how quickly he could dissolve his deceased wife's assets into ready cash. He fell asleep at the cottage's tiny kitchen table with a smile on his face.

Even TooFoo was restless, pacing by the front door of Janie and Jimmy's cottage crying pitifully. At five in the morning, he finally gave in to Janie's pleas, curling up beside her on the bed, his feet twitching in restless dreams.

The deputies working third shift at the station kept busy correlating the growing accumulation of data that had been collected in the case.

Sheriff King spent the night doing research on poisonous mushrooms.

By seven the next morning everyone had their battle plans drawn.

*****

Jimmy had found a hand drawn brochure advertising fresh produce from the Sunshine Commune in the glove compartment of Bosco's van. There wasn't a phone number, but there was a map showing how to get to the market. Up bright and early, he and Janie headed off to find themselves some hippie radicals.

Bosco had tapped out a message to Isis in the old code they'd invented in their Berkley days. Both were all smiles when the jailer brought their breakfast trays. They accepted them without comment and then promptly dumped them on the floor. The hunger strike had begun.

Carter headed back to the home he had shared with Lydia armed with duplicate copies of his wife's autopsy report. He could not only prove that she was dead, but that she had been murdered with poisonous mushrooms by person or persons unknown. He filled the long drive with phone calls to his attorney, local realtors, and the closest Porsche dealer.

Sheriff King got to his office an hour earlier than usual having spent the night tossing restlessly waiting for morning. His night shift deputies brought him up to speed on their unusual prisoners. They showed him the two-inch thick folder that sat waiting for him in the middle of his desk, filled with the research he'd asked them to complete. Slipping into his chair, King began pouring over the data. He never even noticed when one of his men slipped into the room, sliding a cup of black coffee and a cheese Danish onto the edge of his desk.

Back at the Marina, Mr. Penderschott was having a dialogue with his newly hired contract attorney. He wanted to know if he could sue someone for loss of income on his boat rental business. The *Hurrah* was still draped in crime scene tape with orders that it wasn't to be moved from the dock. Repeated calls to the Coast Guard and the local Sheriff's office went unanswered. He'd had to cancel three reservations and refund the reservation money. If word got out that the *Hurrah* was a 'death boat' he would lose more business. Or even worse, attract all the paranormal nut cases within a hundred-mile radius wanting to contact the dead woman's ghost. They were the kind of clients who scared off the better paying customers with their mumbo jumbo. Plus, the authorities still hadn't come to remove Bosco Blue's broken-down van from the parking lot. The thing was a real eye sore with it's rusted out fenders and multi-hued paint job. Though the attorney commiserated, he told Penderschott that he couldn't fight city hall, until the Sheriff's department released the scene, all he could do was wait.

The day wasn't starting out good for anyone, well, except maybe for TooFoo. The tiny dog had slept snuggled up in bed until Janie brought him a strip of crispy bacon from her breakfast plate. Petted, fawned over, and given treats all morning long, he didn't miss his old life one little bit.

Chapter Twenty-six

The miniature map on the brochure from Bosco's van was a bit hard to follow. Jimmy got lost twice. Janie grumbled at him to stop and ask directions, but Jimmy swore they were "almost there" and kept driving. When they circled back past the same faded red barn for the third time, he finally admitted defeat. Pulling into a gas station up on the main highway he grudgingly asked for directions. The clerk inside knew exactly where the commune market was located and gave them great directions. They were at the main entrance in a matter of minutes.

The Sunshine Market sat back from the edge of a dirt road on a thick patch of grass. An ancient oak provided shade for half of the market's grounds. Rickety booths that looked as if they were built from salvaged boards stood in neat rows under the shade. Fresh produce, displayed in rustic bins and hand-woven baskets, looked vibrant and delicious. There were piles of medium sized pumpkins stacked atop larger ones sitting on the ground. Colorful gourds in every size imaginable were tucked in and around the pumpkins. Several varieties of both red and green apples overflowed their baskets, spilling out across the countertop. Another stand held fanciful baskets woven from straw, pine needles and grapevines. There was also an eclectic assortment of used items like books, baby clothes and old records.

The people staffing the tables were as colorful as the wares they were selling. Ranging in age from early teens to late seventies, most were dressed in jeans and bright tie-dyed shirts. One woman had on an ankle length dress of snow-white cotton laced with rainbow-colored ribbons along the hem. Though the weather was a bit chilly, she was barefoot, with lavender painted toenails. A big bear of a man with a thick, tangled, coal black beard sported a pair of bib overalls splattered with dabs of paint. Peace symbols and doves decorated every sign advertising the items for sale. Music wailed from a small stereo; old folk tunes interspersed with sixties anti-war protest songs. An atmosphere of gaiety clung to the market, just what Jimmy and Janie needed to bolster their spirits.

Janie chose the friendly looking woman in the long white dress to approach first. "Excuse m-m-me," she nervously stammered "We're hoping someone here can help us."

"What do you need, child?" the woman asked, her eyes dancing with a smile.

"Um, does anyone here know Isis Winters or Bosco Blue?"

The woman chuckled shaking her head. "What kind of trouble have that disreputable pair of old codgers gotten themselves into this time?" She was surprised when Janie burst into tears.

"They're in jail," Janie wailed, turning to collapse into her husband arms.

"What jail? Where? Why?" the woman demanded, her face now sporting a deep frown.

"The county jail over in Jo Davies," Jimmy blurted out. "Bosco got arrested for resisting arrest. Isis is in for murdering someone."

Stunned by Jimmy's words, the woman gaped at him in disbelief. Then she turned and sprinted over to the bearded man in the bib overalls. She leaned in to whisper in his ear. His face clouded like a summer sky ready to storm. He dropped the big pumpkin he was holding, which smashed into pieces on the ground, spraying several nearby shoppers with pumpkin guts. He strode towards Jimmy and Janie, anger contorting his face.

"What the hell do you mean, Isis is in jail for murder?" he bellowed at Jimmy.

Stammering and stuttering, Jimmy told the man the whole story. By the time he was done a small crowd had gathered round them.

"Go back up to the main house and rouse everyone," the woman in white ordered the big man. Turning to face Jimmy she said, "My name is Raven Night. Bosco and Isis are dear friends of mine, of all of us. What can we do to help?"

Jimmy outlined the ideas he and Janie had formulated on the drive up. They needed people to act as character witnesses.

They needed to talk to the woman whose baby Isis had delivered. And they needed help with money to pay for a lawyer.

Putting an arm around each of the young people's shoulders, Raven drew them up a narrow path towards a distant circle of buildings. She assured them that they had come to the right place. Everyone at the Sunshine Commune knew, respected, and loved Isis and Bosco. She assured them that they would get all the help they needed.

Chapter Twenty-seven

Carter Williams stood outside the gargantuan monstrosity of a building he and Lydia had called home. Sixteen rooms of over-the-top opulence situated on twenty-seven acres of landscaped perfection. It boasted a tennis court, pool with spa, mini lake with swans, a gigantic greenhouse, and an eight-car garage. It took a staff of thirty people to keep it up and to look after Lydia's needs. The land had been portioned off from the larger estate of Lydia's father, Arthur Stanley Jackson. The man had died a multi-millionaire, leaving half his estate to his third wife Babette, the other half in trust for Lydia. They'd gotten only a monthly stipend from the trust until Lydia had her fortieth birthday. After that she had access to the full amount, close to thirty million dollars. That landmark birthday had occurred three months ago. It was the catalytic event Carter had been waiting for to decide the fate of his darling wife. Either she loosened up the purse strings, allowing Carter to live in the fashion he felt he deserved, or else...well, really, there had been no choice. The 'or else' couldn't be a divorce, because of the prenuptial agreement he'd stupidly signed. If he divorced Lydia, he left with only what he had brought into the marriage - a whole lot of nothing. Staying married to her any longer was just too horrible to contemplate. *Too bad she couldn't see fit to give me my due*, Carter bitterly mused.

Letting his eyes sweep over the house he felt his stomach clench in a knot. How he hated all the gilded opulence of it. He hated the pretentious artwork, fake Greek columns and marble floors. It was all gaudy beyond belief. Now that it was his he could sell it, lock, stock, and barrel, and move to a location with more class. Maybe he would buy a nice place on the beach in Boca Raton. Oh, or a rustic ski lodge in Aspen. *Hell, I might just have to buy a house in both locations*, he chuckled to himself. He couldn't help whistling as he strolled through the huge house, mentally labeling each item inside with a bright yellow 'for sale' tag.

Exhausted from the three-hour drive home, Carter used the house intercom to call back to the service area, ordering one of the staff to come draw him a bath in the big marble tub in Lydia's bathroom. When his wife was alive, he'd never been allowed access to her inner sanctum, they'd had separate rooms at opposite ends of the upper floor. Lydia would come to his room down the hall if she felt like being intimate, a rare occurrence Carter both dreaded and longed for in equal measure. Stalking into Lydia's bedroom he stripped off his clothes, tossing them on the floor. Strutting across the shiny marble floors of the oversized bathroom, he sank into the sweet-smelling bubble bath that had been run in the sunken tub. Picking up the French style phone on the shelf next to him he punched O for the operator, demanding someone connect him to the local real estate office he had scoped out early that month. *Time to unload this pathetic excuse for a home,* he smiled as his aching muscles began to respond to the steaming water.

*****

The next two days moved along at a snail's pace, keeping Carter Williams on edge, trying to move his plans forward without raising suspicions. He thought he had everything covered. Unbeknownst to him, fate was going to step in and blow all his carefully crafted plans right out of the water.

Chapter Twenty-eight

Friday morning found Carter Williams sitting impatiently in the offices of Caldwell & Caldwell, waiting to hear his late wife's will. The legal firm was one of those old school types with a short, but prestigious, client roster. They had overseen the affairs of the Jackson family for four generations. They took their jobs very seriously.

Carter was just starting to get miffed over his long wait in the outer office when a rail thin young woman stepped out of the inner sanctum, calling his name. She led him down a long corridor lined with thick royal blue carpet. Stopping outside a set of double doors labeled *Conference Room A* she rapped sharply one time. Carter did not hear a reply, but the woman must have as she pushed one of the doors open, gesturing for him to step inside.

The room held a ponderous table made of heavy oak, surrounded by six over-sized armchairs. A small microphone hung on a thin cord from the ceiling, dangling inches above the center of the table. Two men were already present at the far head of the table. Carter recognized the elder one as Michael Caldwell, second in command of the firm. He was the one who had handled the prenuptial agreement which Carter had reluctantly signed two days before his wedding. The other man was a stranger to Carter. *Probably some underling in training,* he reflected, immediately dismissing the man's presence.

Moving forward, Carter began to pull out the chair at the opposite end of the table but stopped when he heard a small cough. Looking up, he saw the younger man gesturing for him to take a seat across from him at their end of the room. Grumping under his breath about young upstarts, Carter took his time ambling up to take the other chair. He seated himself, ignoring the proffered hands of the two attorneys. "Let's get this over with," he snapped. "I have arrangements to make for the interment of my wife's body." Busy looking around the room, with an expression of boredom on his face, Carter didn't notice the look that passed between the two men. Their obvious loathing would have surprised him.

"Yes, let's get this out of the way," Michael Caldwell sourly said. "The will is quite simple, so this won't take up much of your time." Pulling a thin sheet of paper from a manila folder on the desk he cleared his throat and began to read... "I, Lydia Collette Jackson Williams, being of sound mind...."

Carter listened impatiently to the legalese required at the beginning of all wills. Trying to keep his face impassive, he crossed his legs, swinging a foot impatiently under the table.

"...do hereby bequeath the bulk of my estate to the love of my life – Too Foolish Jackson Williams, otherwise known as TooFoo. I direct the firm of Caldwell & Caldwell to hire the best-qualified person or persons to care for my darling TooFoo in his own home until he passes on from natural causes. Upon his death they will inherit what is left of the estate as payment for their services."   Mr. Caldwell smiled as he laid the document back down on the tabletop.

It took a moment for the words he had just heard to sink into Carter's head. The dog? She left everything to the dog? Carter figured he must have heard wrong. Of course, the dumb ditz probably left a considerable sum for the care of that horrid mutt, however, he doubted she was mean-spirited enough to leave it the entire estate. Looking at each of the men seated at the head of the table Carter cleared his throat and asked, "Could you read that last part again?"

"It's quite simple, Mr. Williams, the entire estate is now part of an irrevocable trust with the animal known as TooFoo being the sole beneficiary," Caldwell dryly said. "Oh, by the way, you have three days to vacate the premises."

"The dog? She left everything to that freaking dog?" Carter screeched, losing any semblance of calmness, shocked by what he had just heard. "That's ridiculous! No, no it's more like unlawful, that's what it is."   Pounding his fist on the table he roared even louder, "This will not stand gentlemen, it will not stand!"

"As I stated, Mr. Williams, it is an irrevocable trust. There is nothing you can do to change it," Caldwell declared with a smirk. He had never liked Carter and was extremely happy to see the man eviscerated.

"The hell there isn't," Carter roared. "That Will is the work of a lunatic. Yeah, that's right, a crazy loon. My attorney will tear that document to shreds."

"No, sir, he will not," Caldwell refuted. "Mrs. Williams anticipated just such a response from you. She saw a mental health specialist before even asking us to change the will. We have a copy of that exam right here. It was completed by a very reputable team of doctors only four months ago. The will is ironclad." Smiling across the table at Carter, Michael Caldwell added, "You have three days to leave the premises taking only what you originally brought to the marriage. Oh, and an extensive inventory was completed prior to the Will's preparation listing which items are legally yours, so be sure you are careful in what you choose to remove from the premises."

Carter spluttered. He squawked. He threatened. When none of that changed the demeanor of the man before him, Carter went berserk. He pounded the table. He screamed until he grew horse. Nothing persuaded the men to waver in their resolve to carry out Lydia's last request. When Carter finally grew silent, having dissolved into tears, Caldwell had one of the firm's security staff escort him from the building.

*****

Cursing under his breath, Carter raced back towards what he still considered to be his home. *I'll have to go back to the marina this afternoon and get that stupid mongrel,* he muttered, taking a curve so sharply his car almost slid off the road. Once TooFoo was in his possession it would be a simple matter for his attorney to declare him the dog's owner thereby giving him access to the trust. Racing through the entry gate of the estate and up the drive he came to a screeching halt in the circular driveway. He was surprised to see two strange vehicles already parked there. The staff knew all deliveries were to be sent round to the back of the house. Glancing at the offending vehicles, Carter noticed that one of them sported county law enforcement tags. *What the hell is going on here,* he mumbled as he made his way towards the front entrance. Before he could even place his hand on the latch the door swung open.

"Ah, Mr. Williams, you're back," a dark suited young man said. "I am James Stoneman from the law firm of Caldwell & Caldwell. I'm here to ensure your compliance with the terms of Lydia Williams Trust." He offered his hand for Carter to shake, but it was ignored. "Oh, and this is Deputy Edwards. He's here to offer assistance if it's needed," Stoneman added.

Carter blinked. This could not be happening. His brain jumped into overdrive scrambling for even a temporary solution. "Just what do you think you're doing inside my home?" he demanded. "I did not give you permission to enter."

"This is no longer your residence, sir," Stoneman calmly said. "You have to vacate the premises. Today would do nicely."

"According to my late wife's will, this house belongs to our darling pup, little TooFoo. Since I will be seeing to his needs, this still is my home," Carter stated. Puffing up his chest, he tried to push his way in the door.

Stoneman stopped him with a raised hand and a harsh glare. "We were informed by a member of your former staff that the dog is not here. That in fact, you gave the animal away."

"That's a boldfaced lie," sputtered Carter. "TooFoo is merely staying with friends while I dealt with some business matters. I will be bringing him home later today."

"Possession of the animal does not mean ownership is implied. Until a decision is made, by Caldwell & Caldwell as to who is best suited to care for the animal, you will not be staying in this house," Stoneman reiterated. "This officer will escort you to the master suit where you may remove your clothing. Since you brought nothing else of record into the home, that is all you will be allowed to take away."

"The Will said I had three days to pack up my things," Carter whined, unable to think of anything to prevent his being ousted from the home.

"When we realized the heir to the estate was no longer here, we felt it would be best if you vacated immediately," Stoneman coldly smiled. "Of course, if you prefer, we can have your things delivered to your new address. Which would be...?"

Since he didn't want the man to know he had no place else to go, Carter had no choice but to comply. Fuming and cursing, Carter packed up his clothing under the watchful eye of the deputy. When he tried to remove several items of jewelry from the wall safe the deputy refused to allow him access. Carter's angry screams brought Mr. Stoneman running. He reminded Carter that Lydia had paid for the jewelry items; they were, therefore, part of the estate. By the time Carter had crammed two large suitcases with clothing he was so angry he could barely speak. He stormed from the house, cursing Lydia, the dog, and every lawyer on the planet. Slamming his car door so hard the windows rattled, Carter screeched out of the driveway in a peel of burning rubber. Turning west at the end of the drive, he aimed his car for Penderschott's marina. Either he would get the damn dog back or he'd see to it that no one else could claim the estate by sheltering the foul little beast.

Chapter Twenty-nine

Jimmy and Janie arrived back at the marina leading a caravan of rag-tag vehicles filled with Isis and Bosco's friends. Mr. Penderschott was kept busy for over an hour assigning cottages and setting up tent camping areas to accommodate the influx of guests. Despite the circumstances that had brought them, he was thrilled to have the money their stay would bring. He just hoped they wouldn't be loudly partying all night or smoking anything illegal.

"We really appreciate you taking all these folks in on such short notice," Janie sweetly smiled as she handed over their credit card to cover another three days.

"Yeah, thanks," Jimmy grunted, when Janie elbowed him in the rib.

"Oh, that reminds me, Mr. Grayson, I have a rather odd message that came in for you," Penderschott said.

"Oh, what's that?" Jimmy absentmindedly mumbled, busy

checking names off the list Raven Night had thrust in his hand before they left the Commune. Jimmy wanted to be sure everyone was assigned quarters before he headed back to his own room.

"A lawyer fella named Caldwell called about that little dog you folks got in your room."

"What did he want with TooFoo?" Janie asked, leaning around her husband's shoulder to stare at Penderschott.

"Seems like that dead lady, Mrs. Williams, left it a pile of money or something in her will," Penderschott replied. "The lawyer wanted to know who had the dog. I told him you two did. He said he would be sending someone to talk to you later today. You're supposed to be sure the dog is here when he comes."

"That horrible Carter Williams told Isis and Bosco that they could have TooFoo," Janie said. "When he got them arrested, they asked us to take care of the poor little thing. I sure hope Carter doesn't think he's getting TooFoo back, he's a horrible man. He doesn't even like the dog."

"I already told that lawyer fella the very thing," Penderschott soothed. "Told him there were about a dozen witnesses that heard Carter Williams tell those hippie folks they could have that dog."

Thanking Mr. Penderschott for all his help, Jimmy and Janie hurried to their cottage to check on TooFoo. Janie was afraid someone might have come and snatched him while they were gone. The tiny dog was waiting for them at the door. He ran in excited circles round their feet, yipping happily. Janie scooped him up, hugging him fiercely and whispering that she wouldn't let mean old Carter near him ever again. Jimmy shook his head in consternation; this was all getting a bit crazy. Storms, a dead lady, dogs inheriting money, it was all just too crazy. Heaving a sigh of resignation, Jimmy figured he ought to go tell the others about this new turn of events. Letting Janie know where he was going, Jimmy went off to find Raven Night.

Chapter Thirty

It was almost dusk by the time Carter Williams came roaring into the parking lot of the Far-A-Way Shores Marina. He'd had to stop off and find a hotel room, since he was no longer allowed to live in the home he and Lydia had shared, and he'd given up his room at the marina. The whole idea of being booted out of his home in favor of some rescued mongrel left a bitter taste in his mouth. Even worse, he'd had to take a room at a flea bag motel out on the main highway, since he had no ready cash at his disposal. He wasn't sure if he could still use the credit cards in his wallet since they were all in Lydia's name, but he'd thrown caution to the wind using them to pay for the room. His situation only got more humiliating as the day wore on. Caldwell & Caldwell called to inform him that the car he was driving was part of the estate and would have to be returned. The Eagle Canyon Country Club called to inform him that his privileges had been revoked. Montfort and Sons, the custom tailor he used for all his clothing purchases, left a message on his voice mail that his new suits were ready, to the tune of three thousand dollars. That was three thousand dollars that Carter didn't have right now. If he didn't get the estate settled in his favor soon, it would spread all over town that he was a deadbeat loser.

The marina office had been closed for several hours by the time he arrived; only a small security lamp burned inside the entryway. Carter spent ten minutes banging on the door. Cursing under his breath he stormed off towards the line of cottages along the slough. Several of them were brightly lit and he knew one of them had to be harboring the mutt. Stopping at the first one, he pounded loudly on the door.

"Who the hell is making all that damn noise?" a bear of a voice roared from inside.

Carter took a step back not sure this was such a good idea. There was no way of knowing who was renting some of the cottages. Still, he needed the dog back, so he plastered a big smile on his face trying to appear small and harmless. Then he knocked again.

The door swung open revealing a man as bear-like in appearance as his booming voice. Stepping out onto the tiny porch, filling it to capacity, he glared down at Carter who had backed onto the narrow walkway that ran past the cottages. The man roared, "Waddaya want mister?"

"So sorry to disturb you, sir, but I seem to have lost my little dog. I was hoping you might have found him," Carter simpered. Thinking fast he quickly added, "There's a reward if you've found him."

"Ain't seen no dog," the man huffed, slamming the door in

Carter's face.

Gathering his resolve, Carter moved off to the next cottage in line. The woman who answered that door was dressed all in white, barefoot, and waving some sort of burning branch over her head. She glared at Carter, mumbling something about "Be gone evil spirit," before slamming the door in his face. Continuing down the row of cottages Carter met several more hostile guests. Soon there were only two cottages left. Carter knew the last one was empty, because it still displayed a ribbon of bright yellow crime scene tape across the front door. It was the one where that hippy couple had been staying. That meant the other cottage had to be those kids from the boat trip.

Knocking on the last cottage's door Carter was relieved to see a familiar face. It was that young man Timmy or Jimmy or something like that from the boat.

"Hello again," Carter cheerily smiled. "It's so good to see you. You haven't seen my wife's little dog, have you? I've come to take him home."

"No chance of that we been warned about you," Jimmy snorted in disgust. "That lawyer Caldwell told us no one was to take the dog. He's on his way to see us right now. You'd better leave."

The ingratiating smile vanished from Carter's face. "Look here you illiterate bumpkin, that dog is mine and I want him returned immediately. If you don't give him to me, I will be calling the authorities."

"Well, you go right ahead and do that, Mr. Williams, I'm sure they won't mind waiting to arrest me till that Caldwell fella gets here," Jimmy snapped. Then he, too, slammed the door in Carter's disbelieving face.

Back at his car, Carter called his personal attorney updating him on the Will and the situation with the mutt. He informed the man that a generous bonus would be his if he found a way to get Carter possession of the dog. Since the man was as sleazy as Carter himself, he readily agreed to investigate the matter.

Pulling up the directory on his cell phone, Carter skimmed the names until he found the one he needed -- Top Notch Investigations. Though he had found the company to be less than their name implied, he also knew they did anything for a buck. When the owner, Buddy Green, answered, Carter laid out his alternate plan for gaining possession of TooFoo. If Green could snatch the dog without getting caught, there would be a hefty reward when he returned the 'lost' animal to its rightful owner. Buddy said he'd need to make a few calls. Carter told him the sooner the matter was settled the more he'd be willing to pay. Buddy said he'd get back to him before noon the next day. Carter felt slightly less queasy after talking to the two men. If anyone could help him, they could.

Then he got another brilliant idea. Hoping out of his car he raced over to the pay phone by the marina entrance. Quickly looking up a number in the directory that hung there from a heavy silver chain, he made another call.

After close to a dozen rings a woman answered,

screeching into his ear. "Daily Inquisitor how may I direct your call?" Holding a handkerchief over his mouth, Carter mumbled into the phone "Breaking news desk." When a man barked "What?" into his ear, Carter quickly stammered out his "breaking news" then hung up before the reporter could ask any questions. Smiling, he slunk back to his car feeling better than he had in days. He was sure that one of his three plans would gain him possession of the mutt, which would in turn guarantee he'd get all of Lydia's estate.

Chapter Thirty-one

"Is he still out there?" Janie whispered to her husband.

Jimmy peeked out the side of the blinds spying Carter's car still in the lot. "He's sitting there talking on his phone."

"Oh, Jimmy, I sure hope Raven can work out a plan to protect TooFoo," Janie softly cried. "You know that if Carter gets his hands on him, he'll do something awful."

"Raven will be here as soon as that jerk Carter leaves. We don't want him to know we have help at least not yet," Jimmy soothed. He kept his eyes glued to the parking lot waiting for Carter to drive off. As soon as he did, Jimmy sprinted off to get Raven.

Seconds after Jimmy left, Janie heard a knock at the door. She knew it couldn't be her husband because he hadn't been gone long enough to be returning already. Terrified that Carter had come back she grabbed up TooFoo and hid in the bathroom. Someone knocked again at the door, the old lock loudly rattling.

Janie ignored whoever it was hunkering down in the tub with the shower curtain pulled. The knocking continued. Finally, a voice called out asking if anyone was home. It was not Carter Williams. Janie left TooFoo in the tub nested in a pile of towels and went cautiously out to open the door.

"Hello, young lady, you must be Mrs. Grayson," the man on the stoop smiled. "I'm Mr. Stoneman, from Caldwell & Caldwell," he added, offering her his hand in greeting.

"You got any ID?"

Stoneman jumped nervously almost stepping backward off the stoop. Spinning around he stared at the people who had quietly snuck up behind him.

"He looks like a lawyer," Raven Night said, taking in the man's dark suit, shiny shoes, and pin-striped tie.

Stoneman pulled his wallet from his pocket showing them his driver's license and his bar association card.

Satisfied that he was who he purported to be, Janie invited him inside. Jimmy and Raven followed, taking seats on the edge of the bed. Three pair of eyes stared at the young lawyer making him feel a bit uncomfortable. Taking a minute to lay his briefcase down on the coffee table, and fumble inside, he pulled out a manilla folder.

"First of all, I have to see the dog to be sure he is actually the one addressed in the late Lydia Williams' will."

Janie hopped up and went to fetch TooFoo from the bathroom. She sat the tiny animal on top of the coffee table. "Here he is," she announced, one hand resting protectively on the small animal's back.

"Good, Lord," Stoneman gasped. "That is one ugly mutt."

TooFoo's ears perked up. He looked Stoneman up and down as if taking his measure. Evidently, he decided he didn't like what he saw and began loudly yapping. The hair along his back stood on end as he slowly edged back towards the safety of Janie's arms.

Stoneman laughed nervously. "Feisty little thing, ain't he." Then he pulled a photo from the folder, holding it up next to TooFoo, carefully comparing the now growling dog with the one in the picture.

"He has a collar and tag, but I took it off to bathe him and forgot to put it back on," Janie rambled. "He really is that dead lady's dog."

Stoneman smiled at her. "I can see from the photo comparison that this is indeed TooFoo. It would be impossible for another dog to look anything like this one. He is quite an odd-looking little thing."

Everyone stared at TooFoo. He was indeed an unusual looking animal. Weighing only four pounds, his legs were thin as toothpicks. They looked barely able to hold up his rotund little body. His head was bulbous in the back, narrow in the front, and sported two extremely large fur tufted ears. There was evidence of Yorkshire terrier in the long silky hair that draped his frame, but instead of the traditional two-tone shade usually displayed by that breed, TooFoo was a rusty reddish brown. Snaggle-toothed, bow-legged, bug-eyed and with a whining bark that sounded like a broken wind- up toy, he presented an image only a true dog person could love.

"So, what's going on? Why did you need to talk to us about TooFoo?" Jimmy asked, bringing everyone's attention back to Stoneman.

The lawyer pulled a single slim document from the manila folder laying it down on the table. Turning it so the bold lettering at the top faced the young couple and their lady friend he waited for their reaction. All three leaned forward to look at the bold printing at the top of the page – Last Will and Testament of Lydia Collette Jackson Williams. Stoneman plucked up the paper before they could read further. Handing it to Jimmy he watched the young man's face go from a scowl to a look of consternation. Jimmy passed the document to his wife. Her face soon registered the same look of shock as her husband's. Finally, the other woman glanced at the will. She too looked stunned by what she had read.

"Am I correct in my information that Carter Williams gave the dog known as Too Foolish Jackson Williams, or TooFoo, to you?" Stoneman asked.

"Um, not exactly," Janie replied. "He tossed it out in the parking lot when we got back here from the cruise. Our friend Isis Winters was horrified and offered to take the dog. Carter told her to go ahead, that he didn't want the mutt. He said she could have him."

"And is this the same Isis Winters who has been accused of Lydia Williams' death?" Stoneman asked.

"She did not kill that woman!" all three yelled in unison.

"Please, please! Let me rephrase the question," Stoneman quickly pleaded. "Is Ms. Winters currently incarcerated?"

Janie began to cry, burying her face in Jimmy's shoulder. Jimmy looked at the lawyer as if he wanted to tear his head off. "Yes, she's in jail, along with her husband Bosco. That lying bastard Carter Williams saw to that."

"When they got arrested, did they say anything about the dog?" Stoneman prodded.

"What do you mean?" Jimmy countered.

"Did Isis Winters mention the dog before she was taken away?" Stoneman calmly asked.

Scratching his head Jimmy replied, "Yeah, but I don't know why you need to know what she told us." Janie nudged Jimmy with an elbow, encouraging him to continue. "Isis told us to look after TooFoo. We told her we would. Is that what you meant?"

Stoneman flashed them a brilliant smile "Yes, young man, that's exactly what I meant. For all legal intents and purposes, you and your wife are now the temporary guardians of the heir to Lydia Williams' estate."

Jimmy and Janie sat wide-eyed, stunned into silence by the lawyers' words. Raven managed a muffled "Oh, my God" before TooFoo began running around the tabletop barking madly. It was as if he understood what the lawyer had said and was thrilled to have become a millionaire.

Before leaving, Stoneman suggested that taking the dog

back to Lydia's estate to be cared for by the servants might be the wisest choice. Janie became almost hysterical at the thought of TooFoo being turned over to someone else. She stubbornly stated that she had made Isis and Bosco a promise to look after THEIR dog, and she intended to keep that promise. Stoneman told her it might be better for the dog to be in familiar surroundings. Jimmy told Stoneman he could stuff it if he thought anyone was taking the dog anywhere without Isis Winter's permission.

"The woman is in jail accused of murdering that dog's owner," Stoneman said. "If Carter Williams has a good enough attorney, he might be able to get custody of the animal. You wouldn't want that, would you?"

"That slime ball shows his face anywhere near us and I'll put his lights out," Jimmy roared.

"You're not listening to reason, young man," Stoneman huffed.

"No one is taking TooFoo from us, no one!" Janie sobbed. "I promised Isis, I gave her my word."

Before things got any more out of hand, Raven interceded with the suggestion that Jimmy, Janie and TooFoo join her at the commune. She told them that a vet lived there, along with a dozen members of a local animal rights group. When Jimmy and Janie had to go off to work TooFoo would be lovingly cared for and quite safe from those who might wish to harm him. After making a quick call to his office, Stoneman agreed with the plan. Jotting down contact information from everyone there, he left feeling confident that the small animal would be properly cared for until his ownership could be proven. Heading back to the office he daydreamed about the big bonus he would be getting by the time this case was over. He'd handled enough estate settlements to know this one was not going to be resolved overnight. Visions of billable hours danced through his head.

While Jimmy and Janie got their things packed, Raven made a quick phone call. Isis and Bosco's young friends would need all the help they could get. Since the commune had been a part of the local community for over thirty years, they had made a lot of valuable contacts. There were favors owed, and Raven was calling those folks to task.

By the end of the day, TooFoo and friends were ensconced in a quaint three-room A-frame at the Sunshine Commune. The entire community had been informed that a friend, needing protection from a 'bad parent' was staying on the grounds. Everyone went into alert mode. No strangers would be allowed into the commune without a thorough search and a damn good reason for being there. Lookouts were strategically hidden around the perimeter to see that no unwanted guests got inside. That night, Jimmy and Janie slept soundly for the first time in days.

Chapter Thirty-two

At breakfast the next morning Raven gave everyone unwelcome news. TooFoo's story was on the front page of the trashy tabloid, *The Daily Inquisitor*. The headline screamed in bold black letters **"Woman Leaves Estate to Beloved Pet Who Mysteriously Vanished."** The brief article told of Lydia's death, Isis's arrest on suspicion of murdering her, and that TooFoo, heir to the Williams' estate, was missing. It went on to say that the paper would run an exclusive interview with the woman's grieving husband in their next edition. In fine print at the very bottom of the story it stated there was a reward for return of the dog, or information that led to its return, 'no questions asked.'

"You know damn well it was that rat bastard Carter who tipped them off," Jimmy exploded. "What the hell do we do now?"

"First, we stay calm," Raven cautioned. "Mr. Stoneman knows you and TooFoo are here at the commune. No one will let anything happen to you or that darling pup."

Janie shook her head. "This is all pretty scary stuff. Jimmy and I have never been involved in anything criminal." Wrapping her arms protectively around her body she closed her eyes for a moment before asking, "Do you think we should tell Isis and Bosco what's going on?"

"I'll get a message to them today. I had already planned on visiting the jail with our attorney, Jay Woods," Raven replied. "You two need to get back to your regular routine. Go to work, live your life and don't worry about a thing."

"I won't stop worrying until Isis and Bosco are out of jail," Janie lamented. "How can anyone think she's guilty?"

"It's easy to misjudge people who are different from the norm," Raven smiled. "Trust me, Isis and Bosco are going to be just fine." TooFoo gave a loud snort, shaking himself all over. Raven reached down to sweep him up in her arms, nuzzling the top of his head. "See, even TooFoo isn't worried anymore."

When Carter Williams glanced at the stack of newspapers lining the check-out lane at the Quick Stop Market his face split into a grin. It would be only a matter of time before that stupid mutt was handed back to him, along with all of his late wife's beautiful money. Adding a copy of the paper to his take-out coffee and muffin he gave the young clerk a brilliant smile. "Glorious day, isn't it?" he said scooping up his change.

Chapter Thirty-three

Sheriff King was at his wits end that morning dealing with Bosco Blue and Isis Winters. They refused to eat, flinging anything they were offered on the floor. At least they were still drinking water which was a good sign at this point. The constant chanting though was getting on everyone's nerves, and King didn't have a clue how to get them to stop. When a deputy came to tell him that several carloads of oddly dressed people had just pulled up in the parking lot, he groaned out loud. All he could think was *why me?* Before he could even walk out front to assess the situation for himself, he heard shouts of "free the innocent" ringing out from the parking area.

Glancing out the front windows, King saw over thirty people marching in a circle around the parking lot carrying signs, yelling at the top of their lungs. Grabbing up a bullhorn he stepped out to face the mob. "You folks need to disperse," he bellowed.

The marchers just yelled louder. As they passed the front entrance of the building, they raised their signs, angrily waving them in the air.

Sheriff King didn't want to inflame the situation, but he couldn't have them disrupting business all day long either. He thought things over for a moment before stepping forward.

"Folks, can't we negotiate a truce?" he yelled.

The marchers stopped in their tracks. A tall dark-haired woman in a flowing paisley dress came forward accompanied by a short man in a faded three-piece suit and red high-top sneakers.

"I'm Raven Night," the woman smiled. "This is Jay Woods, legal representative for the members of the Lasting Sunshine Free People's Commune. We wish to discuss the illegal incarceration of Bosco Blue and Isis Winters."

"Come on in and we'll talk," Sheriff King sighed. "I'm sure we can reach an equitable solution to this situation."

After settling Ms. Raven and her attorney, Jay Woods, in his office, Sheriff King offered them coffee, which they declined. He pulled out the arrest reports for Bosco and Isis, shoving them across the desk for Mr. Woods to read. Settling back in his chair he waited to hear what they had to say after reading the reports.

"What further evidence do you have against my clients?" Woods asked as he tossed the report back on the desktop.

"Well, as far as I can tell they aren't your clients yet," Sheriff King replied. "Would you like to speak with them before continuing our conversation?"

"Oh, but they are my clients, sir. Everyone who chooses to live at or work for the commune agrees to be represented by me in case of any legal troubles," Woods stated. "So, let's get on with this. Bosco Blue has only been charged with a misdemeanor offense of resisting arrest. Why hasn't he been released yet?"

"Because he's refused to cooperate with us, that's why," snapped King. "He and his wife are on a hunger strike, chanting and refusing to respond to any of our questions or procedures."

"If you will direct me to a conference room and bring in my clients, I will get the situation resolved," Woods confidently said.

Sheriff King took the attorney to an empty interrogation room, instructing a deputy to go get the prisoners. He told the Deputy to be sure to inform the pair that their attorney, Mr. Woods, was here to see them.

Bosco and Isis were elated to see their friends. After exchanging brief hugs, they quickly got down to business. Their first concern was about Jimmy, Janie and TooFoo. When they learned what had been happening since they'd been jailed, they were stunned. Raven told them about Carter's underhanded attempts to get the dog back. She assured Isis that TooFoo was safely hidden away at the commune. Then she handed her a copy of the *Inquisitor*. Isis was horrified to see herself portrayed in the press as a murderer, even if it was just a tabloid rag. They all figured it wouldn't be long before the regular papers and local news stations picked up on the story. Having taken possession of the tiny dog from Carter only made Isis look even guiltier. People would assume she'd had a motive for doing away with Lydia Williams - all that money. They wouldn't care about the fact that Isis had only met the woman when they all took that fateful river cruise.

"Bosco, we need to get you bonded out today," Raven said. "We'll need your help in dealing with Lydia's attorneys."

"What about Isis?" Bosco demanded. "Can't you get her released, too?"

"Now that may prove to be a little more difficult," Woods sighed. "She's being held on a capital offense. What I can do is demand that a Grand Jury be convened as soon as possible. They can then ascertain if there is enough evidence to hold her over for trial, but that's the best I can do at this point."

"I don't want to leave her here all alone," Bosco adamantly said. "We've never been apart for even a day in the last thirty years. It just ain't right."

"Honeybear, they'll need you to help plan strategy," Isis smiled patting her husband on the arm. "I'll be fine. You know I will."

After much grumbling on Bosco's part, they all finally agreed that getting him out would be a boon to their cause. Jay Woods stepped to the door calling out for Sheriff King.

"Here are my clients' terms," Woods said as soon as the sheriff walked through the door. "Bosco will pay his fine and be released today. You'll notify the District Attorney that we want a Grand Jury seating as soon as possible to determine if there is sufficient evidence against Miss Winters to warrant a trial. My clients agree to abide by the rules for Miss Winters' continued incarceration. Does that sound acceptable?"

"That sounds more than reasonable," Sheriff King sighed with relief.

Several hours later Bosco was a free man. Fiercely hugging his wife, he promised to come back for her as soon as he could. He left with the group from the commune, still unhappy about the enforced separation from his spouse. Isis kept her part of the bargain, returning quietly to her cell and accepting her lunch tray with a smile.

Chapter Thirty-four

Carter Williams carefully prepared for his second interview with the reporter from the *Daily Inquisitor*. Dressed in a drab black suit, his tie undone, scuffed loafers on his feet -- he looked the epitome of a grieving husband. His hair was tousled, his face unshaven, his eyes red rimmed and watery. He had found that a bit of soap worked wonders if applied to the edge of one's eyes. He had placed pictures of Lydia and the mutt on the nightstand next to the bed. The frame draped with a length of black ribbon. When the knock came on the door to his motel room, he was ready. Slowly opening the door, Carter swiped at his still watering eyes, snuffling loudly. "Oh, it's you," he sighed, ushering the reporter and camera operator inside.

Meanwhile, at the Caldwell law offices, James Stoneman was busy bringing his bosses up to speed on the Williams estate situation. Not only had he spoken with the young people caring for the dog named Lydia's heir, but he had also canvassed the marina. He had ten affidavits from witnesses who had heard Carter Williams tell Isis Winters that she could have TooFoo. He also had three statements confirming Ms. Winters' comment to the Grayson couple about them taking care of the dog in her absence. He had worked well past midnight, all billable hours of course, researching Isis Winters and her husband Bosco Blue. The file on them was not only extensive, but extremely helpful. Stoneman had learned that they were both animal rights activists, ran a successful farming operation, and had rescued dozens of stray animals, many of whom had been given a home with the couple, living to ripe old ages.

"Excuse the impertinence, but if this Winters person is the legal owner of the dog now, how does that help our law firm?" Stoneman curiously asked his bosses.

"As executors of Lydia Williams' will and holder of the trust, we earn a handsome annual fee for overseeing that trust, that is, if we are allowed to continue representing the estate in legal matters. Now that we know the background of this Winters woman and her husband, we can see that they will surely have need of our continued services." Mike Caldwell smugly added, "Just think of all the lovely billable hours that will be needed to reassure them that little TooFoo's money is being wisely looked after."

"Sounds like you've thought of everything, Mr. Caldwell," Stoneman patronized. He smiled broadly, already planning on how he could continue to be part of those expensive billable hours. "Have you heard anything from Carter Williams or his legal counsel since he was booted off the estate?"

Michael Caldwell frowned with distaste. "No, we have not,

but I'm sure it's just a matter of time before we do. The man will not take the loss of such a rich prize lightly; he'll fight tooth and nail to get it back. Since I believe it is in the best interest of this firm to deal with the dog's new owners, we will just have to distance ourselves from Carter Williams, and stay one step ahead of his attorney."

Chapter Thirty-five

Buddy Green had been camped beneath a stand of oaks just down the road from the Sunshine Commune all morning. The place was swarming like a busy hive. People were working in the gardens, plowing fields, and cleaning out animal pens. A small group of women were busy hanging laundry on long rope lines. About a dozen children were running around the main building area, darting in and out of houses at random. As for the dog he was supposed to find - he hadn't caught even a glimpse. He had heard barking earlier, but it sounded as though several animals were contributing to the mayhem. Figuring he'd have to wait until nightfall to sneak onto the grounds, he left to get himself some breakfast at the café down the road. Carter Williams had assured him that any reasonable expenses he incurred trying to get this stupid dog back would be covered, and Buddy figured breakfast counted as one of those expenses.

The Dew Drop Café was one of those deceptive hole-in-the-wall places, the exterior a bit shabby, the interior outdated, with no specific decorating style. Mismatched wooden chairs, painted sunny shades of yellow stood round an equally odd assortment of tables. Red and white checked oilcloths tried to make them match. Mason jars filled with autumn leaves graced each one while sparkling cut glass shakers held the usual assortment of condiments. Homemade wooden holders painted with glittering blue raindrops kept the menus readily at hand. The daily special was chalked on a board by the front door. Buddy Green knew that the food would be simple homestyle cooking, but that was just the sort of food he enjoyed. This was the kind of place where the locals tended to linger after a meal, free refills of coffee and local gossip keeping them in their seats.

The scruffy man who jangled the bell over the front door of the Dew Drop at nine that morning was a stranger. The locals had been given a heads up on the situation with Isis and Bosco, so the stranger was heavily scrutinized. Every eye in the place watched him take a seat at the only empty table by the front door. Stopping at the man's table, server Rose Night smiled, asking if he'd had a long drive. The man just mumbled at her that he wanted coffee. He pulled a menu up in front of his face not bothering to even look up at her. When she brought his coffee over, he barked out an order for ham and eggs, telling her to "leave off the damn grits."

Still smiling Rose told him, "Okey-dokey." Moving back behind the main counter, she gave a nod to a group of men sitting in one of the side booths.

Hoping he was right, that the food tasted better than the run-down place looked, Buddy Green gazed morosely out the front window. He hated taking jobs like this one, dog napping was a new low even for him. Still, Carter had promised him a hefty fee for the dog's return, and he desperately needed the money. It looked like his current wife, number three, was serious about wanting a divorce. Though he didn't have much, Buddy knew she'd still want half of everything. Lost in thought he didn't notice the group of men approaching his table. Suddenly they were just there, swarming around him like angry bees. They snagged the three chairs around the table pushing them closer, pressing him up against the plate glass window.

"Howdy, Mister, what ya doing here?" the one with a thick black beard asked, having squeezed uptight against Buddy.

"Look, I don't want no trouble. Just stopped to get breakfast," Buddy nervously replied. "Just passing through."

"He just stopped for some breakfast," the man snorted to his friends. "Wrong answer, mister. Lots of folks seen your car sitting out on Willow Hollow Road since sun rise."

"Like I said, I'm just passing through. Just passing on down the road. Don't know the names of the roads around here though, so I got a bit lost," Buddy rambled. He smiled, trying to look like he was still a bit confused. "Figured I'd have some grub, ask directions, and be on my way."

"Thing is, mister, you were seen out that way by a lot of people. They all saw ya at a different time of morning, too. Long time to be lost in one spot." The man leaned into Buddy, pressing him tighter against the window. "You know someone who lives out this way?"

"I told you, I'm just passing through. Was looking at leaves and stuff, that's all," Buddy muttered.

"That right?" the man asked, moving his face to within an inch of Buddy's. "Ya wouldn't have been looking for a little doggie, now would ya?"

Buddy began to sweat. *How the hell do they know I'm looking for the dog*, he wondered. "I'm just going to eat my breakfast and be on my way," he quietly said. His head was beginning to ache from being scrunched up against the window. All he wanted to do was leave in one piece. "Don't think I'll be back this way again any time soon," he added with what he hoped was a reassuring smile.

The big man patted Buddy's head, rocking it as if it were one of those bobble head dolls. Then he smiled, pushing back his chair, getting to his feet. He gave the other men a nod, they all stood, moseyed back to the other side of the room where they resumed their seats glaring angrily back at him.

Buddy eased upright, softly cursing small town busy bodies. Grumbling under his breath about *"inbred rednecks not minding their own business"* he jumped when the waitress slapped a platter of food down in front of him. He mumbled a thank you, waiting for the young woman to walk away before digging into his food. He sprinkled a dash of salt and a bit of pepper on his eggs, irritated to see that they had gotten his order wrong. A butter drenched mound of grits glistened next to his slice of ham. He scraped the pile of wet corn goop off his plate into an empty coffee mug from the place setting beside him, leaving a slime trail of butter in its wake. Shoveling up a mouthful of eggs his eyes bulged, and he began to choke. They were so salty his tongue felt pickled. Gagging, he spit them out, gulping the last of his coffee trying to get the taste out of his mouth. He heard loud rings of laughter from across the room. Grabbing up the check, he raced over to the cash register, paid the bill, and dashed for the door. *These folks are scary, damn scary*, he mumbled as he headed for his car. He decided that if Carter Williams wanted that dumb mutt back, he could come get it himself. Even though the recovery fee was a good one it wasn't enough to warrant taking a beat down. Buddy squealed out of the parking lot without a backward glance.

"Dang, that fella didn't eat his delicious breakfast," Rose Night chuckled to her friends. "Wonder why he was in such a hurry? He even forgot to leave me a tip. Now that is just rude. Gee, you don't think it was something we said, do you?" The entire café roared with laughter.

Chapter Thirty-six

Bosco was mostly silent on the drive back from the jail, lost in his own thoughts. He hated leaving Isis behind even though he knew she was fully capable of holding her own. Still, it seemed strange not to have her sitting at his side. They had been together for so long it felt as if he were only half a person without her. She was right though about the others needing him to help mount her defense and protect TooFoo. He still couldn't believe that crazy Lydia Williams had left her entire estate to the dog. Bosco didn't really care about the money. He and Isis had never been into material things. Although, he could think of a lot of worthy causes it could be used for at the commune. He did care deeply about Isis, and in turn the dog, because she had grown attached to the ugly little yapper. At least she'd have someone to console her if those medical tests he'd had came back showing what he feared they would.

When they arrived at the commune Bosco couldn't help but smile. The place had always been a haven, but now it offered more than just its usual brand of welcome. The folks here guaranteed the safety of all those who lived within its confines. No amount of pressure or bribery from Carter Williams would make any of them betray their friends.

Bosco could see that new safety measures were already in place. He spotted his friend Creek up the old walnut tree by the main gate, crossbow in hand. Not too many people would have noticed the man, but Bosco did. He also found the other three members of the commune's security group hugging treetops on each end of the compound. Though the people living here preferred peaceful resolutions to situations they could, and would, use force to protect their loved ones. Jimmy, Janie and TooFoo were in the safest place possible.

Speak of the devil, Bosco softly chuckled to himself, spotting Janie racing towards them, TooFoo tucked up in her arms. A glowing smile lit the young woman's face when she saw Bosco step out of the lead vehicle. She ran to bear hug him as usual, jabbering on and on about all that had been happening.

"Glad to see you too, kid," Bosco beamed. "Yeah, and you too, ya mutt," he laughed, knuckle rubbing the little dog's head, which got TooFoo whining and drooling with pleasure. "Let's get to pow-wowing, I want my wife home as soon as possible. Raven, call in the troops."

Raven Night let out an ear-splitting whistle that could be heard all over the commune. Soon there was a crowd of people all yelling in delight at the sight of Bosco standing there a free man. After much hugging and backslapping the group moved off to the main dining hall.

The men up in the trees turned their eyes back to the

road, keeping careful watch for anything suspicious.

Chapter Thirty-seven

Carter Williams was so angry with Buddy Green that all he could do was sputter at him. Not only had the man not retrieved the stupid dog, but he had just told Carter he was quitting.

"I'm not paying you a dime," Carter bellowed.

"That's fine by me. Ain't no amount of money worth going up against that group of whack jobs," Buddy barked back. He hated how things had soured on this job. He didn't want to lose Carter as a client, since he had so few. If only he could think of a way to get that stupid dog back without putting himself in harm's way. Suddenly a name popped into his head - Josh Groder. Even though Buddy did stuff a bit on the shady side occasionally for the most part he was an honest guy. But Josh Groder...now there was a man who would do anything for a buck. He was even sleazier than Carter. Though Groder wasn't the brightest crayon in the box, once on a job, he was tenacious. Buddy quickly told Carter about Groder, and for a hundred bucks gave up Groder's cell number. He thought about calling Groder himself, asking for a referral fee, but decided cutting his loses and walking away unscathed was the better choice. Something about the whole deal had the hairs on the nape of his neck standing up – a sure sign of trouble.

When Buddy got back to his office at the strip mall, he carefully removed every reference to Carter Williams from his office files. He called his sister Louise to cat sit his feline pal Rusty, telling her he was going on vacation for a few weeks. Better to be safe than sorry. This whole mess looked like it might just blow up in Carter's face. Buddy didn't want to be around when it did.

*****

Carter Williams got a chill down his spine talking to Josh Groder, the man Buddy Green had recommended he call to get TooFoo back. The man sounded like the kind of guy who would eat broken glass just for fun. However, Carter needed that damn dog back and soon. He promised Groder that he would leave $500.00 and a picture of TooFoo at the front desk of the South Side Motel out on Highway 20 by noon. The guy said if the money wasn't there as promised, he'd be around to see Carter to collect it. "A promise is a promise," he'd rumbled at Carter, before hanging up with a growl.

Carter checked his dwindling stash of cash before dashing off with barely a minute to spare. He did not want to test Josh Groder's resolve.

Chapter Thirty-eight

Jay Woods looked like an unsuccessful street front lawyer, the kind who chased ambulances to make an easy buck. His suits were off the rack, usually bought on sale, and he always wore them with his favorite high top red sneakers. Shorter than average, with a roly-poly shape, he wore suspenders rather than a belt for the sheer comfort they afforded. Busy to the point of distraction, he often forgot to get his hair trimmed so it dusted his shoulders and straggled over his ears. He looked as if he barely had two nickels to rub together. Having a generally cheerful disposition kept a smile on his face, which made him appear a bit dimwitted. That misconception on the part of his opponents served him well. In the top ten percent of his graduating class from Yale, he boasted both a genius IQ and a keen sense of morality. Having inherited a generous trust fund from his maternal grandfather he didn't have to worry about things like billable hours or political correctness. Most of his expertise was used on behalf of several environmental groups. He kept other clients, like the Sunshine Commune, simply because he liked what they stood for - freedom.

Arriving at the District Attorney's office precisely at nine, Jay charmed the receptionist into listing him first on the morning agenda. His natural clumsiness and downtrodden appearance brought out the mothering instinct in most females, and this woman was no exception. Sitting on the edge of one of the hard leather chairs, Jay clutched his brief case to his chest, an angelic smile plastered on his chubby face.

When District Attorney Mark Casten arrived at work, gliding through the front doors at a quarter past nine, he barely noticed the man in the wrinkled suit. Barking an order for coffee to his secretary he sailed through to his office. A moment later the nice young woman at the reception desk told Jay he could go back.

"Good morning, sir," Jay called out as he popped his head in Casten's door. "How are you this fine morning?" he added, precariously balancing two cups of coffee in his left hand.

"Who the devil are you?" Casten snapped.

Continuing to smile Jay replied, "I am Jay Woods, legal counsel for Isis Winters. We need to talk about convening a Grand Jury as soon as possible. My innocent client does not deserve to spend one more day than is necessary incarcerated."

Casten glared at the man. "I don't remember having your name on my appointment list for today. And I don't know who this Isis Winters person is supposed to be."

"The lovely young woman out front penciled me in," Jay cheerily replied. "As for Isis Winters, she is in jail on the charge of murdering Lydia Williams. She's totally innocent of course, so we need to get her released as soon as possible."

Accepting one of the coffee mugs from Jay Woods, Casten tried to recall the particulars of the Williams case. Motioning for Jay to take a seat, he pulled a thin folder from the thick stack of files on his desktop. Looking over the enclosed papers about the arrest, his memory of the case sharpened. As far as he was concerned it was a done deal; the woman was guilty.

"It looks like we have motive, access and witnesses," Casten stated. "Seems cut and dried to me. Did you want to talk about a plea bargain?"

"No, Mr. Casten, I did not," Jay firmly stated. "The evidence is circumstantial at best. The witness statements are not definitive. And the motive is pure speculation."

"So, a plea bargain is out of the question?"

"Yes. My client is not guilty."

"The District Attorney's office would be willing to accept a plea of involuntary manslaughter with a minimum sentence."

"No, thank you. My client is innocent," Jay Woods stubbornly reiterated.

Remembering some of the water cooler gossip he'd heard over the years about Woods, Casten sighed in resignation. The man was a bulldog when he sank his teeth into a case. "Well, let me call Judge Andrews then, see how soon he can convene the Grand Jury. I'll have someone call your office once the date is set."

"When can I expect all materials and statements pertinent

to the case for review?" Jay countered.

"If you can wait a few moments, I'll have my secretary give you copies of everything we have so far." When Jay nodded. Casten buzzed the front and asked for copies of everything in the file.

Thanking him for his time, Jay shook Casten's hand. Shuffling back out to the reception area he took a seat once again on the uncomfortable leather chair. The same smiling secretary brought him a fresh jelly donut and more coffee. Jay thanked her profusely, he loved jelly donuts.

Chapter Thirty-nine

The money was exactly where it was supposed to be which made Josh Groder a happy man. Studying the picture of the dog he had been hired to grab, he grunted. The thing was butt ugly. He wondered why anybody would want it in the first place, let alone be willing to pay $2,500 to get it back. Rich folks were just too damn weird. What the hell it didn't matter if the dude was crazy nabbing the dog would be easy money. Josh hopped into his battered old pickup truck heading off to find the Sunshine Commune. He'd already put a pillowcase, a box of dog biscuits, and his nickel plated 45 in a duffle bag stowed behind the front seat. Turning on the radio, he whistled along to a Waylon Jennings tune about mommas and cowboys. *Yupper, it's gonna be a frigging nice day,* he smiled.

The traffic on the main road that ran past the Sunshine Commune was heavier than usual that morning. The place had been easy enough for Josh to find. Folks back down the road at this little diner had told him how to get out here. They'd been a bit closed mouth when he'd first walked in, but his dimwitted country boy act soon won them over. Though he didn't have an honest bone in his body, Josh did have the face of an angel. Thick golden blond hair fell to his shoulders in soft curls. Baby blue eyes fringed with thick lashes gave him a wide-eyed expression. Though his lumbering gait seemed awkward, it belied an underlying cat like grace. Broad shouldered and barrel-chested with muscles honed by heavy labor jobs, Josh Groder was not a man to mess with unless you had a death wish. Josh had limitations, but he knew what they were and had learned early on in life to compensate for them. He wasn't the smartest guy around, but he possessed something far more valuable than brains to a man in his line of work - he was a born liar. Josh Groder could not only tell the most complicated lies one could imagine, but he was able to remember them and keep them all straight never forgetting who he told what, an invaluable tool for a criminal to possess.

Some girl named Rose at the diner had fallen for his act right away. He'd bumped into her on the way in the door, 'accidentally' spilling the tray she carried. He'd stammered, stuttered, blushed, and dropped to his knees trying to clean up the mess. She had patted his arm, cooing that it was all right, she'd get it. When she came to take his order, he had quietly asked about the commune. The girl's face had gone perfectly still. She'd asked him why he wanted to know about the place. He'd hesitantly given her the story he'd thought up before leaving his house, stammering and stuttering as if embarrassed to tell it to a stranger.

"My grandmother lived there years ago when it first

started," Josh told the girl. "Now she's very ill, not long to live, and wants pictures of the place." He'd been slick enough to stop and buy a cheap camera at a discount mall along the way. Picking it up, he'd waved it under the waitress's nose. "I promised her I'd come take some photos, ask around and see if any of her old friends still live there."

The girl had looked a bit wary asking him for his grandmother's name.

"Shirley Wagner," Josh told her. "But everyone called her Sunshine." It had been easy enough to dig up the name of the commune's founding member on the internet. Shirley Wagner had mysteriously disappeared years ago so there was no chance Josh would run into her. The name worked wonders as the girl waiting on him had gasped aloud, taking a step backward. Then she began babbling on and on about her mother and how she was always talking about Sunshine. Seems no one had known where Sunshine had gone when she left the commune. The server asked Josh if he knew that the commune was named after his grandmother. He acted all surprised, started stammering and blushing again. After that, it was like taking candy from a baby. The girl had not only told him how to get to the place but had added a free stack of pancakes to his breakfast order.

Turning down the road the girl had told him about, Josh saw a row of brightly colored buildings up ahead. People were wandering around all over the place. Kids, dogs, goats, and a bunch of chickens all running wild from one grassy spot to another. Josh hoped it wasn't going to be too hard to find the Williams mutt before someone caught on that he really didn't know anyone named Sunshine.

"Hello! Welcome to the Lasting Sunshine Free People's Commune," a group of young women called out. They waved to Josh as they walked off down a narrow dirt path that disappeared behind a thick stand of pine trees. Josh assumed their friendly tone was due to the woman at the diner calling ahead to tell people he was coming. He hoped he wasn't going to have a problem with choosing to tell her about knowing Shirley Wagner.

Josh wandered around for a bit; peeking in the windows of each building he passed. Remembering his cover story, he stopped a few times to snap a photo. Though he wasn't positive he was being watched, he continued to act out the role of astounded visitor. Every time he saw a dog, he would call out "here puppy" making a big deal of petting the mutts. If anyone were standing nearby, he'd ramble on and on about how much he loved dogs. Several of the mangy beasts licked his hand. It was all he could do to keep from kicking them and wiping off the slime on his pant leg. *Flea ridden dirt bags,* he thought. Josh had never owned a pet. He didn't like dogs. He thought only animals you could slaughter for food should be allowed to live - temporarily.

After he had been roaming around the place for over an hour with no luck spotting the dog he was after, he sank down onto a bench with a heavy sigh. This was not proving to be as easy a task as he had expected. Letting his eyes roam around the compound he noticed a tall, dark-haired woman poke her head out of one of the nearby buildings. She gave him a quick once over before calling out to ask if he was hungry. Josh told her no, but that he sure could use a cold drink. She smiled and gestured for him to follow her. When Josh stepped inside the lavender painted building, he found a one room interior filled with mismatched furniture. The walls were each painted a different pastel color and hung with bright posters. A partially open door revealed a quaint bathroom with a claw footed tub. The woman said her name was Raven. She gave him a bottle of peach flavored tea. It was so sweet it almost made him gag. Josh nodded, thanking her, pretending to sip the tea. He soon discovered that the woman was a real jabber-jaws. She went on and on about his fake grandmother, Sunshine. Just when he thought her yammering would drive him crazy a little girl about eight years old showed up. She told the woman that she was needed at the honey barn. Apologizing, the woman headed out, saying she'd back in a moment, that if he had time to wait, she'd bring him a jar of fresh honey. Josh just nodded and smiled.

The kid went outside with the woman but popped back in a minute later carrying a furry brown bundle in her arms. Josh thought he'd shit a brick. It was the damn dog! Telling the kid how much he loved dogs, he convinced her to let him hold the squirming hairball. As soon as he had it in his hand, Josh grabbed the kid by the scruff of her neck. She barely managed to squeak a protest as a look of sheer terror washed over her face. Dragging her backward, Josh shoved her into the bathroom. He dropped the dog in the sink so he could tear down the shower curtain still keeping a grip on the kid. Ripping strips of the flowered material, he tied up the trembling child making sure he fitted a gag in her mouth. Wrapping the now yipping dog in a towel, he stuffed it under his shirt.

Outside, he scurried back to his truck trying to look

nonchalant. When he heard the Raven woman calling for him to come back, he ran the last few feet. Leaping into the driver's seat, he tore out of the parking area in a cloud of dust. Glancing in the rearview mirror he saw several men come running toward where the woman stood waving her arms and loudly yelling. Josh's truck may have looked old, but it had a souped-up V-8 under the hood. He was long gone before anyone from the commune could get to a vehicle and try to follow him.

Jerking the stolen dog out from under his shirt, Josh tossed it onto the passenger seat. It let out a small yelp, before cowering against the far door. Yanking out his cell phone Josh called Carter Williams. Once the guy stopped shouting hooray Josh told him to have the rest of the money ready by four that afternoon. He'd meet him at the rest stop out on the highway to make the exchange. Both men hung up from the call feeling elated.

Back at the commune everyone was still in shock. The men who had driven off to follow the thief came back empty handed. They reported that there was no sign of the truck anywhere.

"How could I have fallen for such a stupid trick?" Raven moaned. "We knew Carter would try to get the dog, and yet I let my guard down. He just looked so innocent!"

The others tried to comfort her, saying that they had all been fooled. The man had seemed so harmless. No one had thought him capable of such violence. Luckily, he hadn't done anything to harm the child except scaring her, which would give her nightmares for weeks to come. Plus, he had taken her beloved furry best friend. Snoopykins, a purebred Yorkie with an unbelievably bad haircut courtesy of his young owner, had obviously been mistaken for TooFoo a Heinz fifty-seven mongrel. They all feared what Carter would do when he realized the wrong dog had been kidnapped.

The members of the commune discussed their options and decided to call Sheriff King. Though they usually preferred to handle their own problems, and not call in the local law enforcement, this situation called for reinforcements. Plus, Raven had an idea on how to insure TooFoo's safety that would require the cooperation of the Sheriff. Bosco had already reluctantly agreed to cooperate, but he wasn't too sure Isis would be as thrilled with the plan as the others were. He crossed his fingers, asking the fates to intervene.

Chapter Forty

The rich dude was late and that pissed Josh Groder off. He didn't like hanging around the rest stop, too many people coming and going. Plus, the stupid mutt had puked in his truck. He thought about charging extra for cleaning it up, but figured he'd be lucky if he got anything out of the deal. He didn't trust rich people as far as he could spit. Scowling across the parking area he figured he would wait ten more minutes before splitting. That rich dude would be so sorry if he did because Josh Groder didn't forgive people who went back on deals. It was the one rule he lived by – a deal is a deal. Reneging on a deal was grounds for reprisal. Josh enjoyed dishing out reprisals.

Just as he was climbing back into his truck, ready to leave, he saw a black Escalade pull into the lot. *Got to be the rich dude,* he muttered. Climbing back out Josh leaned against his door a frown gracing his face. *About damn time,* he thought, the frown turning to a scowl.

Carter figured the big blond man in the ragged jeans and flannel shirt had to be Groder. The look on the guy's face could have frozen water. Carter was glad they were meeting in a public place; the guy gave him the creeps. Carefully parking two empty slots down the row, Carter patted the envelope of cash in his inside jacket pocket. Faking a smile, he approached the idling truck.

"Have you found him? Have you really found my darling little lost doggy?" Carter crooned, figuring he was covering his ass if anyone was watching the exchange.

"You got my money?" Groder grunted.

"Let me see my little puppy wuppy first," Carter simpered, acting like a doting pet owner.

Groder walked around and yanked the passenger side door of his truck open pulling out a furry brown bundle. "Here's your stupid dog, mister," he snarled shoving the mutt into Carter's arms.

Carter's elation turned to anger the smile quickly slipping from his face. "This is not my dog you idiot."

Josh glared at Carter then down at the dog before roaring, "You trying to juice me?"

Sighing in exasperation, Carter pulled a picture of TooFoo from his jacket pocket. "This is what the dog looks like, he's a mongrel. That is a purebred Yorkshire Terrier with a bad grooming job. I gave you a picture, how could you mix them up?"

Josh snatched the dog back. Yanking the photo from Carter's hand he held it up next to the dog dangling from his fingers letting out a groan. Damn! The dude was right it wasn't the same dog.

"I am not paying you one red cent," Carter snapped, snatching the photo back.

Josh took a threatening step towards Carter, who cringed, but held his ground. The little pup wriggled whining with fear. Groder tucked it up under his left arm before moving closer to Carter, his face red with anger. The situation didn't get a chance to turn ugly though as a van from some church group pulled up next to Josh's truck. It was filled with little old ladies who immediately began pointing at the dog in Groder's arm. Both the men knew not to let the situation escalate with so many eyewitnesses present.

"This mutt looks almost like the other one," Josh complained. "You can have him for half the money."

Carter closed his eyes shaking his head in exasperation. "No, you idiot. It's got to be the right dog. This one will not do. Even if this dog looked like the other's twin, it still wouldn't work. TooFoo, the right dog, has a microchip in his shoulder. They'll scan this flea bag and know it's not the right dog. No TooFoo, no money."

Groder gave Carter a menacing glare. He really wanted the money he'd been promised. He had to think of another angle and fast. "Fine, mister, I'll go back after your dog, but the folks at that commune place are on to me now. It's gonna be a lot harder to get back in there. I think I'll need a bit more incentive to try dog napping again."

"Not one more dime," Carter adamantly said. "I am not

paying for your mistake."

Glaring and snorting like an angry bull, Josh Groder stomped up and down the parking lot, cussing up a storm. When the little dog in his arms began to whimper, he tossed it down in the grass. Slamming back into his truck, he yelled out the window at Carter. "I'll be in touch, mister, soon as I get your dog. You'd better have my money ready." He hacked a thick wad of spit out his window before screeching out of the parking area.

Carter walked back to his car on shaky legs. With every step he cursed Lydia, the dog, and life in general. *I should not have to deal with lowlifes to get back what is rightfully mine*, he grumbled.

Neither Carter nor Josh Groder gave a thought to the dog they had so callously ripped from its home. It lay shivering under a holly bush, whimpering for its owner.

Chapter Forty-one

Sheriff King was dismayed to look out of his office window that morning and see Bosco Blue trooping through the parking lot, followed by that Night woman and their pudgy little attorney Jay Woods. King knew that whatever they wanted it meant another headache for him.

"Good morning sheriff," Raven Night called out as she popped in the front door. "We need to powwow about a problem."

"Good morning, Miss Night, what can I do for you folks?"

Raven launched into a brief replay of the incident with the horrible man who had come to the commune and stolen Snoopykins. The others added their sentiments none of which could be repeated in public. They were all mad as hell.

"So, do you want this office to start an official investigation into the theft and assault? Sheriff King asked, looking from Bosco to Raven to Jay Woods.

"What we want," Raven stated, "is a way to protect

TooFoo and our friends at Sunshine."

"Afraid I can't assign my men to patrol the place without getting an okay from the County for the extra funds."

"Oh, we've got that part covered," Bosco grinned.

Sheriff King got a sick feeling in the pit of his stomach wondering what Bosco meant. He wasn't sure if he should ask for clarification or ignore the comment, so that way when things blew up, he could claim ignorance.

"Don't look so worried, Sheriff," Raven laughed. "We aren't planning anything illegal."

Managing to smile despite his misgivings King directed them to one of the interrogation rooms. "Okay, tell me about this plan of yours."

The group quickly outlined their idea for protecting TooFoo and the folks at the commune. Sheriff King had to admit it was almost a perfect plan. Now if they could just convince Isis Winters to go along with the idea then it would be a perfect plan.

When one of the deputies brought Isis her breakfast, she knew something was up because instead of the usual watery scrambled eggs, pasty white bread toast and blackened bacon, there was a flaky golden croissant, a small pot of raspberry jam, and a large carafe of what smelled like chamomile tea. Though her stomach growled with pleasure, Isis left the meal untouched, worried what unwelcome news would be forthcoming. Unwelcome news was the only reason she could think of for the change in prison fare. They were trying to soften the blow by appealing to her baser needs. Nervously pacing the small cell, she waited for the bomb to drop.

An hour later she was surprised when the door opened to reveal Sheriff King flanked by a group of her friends. A smile freezing on her face, Isis glanced from Bosco to Raven to Jay Woods, a wave of nausea washing over her. Bosco looked guilty. Raven looked smug. Jay was frowning and Sheriff King was smiling. None of their expressions improved the queasy sensation rolling around inside her stomach. "Okay, give me the bad news," she demanded, planting her feet in a wide stance, coiling her arms around her body as if they were armored protection.

When Raven told her about what had happened at the commune, that Snoopykins had been stolen, Isis was just heartsick. *This is my fault,* she softly moaned. Before she could totally dissolve into tears, Bosco pulled her into his arms. His loving warmth coursed through her, keeping the tears at bay.

"We've got it covered," Raven assured her friend with a glowing smile. "Don't worry about a thing."

"How can you even say such a thing? Everything has gone horribly wrong and I'm to blame. I never should have kept TooFoo. If I had given him back to Carter Williams everything would be fine."

"You know that's not true," Bosco said, tightening his embrace. "If you hadn't taken that poor mutt home, he'd probably be at some animal control place waiting for the grim reaper."

"Listen to your friends," Sheriff King pleaded. He hated seeing Isis so stressed out thinking she had done something wrong. Shortly after meeting Isis, he had figured out that she had a heart of gold, one that was easily bruised. "Your friends' have a plan that should solve everything. Just try to pull up some of that good karma you're always talking about."

Despite her worries, Isis had to smile at the staid sheriff's use of such an esoteric idea as karma. "Fine, I will try to pull up some karma, but you'd better have some good news for me soon." Untangling herself from Bosco's arms, Isis took a seat on the edge of her cot. "Before all of you start yammering at me at once, do you suppose I could get a cup of chamomile tea?"

"That sounds like a wonderful idea," King said, "since we'll have a bit of a wait for the others to join us let's all have some tea." When the sheriff didn't elaborate on who was coming Isis gave him a sigh of frustration. King patted her shoulder and said, "Believe me the surprise will be worth the wait."

Chapter Forty-two

Looking through the high-powered binoculars he had borrowed from his neighbor's storage shed, Josh Groder cursed under his breath. He'd been right in telling Carter it would be a lot harder to get back into the commune. On his first visit the guards had been minimal and in hiding. Now there were more of them, and they were armed and in plain sight. Plus, there was a county patrol car parked next to the purple house where he'd snatched the first mutt. Josh saw a uniformed man came out of the purple building, closely followed by a big bear of a man with a tiny furry bundle resting in his arms. Josh swore out loud. That had to be the rich guy's dog. When the men piled into the patrol car and pulled out on the main road, Josh raced back to his vehicle. He had to follow and see where they were taking the mutt. Letting a minivan and an old truck pass him before he pulled out onto the road, Josh swung in line behind them. He could just make out the patrol car up ahead.

Parking two streets down from the jailhouse where the

patrol car had finally stopped, Josh watched the men enter the building. They toted the little dog in with them. Donning a quick disguise from his glovebox, black framed glasses, a ball cap and a fake mustache, Josh hopped out of his truck and moseyed down the sidewalk. Ducking down a cross street, he circled back to an alley that ran behind the jail. Peeking in windows, he searched for the man with the dog.

Sheriff King asked Isis Winters and the others to follow him up to the conference room. He stood at the open door waiting to usher them inside. He couldn't keep the smile off his face.

Isis squealed with delight when she saw her friend Bear waiting there with tiny TooFoo cradled in his arms. She hastily pecked Bear on the cheek, before scooping the little dog from his arms, laughing as it licked her face.

"Oh, I missed you, you little dickens," Isis crooned. "Yes, darling, I love you, too."

"If I didn't know better, I'd think you liked that mutt more than me," Bosco grumbled watching his wife fawning over the ugly little mutt.

Isis turned to grace Sheriff King with a dazzling smile. "Sheriff, I don't know how to thank you." Returning her attention back to the dog, she rubbed its fuzz covered belly. "Oh, who's a good puppy? Who's a good puppy?" TooFoo wriggled so hard he almost flipped himself on the floor.

"What would you say if I told you that TooFoo could stay here with you?" Sheriff King said. "Until we get things cleared up and spring you."

Turning to stare at him with a look of confusion, Isis set TooFoo down on the floor. "Why would you want to lock up a poor little dog in this sterile, cold box? Do you hate dogs?"

"Babe, we got us a plan," Bosco intervened before Isis could get on her soapbox about inhumane incarceration methods used to house criminals. It was one of her pet peeves. She thought they should live in security communes, faming the land and maintaining a useful role in society. To think that someone would recommend subjecting a dog to the same treatment reserved for hardened criminals had her bristling with indignation.

"Spill it, Bosco," Isis demanded, crossing her arms and scowling.

"Dognapers would never be able to get into the jail, would they?" Bosco grinned. "Where better to stash the mutt then right here with you?"

"You want to incarcerate TooFoo?"

"Yeah, Babe," Bosco replied his grin slipping a bit. "Just till we can think of somewhere safer for him."

Isis turned to glare at Sheriff King. "This was your idea? This was the 'big plan' you were all yammering about this morning?"

"We talked it over and decided it was for the best," Jay Woods chimed in, trying to deflect some of Isis' anger from the now frowning sheriff.

"Isis, it just seems like it would solve a whole lot of

problems for a whole lot of people," Sheriff King sighed. "Think about it first before you go blowing a gasket."

Rolling her eyes, Isis strode over to the barred window that looked out on the street. She stood there a long time staring out, running their plan through her head. Turning back to face the room, Isis bent down and scooped TooFoo up in her arms, crooning in his ear. "Would you like to stay in this nasty old jail? Would you like to stay here with me?" TooFoo promptly licked her face. "Hmmm, I guess that settles it then, he agrees with all of you. Oh, Bosco, did you think to bring along his bed, toys, brush…"

Interrupting his wife's litany with a grunt, Bosco sighed. "Yeah, Babe, it's in the car. I'll run out and get it before we leave."

"Now that we have that settled, I have more good news," Jay Woods smiled. "Or at least I think it's good news. The Grand Jury will be convened this Friday."

"Does that mean Isis will be able to come home?" Bosco excitedly asked.

"Based on the initial evidence, I think it will mean not only will she be home, but that she will no longer be a suspect," Woods confidently replied.

Bosco hooted out loud, which got TooFoo yapping and Isis laughing. Even Sheriff King had to smile thinking about getting his normal, quiet jail back.

Josh Groder watched through the window dumbfounded as a deputy returned the hippie woman to her cell, along with the hairy little dog. Damn, this job just wasn't working out. If he couldn't get the dog back, he'd have to think of another way to get money out of Carter Williams. Cursing under his breath Groder stomped back to his car.

209

Chapter Forty-three

Always looking out for number one, Carter had gone back and picked up the stupid mutt the moron had stolen. Even though it was the wrong dog it might still help Carter's case for getting custody of the right one. Glaring down at the cowering animal on the seat next to him Carter sternly admonished it to behave. Turning up the stereo so he wouldn't have to listen to it whimpering, he headed for the offices of Caldwell & Caldwell.

*****

James Stoneman was a bit surprised when his secretary announced that Carter Williams was waiting in the outer office. He was even more surprised to hear that Williams had a dog with him. Striding out to the reception area he paused to take in the scene. Williams was indeed sitting there holding a small brown dog that was whimpering pathetically. Carter wore a forlorn look, absent-mindedly stroking the dog squirming around in his lap.

"Mr. Williams, what can we do for you today?" Stoneman asked, moving to hover over Carter.

"Oh dear, this is so surreal," Carter sighed. "I'm not sure you can help me. Maybe you will know what I should do though." Carter quickly told Stoneman about getting a mysterious phone call from a man saying he had TooFoo. The man wanted money of course, for the dog's safe return. Carter said he rushed right out to the designated meeting place without giving it a second thought, his only concern having been for darling TooFoo's safety. At this point he held up the dog in his lap. "The man had this poor little thing in a pillowcase."

"That is not TooFoo," Stoneman bluntly said.

"Yes, I know," Carter irritably snapped back, forgetting for a moment to act the role of confused and grieving widower. Mentally berating himself he quickly added, "But it belongs to someone. That someone is missing it as much as I miss my doggie. I gave the man the money he asked for so I could get this poor, sad creature away from him. What do I do now?"

Before Stoneman could reply the main door of the law office came crashing open. A crush of reporters with camera operators in tow burst into the waiting area. They all began clamoring for a statement from Carter about finding his dead wife's lost dog.

Huge tears streaming down his face, Carter sadly replied, "I was coerced into paying for this dog." He held up the shivering animal as cameras swung his way. "It's the wrong dog. My TooFoo is still missing." As the cameras whirred, Carter dissolved into tears, hugging the little dog up to his chest.

Everyone began yelling out questions; it was pandemonium. Carter just sat there hugging the squirming dog, crying big crocodile tears. Stoneman was furious. He was sure that

Carter had tipped off the news people himself. By the time some semblance of order was restored the reporters were sympathizing with Carter, glaring accusingly at Stoneman. It was too late to prevent the inevitable; live feeds were going out to the local news stations telling how Carter had rescued the adorable dog in his arms, knowing full well that it wasn't his dog. Carter made a tearful statement begging for help to find the dog's rightful owner. He said that even though he had already paid a sizeable ransom for the wrong dog, he would pay an even larger reward to anyone who found its rightful owner. "This little pup will be cared for at our family vet's office until its owner can be found," he choked out with a small smile.

The receptionist ran to hug him, crying softly about what a wonderful thing he was doing. Carter kept his sad face on for the cameras, but he was smiling smugly on the inside. This was just the kind of publicity he needed.

Chapter Forty-four

Raven Night got an unexpected call from the folks who lived two farms over from the commune. They had seen a story on the evening news about a dognapping. They said the pup looked like one they had seen a few days ago at the commune market. Raven thanked them, hung up, and raced over to the main building. She told Woods and Bosco about the call, dancing nervously from foot to foot. Since there were no televisions at the Commune, Woods called the TV station to find out what kind of dog had been found. After hearing a description, he knew the dog was Snoopykins. He and Bosco immediately headed out to collect the pup and return him to his anxious young mistress. They were both in such a hurry neither of them was aware of the small dark colored car that dropped into position behind them as they left the commune.

*****

Hugging the reclaimed Snoopykins to his chest, Bosco tried to keep the puppy from licking the beard off his face. Chatting amiably with Jay Woods as they walked back to Jay's car, he didn't hear the approaching footsteps until it was too late. Out of the corner of his eye he saw a flash, and then felt a heavy jolt to the side of his head. He dropped to the pavement like a sack of wet cement. Jay Woods turned too late to help his friend or save Snoopykins. The masked assailant had already scooped up the dog and run off. After helping a stunned and bleeding Bosco to his feet, Woods walked him back inside the Happy Valley Pet Clinic before calling Sheriff King.

Arriving within minutes of receiving the flustered call from attorney Jay Woods, Sheriff King strode into the vet office already frowning. "What the hell is going on here?" he demanded.

"We've been dognapped – again," Woods replied with a sigh.

"Some crazy bastard bashed me in the head and stole Snoopykins," Bosco growled.

Sheriff King could not believe his ears. So much trouble over one tiny mutt. Pulling out a notebook he took Bosco and Jay's statements, then called in a B. O. L. O. (be on the lookout) for the man in the dark colored compact car. Since Bosco refused any type of medical attention Sheriff King could do nothing more at the scene and headed back to the office. Bosco and Woods drove slowly towards the commune, dreading telling everyone that Snoopykins was missing again.

Chapter Forty-five

Carter Williams was pulled from a sweet dream about buying a new Porsche by his loudly ringing phone. Grabbing up the receiver he barked a gruff, "What do you want?"

"I got that commune's dog," a hoarse voice hissed. "The one you offered a reward for finding its owner. I want that money or the dog's gonna be roadkill."

"What do you mean you found the dog? It wasn't lost, it was at the vet's office," Carter snapped into the phone.

"Two hoodlums come for the dog, I had to rescue it. I'll take it back to its owner as soon as you drop off the reward money," the voice instructed.

Carter wanted to scream at the man, *"keep the damn mutt, you aren't getting a dime from me,"* but knew he couldn't say anything that would put him in a bad light. He needed all the good publicity he could get. Rescuing the commune mutt - again, would show his good intentions. "How do I know you will return the dog once you have the money?" he asked, stalling for time to think of a better plan.

"Fine. Meet me on the back road outside the place where the dog lives. I'll exchange the dog for the reward. Then you can personally hand it over to its owner."

Carter, annoyed by having to pay for the wrong dog a second time, almost hung up. But reason won out when he realized what a fantastic opportunity this could be to advance his case for ownership of TooFoo. Agreeing to the time and place, and swearing not to tell anyone, Carter hung up and set his plan in motion.

Raven Night was so surprised to get a call from sleezy Carter Williams she almost hung up on him. If he hadn't slipped in the name Snoopykins, she would have. He told her that some horrible person had called him to demand the reward money, saying that he had the dog. Since Carter had left it at the vet clinic, he thought the man was lying, until he heard a puppy crying in the background. He told Raven he had agreed to meet the man down the road from the commune. He suggested that they have people hidden there to protect him and the pup. Raven told Carter not to worry; she would take care of everything.

Wondering if Carter was trying to pull a fast one, Raven felt she had no choice but to meet him; Snoopykins was sadly missed by his young mistress. To be on the safe side, she called in a few commune members to join her.

Chapter Forty-six

Josh Groder was in such a good mood he sang all the way to the meeting spot. It had been so easy to grab up the stupid mutt from that vet place, call Carter, and arrange the exchange. He knew Carter was terrified, so he figured the guy would follow instructions to a T. Josh glanced down at the box in the passenger seat, hoping he had put enough holes in the top so the mutt could breathe. No way was he letting it ride on the seat so it could upchuck like last time.

Easing his car down a rutted dirt road just past the Sunshine Commune, Groder parked beneath an old elm. Getting out to stretch his legs he was unaware that his every move was being watched. Before he knew what was happening three large men leaped from the ditch that ran alongside the road, each armed with a shotgun, all of which were trained on Josh Groder's chest. The largest man, with a tangled black beard, ordered him to lie down on the ground with his hands behind his head. Josh had no choice but to comply. They trussed him up like a holiday turkey before dumping him in the bed of his own truck. They tossed a musty smelling old tarp over him and admonished him to "lie still if he knew what was good for him." He felt the truck start up, bump down the road, and then turn out on the smooth tarmac of the main highway. Within minutes they stopped again, and the tarp was yanked off his head. Josh squinted up at the circle of faces glaring down at him. He recognized most of them from the day he first snuck into the commune to snatch the wrong dog. None of them wore welcoming expressions. For the first time in his life, Groder was happy to see that one of them was wearing the uniform of a local law enforcement officer. *These old hippie wackos might get it into their heads to hand out some vigilante style justice*, Josh thought with a shudder. He felt he stood a better chance of surviving if he was hauled off by the cop. "I got nothing to say so just arrest me," he barked

As members of the commune helped lift the trussed man from the bed of the truck, half a dozen news vans came roaring down the highway taking haphazard parking spots in front of the commune. The news crews leapt out of their vehicles, screaming a tirade of questions.

"Do you have the missing dog?"

"Is that the dognaper?"

"Where's the grieving widower?"

The commune members ignored them circling around Josh Groder like wagons waiting for an Indian attack. No one said a word which only got the reporters agitated. They stomped and snorted, braying out more questions, their voices growing louder and louder. The three men armed with shotguns were the only thing keeping off commune property.

When Carter Williams arrived on the scene it only inflamed the chaos. Carter made a show of surprise over the second theft and ransom demand for the child's dog, Snoopykins. He stated he'd had no intention of paying ransom money to a hoodlum. He added that he would be handing over the thousand-dollar reward check to the child, along with her puppy, saying she deserved it for all the horror she had been put through. Then he made a tearful plea for the return of his own darling TooFoo. The reporters lapped up his drivel as if it were nectar from the gods.

Chapter Forty-seven

Early the next morning Jay Woods packed up his briefcase, grabbing a travel mug of black coffee, before heading to the Courthouse. Today the Grand Jury would decide if there was sufficient evidence against Isis Winters to call for a trial. He planned to be the first one seated in the courtroom calmly waiting for his sweetly smiling client to be brought over from the jail. He was a bit dismayed to find Bosco Blue waiting for him outside the courthouse. If Bosco couldn't keep his usual short-tempered exuberance under control, it might ruin everything.

"If you open your mouth one time once we get inside, I will personally ask the bailiff to remove you from room. Is that clear?"

Bosco scowled. "I'm just here to be sure my wife doesn't get railroaded for something she isn't guilty of doing."

"If you let me do my job, she'll be home by this

afternoon."

Woods' confidence in his client's innocence was quickly affirmed. The prosecution's case hinged solely on circumstantial evidence and hearsay. The District Attorney's assumption that Jay Woods was an inexperienced bumbler was the coup de grace. Woods tore the prosecution witnesses to shreds. Not only did he cast a long shadow of doubt on Isis Winter's guilt, but he gave ample reason to suspect Lydia's husband, Carter Williams, of the crime. The verdict was returned in less than an hour – there was insufficient evidence to advance to trial. Isis Winters would soon be a free woman.

Once the verdict was rendered, Bosco ran for the Sheriff's office dragging Woods behind him. Isis had to complete out-processing before she would be released. Bosco wanted to be sure that the first smiling face she saw would be his.

Pacing the reception area like a caged beast, Bosco waited for Isis to appear down the hall from the holding area. When he saw her, he leaped across the service counter, scaring the pants off the young woman sitting there. He raced down the hall scooping Isis up in his arms letting out a victory yell, swinging her around in circles.

"Babe, I've missed you so much!"

Isis took Bosco's smiling face in her hands. "Not near as much as I've missed you, Pookie Bear."

Sheriff King hated to break up their reunion, but he had business to conduct. He ushered them out to the front desk to sign papers and pick up Isis's personal effects.

"Don't forget your cell mate," King reminded Isis. "Deputy Harris will be back in a minute with TooFoo." The little dog had needed his morning walk.

"Sheriff, I don't how to thank you for all you've done," Isis murmured.

"Yeah, never thought I'd be saying this to some establishment oinker, but you're alright man," Bosco blustered, shaking Sheriff King's hand.

King had to laugh before muttering to himself, *I'm actually going to miss having these two old reprobates around, they kind of liven things up.*

After collecting their paperwork and TooFoo, Bosco and Isis gave out one more round of thank you hugs. Sheriff King reminded them to keep out of trouble as he ushered them out of his jail.

Chapter Forty-eight

Unbeknownst to Carter Williams, Jay Woods had an appointment set up with Caldwell & Caldwell first thing that afternoon. The issue of TooFoo's ownership was going to be settled once and for all.

When Bosco and Isis pulled up outside of the Caldwell & Caldwell law offices a small group of smiling faces were already on hand to greet them. Nodding brusquely, Woods led the group through the main lobby and up to the reception desk. He announced his clients, suggesting the young woman behind the desk show them to a conference room immediately. A bit flustered by the oddly dressed group the woman pointed at a door on the left, telling them they could wait in there. *Really,* she shuddered, *socks with sandals and tie-died shirts?* She scurried off to tell her bosses about the strange people waiting to see them.

Richard and Michael Caldwell figured their absence from the initial session with the claimants and their attorney would give them the upper hand. So, they sent their underling, Stoneman, to begin dealing with them. Plus, they both knew that the longer they drug the situation out the more billable hours they could charge to the late Mrs. Williams' estate.

James Stoneman took his time getting to the conference room. These people and their storefront attorney needed to realize who was in charge of the meeting. Walking into the room he ignored everyone. Moving over to the head of the table he laid out several folders and an ostentatious silver and black onyx pen. Bellowing for the receptionist to bring him a mocha latte, Stoneman eased into one of the stiff leather chairs. Plying more strategy, he waited until his coffee was in front of him before addressing the people seated at the other end of the table.

"Ahem. Let us get down to business. First, we must ascertain that the animal in your possession is, indeed, Too Foolish Jackson Williams." Punching a button recessed into the tabletop, Stoneman ordered someone to bring in Dr. Prior. Steepling his fingers, he sat back in his chair staring around the table with an expression of total boredom.

A moment later the door opened revealing the receptionist and a tall, thin man in a gray striped suit. The man introduced himself as Dr. Clinton Prior, head veterinarian at the Classy Canine Clinic and Pet Spa. He sat a small silver case on the table and then asked that TooFoo be brought closer. Isis complied, holding the little animal protectively against her chest, moving to stand next to the veterinarian. Dr. Prior lifted a pen like device from the silver case running it over the dog's head and shoulders. A beep sounded and data began flashing up on the LCD display in the silver case's lid. Prior turned the case for Stoneman to read.

"Please see that the receptionist gets a copy of the data for our files," Stoneman said, dismissing the veterinarian with a curt nod. Then he turned to face the people around the table.

"The microchip implanted in this dog's shoulder confirms that he is indeed, TooFoo. It also confirms that he was the property of the late Lydia Williams, since she was the one who registered the microchip. This means the dog in your possession is the legal heir of Lydia Williams' estate." Not waiting for any comments, Stoneman pulled a sheaf of papers from the folder in front of him. "The problem before us now is the current legal ownership of this animal," he continued. "Let us look…"

Before he could go any further, Jay Woods stood up and interrupted him. "I have signed affidavits here from several witnesses stating that Carter Williams gave possession of TooFoo to my clients, Isis Winters and Bosco Blue."

"That's all well and good, but there is the small matter of Ms. Winters' implication in Lydia Williams' death. If found guilty she cannot profit from her criminal act," Stoneman bluntly stated.

"Earlier this morning the Grand Jury found insufficient evidence to hold Ms. Winters over for trial," Woods replied. "Plus, Bosco Blue, who was not implicated in Lydia Williams death, is more than willing to take on the role of TooFoo's guardianship."

"Yes, we already assume that Mr. Blue would be willing to take over the animal's care. However, we must determine that whoever has possession of the animal is qualified to provide the best possible care; it was Lydia Williams' main stipulation in her will. She wanted to ensure whoever was assigned the role would keep TooFoo's interests at the forefront when accessing funds from the Trust," Stoneman haughtily said his nose in the air. "Not just anyone can be considered adequate to perform the task."

"Why that's no problem at all," Woods brightly smiled. "On behalf of my clients allow me to introduce Professor Robert Cannon from the local veterinary college, Mrs. Estelle Withers president of the local chapter of Pups-n-Pals pet adoptions, and Jason Bell vice president of the local chapter of P. E. T. A., People for the Ethical Treatment of Animals. They are all here to attest to the qualifications of both Isis Winters and Bosco Blue to act as caregivers for the dog known as TooFoo."

Stoneman frowned. His bosses had not said a word about any of these witnesses. He demanded to see each person's credentials. He took a long time looking them over. When he finished, he buzzed out to ask that Michael and Richard Caldwell join him at once. Steepling his fingers, he closed his eyes waiting for the others to join him. He groaned softly, knowing his bosses would not be pleased with this turn of events.

When the conference room door opened it revealed two men who were obviously related. Each had a head of silver-gray hair and a thick bushy mustache. Both wore the same somber black suit and stiff white shirt, with pearl gray striped ties. They looked like bookends. The men strode to the head of the table where they held a whispered conversation with Stoneman. Stiff smiles slid across their faces as they took a seat on either side of their protégé.

Once seated the men introduced themselves as Michael and Richard Caldwell. They asked several polite questions of each witness, nothing of real importance, as if their minds were already made up.

"It seems that further investigation into this matter will be unnecessary," Michael Caldwell finally said. "We concede that Ms. Winters and Mr. Blue are now the legal owners of the animal called TooFoo. We also agree that they are ideal candidates to care for Lydia Williams' heir."

"There are a number of items we wish to discuss about the handling of TooFoo's inheritance," Richard Caldwell added. "Shall we meet back here again tomorrow to begin laying out a health care visitation schedule and a review of the financial portfolio?"

"That won't be necessary," Isis sweetly smiled at him. "Our attorney, Jay Woods, will be taking over the handling of TooFoo's inheritance."

"Yeah, we aren't gonna be needing your services anymore, so cough up the paperwork and let's get this show on the road," Bosco grunted. He could smell shysters when he met them, and these two reeked.

Stoneman and the Caldwell brothers all began talking at once, trying to convince Isis and Bosco that their services were still needed. They were shocked into silence when Isis, Bosco, and the rest of their entourage got up and walked out of the office. Jay Woods stopped long enough to slide duly notarized documents appointing him legal counsel for the Lydia Williams Trust across the table to the three still sputtering men.

Chapter Forty-nine

Carter Williams wondered why the bellman seemed so nervous when he arrived with the breakfast trolley. Since he had paid for the room in advance, in cash, the man could not know that Carter was almost dead broke, and that he wouldn't be getting any large tips for his services. *Really,* Carter muttered under his breath, *I thought this hotel would have better service.* Figuring it was only a matter of days until he could put his hands on Lydia's estate, Carter had moved out of the flea bag motel he had been staying in, opting for classier quarters at one of the finer hotels in town. He'd paid for one more week at the flea bag place just in case he needed to use it for a meeting or publicity purposes. Ignoring the bellman's outstretched hand; Carter busied himself with pouring coffee and buttering toast. The disgruntled bellman stomped out the door a scowl on his face.

It was several minutes before Carter's eyes caught the headline on the morning paper tucked along the edge of the serving cart. ***"Local Couple Appointed Guardians of Millionaire***

Dog" the bold print screamed. Below the headline was a picture of the hippie couple from the boat cruise and his late wife's stupid dog. Carter almost choked on his coffee. Slamming the cup down he strode across the room, snatching up the phone, angrily punching in the number for Caldwell & Caldwell. If this was some sick joke, there would be hell to pay.

"Good morning, you have reached the..." was all that Carter let the woman who answered say before he began bellowing at her. "This is Carter Williams and I demand to speak with Caldwell."

When the woman calmly asked him which Caldwell he wished to speak with, Carter let loose a string of expletives unfit for even the ear of a hardened sailor. The woman hung up on him. Raging in disbelief Carter redialed the number. This time he used his most unctuous voice to request a connection to Richard Caldwell. The woman recognized his voice despite his more pleasant tone, calling him on his poor manners before putting him on hold. *She'll have to be dismissed before I continue using their services,* Carter huffed to himself. The minutes dragged by. He had just heard the same old rock ballad piped into his ear for the second time around before anyone came back on the line.

"This is Mr. Stoneman; how may I help you?"

"I asked for Richard Caldwell," Carter snapped.

"Mr. Caldwell is unavailable."

"Have you seen the morning paper?"

Stoneman sighed into Carter's ear. "Yes, sir, I have." He

mentally braced himself for the onslaught he knew would be coming.

"Well, what do you plan to do about it?" Carter screeched. "Those damn low life hillbillies are probably already up at my house robbing me blind."

"There is nothing to be done, Mr. Williams. Ms. Winters and Mr. Blue are the legal owners of the dog and have been deemed the best qualified to care for said animal," Stoneman sighed. "This firm's representation of the estate of the late Lydia Williams has been completed to the satisfaction of State law. Our services have been terminated by TooFoo's new owners. Good day, sir."

Carter sat in shocked silence listening to the dial tone buzzing in his ear. Furious, he slammed the phone up against the wall. Not bothering to finish his breakfast or even take a shower, he threw on his clothes and headed out for a face-to-face confrontation with the idiots at Caldwell & Caldwell. On the way down to the parking garage he called his own attorney, ordering him to get over to the courthouse to check on the situation. He was so angry he almost mowed down two incoming guests who were unfortunate enough to be crossing the parking lot as he went roaring out.

Chapter Fifty

Bosco called Janie and Jimmy Grayson to share the good news about TooFoo. He asked if they would like to join him and Isis for their first look at TooFoo's home. Smiling broadly at Janie's squeal of delight, Bosco had to hold the phone about a foot from his ear to keep from going deaf. They agreed to meet up outside the house on Pennyroyal Road at noon.

*****

When the Graysons pulled up in front of the late Lydia Williams' estate, they found Bosco and Isis waiting for them, standing outside an ornate wrought iron gate. They exchanged hugs before Janie stepped back to their jeep to pull out the junior cheeseburger she had brought for TooFoo. She barely managed to lay the burger down on the grass before the little dog snuffled the wrapper, his eyes shining with delight. Nosing aside the top bun, lettuce leaf and slice of tomato, he woofed down the cheese topped burger in three giant bites.

"Man, TooFoo, you are one burger loving dog," Jimmy laughed.

Scooping up the wriggling mutt Bosco plopped it in his wife's waiting arms.

"Who's a good doggie?" Isis crooned, hugging TooFoo to her chest. "Let's go see your big old house, shall we?" Turning to smile at Bosco Isis said, "Have you figured a way in yet?"

"You see any kind of doorbell or something on this thing?" Bosco asked Jimmy, his eyes running up and down the monstrous gate.

"There's probably a call box or speaker button somewhere," Janie said.

"Here's a button," Isis called out pointing to a shiny brass circle set in a recess of one of the rock columns supporting the gate. The button gleamed like a new penny. She gave it a couple of quick jabs.

"May I help you?" a mechanical sounding voice wheezed out of a tiny grate below the button.

"It's TooFoo Williams and his friends," Isis loudly yelled.

There was a moment of silence before the huge metal gates began to retract, rolling smoothly back beside the stone columns. The group climbed into their vehicles and drove slowly through the massive archway. All of them took a cue from TooFoo, hanging their heads out their windows, gaping in awe at the wide expanse of slick black driveway. The edge of the drive was bordered with flowerbeds over ten feet wide; each filled with a seasonal planting of bronze and deep yellow mums. Backed by a wide strip of emerald lawn the flowerbeds gave way to a thick stand of mixed hardwoods. The road curved around a corner before opening into a circular drive complete with a splashing mermaid fountain.

"Holy crap on a cracker would you look at this place," Bosco whooped as he climbed out of his van.

"My Lord, it's...it's... so big," Isis stammered.

"There have to be about fifty rooms inside," Janie gasped.

"Daaaang. That is one butt ugly house," Jimmy snorted. His comment brought gales of laughter from the others, and a few yaps from TooFoo.

The group stood there for several minutes taking in the gargantuan proportions of the house. Their eyes roamed over the Greek columns holding up the front entry porch, rising to take in the two stories that stretched above it. A creaking sound drew their attention to the massive carved oak doors at the center of the house. Silhouetted in the now open doorway stood a slender man in formal butler attire. He motioned them forward into a massive entry hall with marble floors, crystal chandeliers and a grand staircase. Two highly polished suits of armor stood at either side of the marble staircase as if protecting the upper floors from intruders. Everywhere the group looked their eyes met ornate gilding, sparkling crystal, multi-hued stained glass, and more white marble.

"My name is Doyle, your personal assistant, Madame Winters. If you would care to meet the staff, they are assembled in the drawing room for your inspection." He gestured to his left, stepping over to fling open a set of double doors.

Grinning from ear-to-ear Jimmy and Bosco swaggered through the doors. Isis and Janie wandered along behind them, too stunned to speak. Stepping inside the room they all froze in place when confronted by the thirty odd members of the estate's staff. The man named Doyle proceeded to rattle off each staff member's name and a list of his or her duties.

"Whoa there, Darryl," Bosco finally managed to sputter. "Are you telling me all these folks work here?"

"The name is Doyle, sir, and yes, they do."

"How many people actually live here?" Isis asked in amazement.

"Counting you, Master Blue, and TooFoo, that would be five," Doyle said with a frown. "Will that be a problem?"

"Well, my goodness...all these people working here... so few people living here...it's just, just..." Isis stammered. "It's just ridiculous."

"If Madame is unhappy with any of the staff, or wishes to hire additional staff, I can arrange that in the morning," Doyle said. Not waiting for Isis to reply he proceeded with the staff introductions. He somehow managed to keep his voice level and bland, even when Jimmy and Bosco began mimicking his nasal tones and roaring with laughter.

"Will you be overseeing the staff, Madame, or will Master Blue?" Doyle asked, raising his voice over the continued laughter. *Really, what heathens*, he thought, waiting for them to get their emotions under control.

"We'll get back to you on that Mr. Doyle," Isis managed to

reply. "Right now, we'd like to find the kitchen, grab a snack, and then stake our claim to a bedroom."

"Very good, Madame," Doyle sniffed. "Please follow me to the dining room."

Trooping after the stiff-backed Doyle the group gawked opened mouthed into each room they passed. Isis kept shaking her head muttering what a waste it was that only two people had lived in the huge place. Janie clung to Jimmy's hand afraid of getting lost and never finding her way back out. Bosco couldn't stop bursting into laughter over the ornate paintings and life-sized statues that filled every nook or large wall space. Jimmy just concentrated on not tripping over his feet, because his eyes were about glazed over from shock. TooFoo was the only one who didn't seem bothered by all the grandeur. He had snuggled down deep into Isis' arms, happy to be back where there were familiar smells. He had promptly fallen asleep.

Doyle seated each of the women at the banquet size dining table, allowing the men to choose their own chairs. He said he would be just a moment, disappearing through a door at the far end of the room. They could hear him calling out orders, followed by the sound of scurrying feet. Before any of them had a chance to comment Doyle reappeared followed by six other staff members. The staff buzzed around them like bees fresh from the hive. The table was set with an array of glittering gold edged plates, crystal stemware, and multiple pieces of silverware. The tall candelabra in the center of the table were lit sending glowing beams of light dancing around the room. Thick burgundy linen napkins folded into crowns were deposited atop the gleaming gold edged plates. Dishes of food were brought in from somewhere beyond the carved oak doors at the end of the room. Each serving dish was paraded past Isis, the covers lifted for her to peer inside, before being whisked off to a massive sideboard that ran the entire length of one wall. Without comment the staff began to dish up the meal, placing filled bowls and plates in front of each of the diners. There was a salad of mixed greens topped with what looked like nasturtiums, along with bowls of steaming hot creamed soup that smelled of cinnamon. Mini sized platters of crispy warm rolls were centered between the candelabra with small blue cut crystal bowls filled with balls of butter tucked up next to them.

"The former Madame preferred her salad course and soup to be served together," Doyle announced. "I hope that is still satisfactory."

Since the man seemed to be waiting for a reply, Isis mumbled, "Yes, I guess that will be fine for today."

"Let me take Master TooFoo back to the kitchen for his meal," Doyle said, scooping the little dog out of Isis' arms. He breezed back through the door at the end of the room followed by all but one of the servers. The young woman who remained behind took up a position against the wall next to the sideboard. Her bland facial expression made Isis uneasy.

"If we need anything else we'll just call out," she informed the girl, who hesitated a moment before nodding and leaving the room.

"Oh .My. God," exclaimed Janie. "This is all just too weird."

"Man, that's an understatement," Bosco snorted. "These people are freaking me out. They just plopped food on the plates and shoved them under our noses. What if I didn't want the stuff?"

"Ugh!" Jimmy gagged, having taken a spoonful of the soup. "What the hell is this?"

Isis dipped her spoon into the creamy white soup and took a tentative sip. "I believe it's cauliflower and white truffle bisque," she replied.

"Babe, we can't live like this," Bosco groaned "This ain't a home. Those people are like robots... or clones... or something. And no one needs this much space, it ain't natural."

"Honey Bear, we have to stay here, it's TooFoo's home. The Will states that he is to live here until, well, you know..." Isis mumbled, uncomfortable speaking about the subject of TooFoo's eventual demise. "It's part of the agreement for caring for him, Bosco, we have to live here."

"Does it say you have to keep the house and people just like they are?" Janie spoke up, a thoughtful look flitting across her face.

"Hmm, I'll have to review the papers with Jay, but I don't think so," Isis replied. "Why?"

"Well, you could share the place. You know, like at the commune."

Bosco visibly perked up. "That greenhouse full of orchids

could probably be changed over to something useful, like a hydroponics garden."

"The garages look like they have some large rooms above them. They would make great art studios," Janie chimed in. "All those windows would let in tons of natural light."

"Oh, that is an excellent idea," Isis agreed. "This place could become an artist enclave, animal sanctuary or. . . my goodness, the possibilities are endless!"

The rest of the meal was spent marveling over the food while making plans for changes to the estate. When a man in a chef's hat brought in a mile high chocolate torte, surrounded by fresh raspberries, the group surged to their feet, giving him a roaring round of applause. Not used to such demonstrative recognition for his services, the man nodded stiffly. Easing towards the door, he double-timed it back to the kitchen to tell the others what had happened and what he had overheard. They all wondered if they would still have jobs as it sunk in that things were not going to be the same at the Williams estate any longer.

Chapter Fifty-one

The receptionist at Caldwell & Caldwell had been given strict orders about former client Lydia Williams' husband, Carter. Under no circumstances was he to be allowed in to see either of the Caldwell brothers. So, when Carter came storming through the entry doors that morning, she steeled herself for the unpleasantness that was bound to be forthcoming.

"You there, girl, tell the Caldwells that Carter Williams is here to see them. And when my attorney arrives, direct him to the appropriate conference room." The young woman just sat there eyeing Carter nervously. "Did you hear what I said?" Carter snapped impatiently.

"Yes, Mr. Williams, I heard you." Gripping the edge of her desk she nervously explained that both senior members of the firm were unavailable. When Carter's eyes squinted down in an angry glare, her fingers dug so deeply into the desktop she felt them go numb. The man went crazy, screeching until his face turned a nasty shade of purple. When she continued to sit there gaping at him, he slammed his fist on top of her desk. Though his behavior scared her out of her wits, none of it did any good. She still had to follow orders, refusing to buzz him through to the inner offices. Not following orders would put her well paid job at risk.

"Your insolent behavior will only result in your being fired!" Carter roared. "Tell those cantankerous old buffoons I am not leaving until one of them talks to me!"

"It's not my fault," the young woman sniffed, on the verge of tears.

Her obvious distress only irritated Carter even more; he began viciously kicking the door that led to the inner office. Just as the receptionist lifted the phone receiver to call for security Carter's lawyer arrived. He managed to quiet the enraged man long enough to ask for Mr. Stoneman. The receptionist said she would see if he was available. She suggested that he take his client outside to get a bit of fresh air while they were waiting. Maybe it would calm him down.

Stoneman kept Carter and his attorney waiting for an hour. When he finally had them shown into his office, he had already formulated a plan that could help them both. Since Lydia Williams' account had been the only one of importance assigned to him for the past five years its loss was substantial. When he complained about the decrease in his income the senior partners threw him bits and pieces of work which were totally beneath his status at the firm. He was afraid they might soon realize that his services were not really needed.

"What the hell have you people done?" Carter sputtered as soon as he walked through the door.

"Please, take a seat gentlemen let us discuss this situation rationally," Stoneman replied.

Huffing and snorting Carter threw himself into one of the leather chairs in front of Stoneman's desk. His lawyer chose to stand behind him, resting a restraining hand on Carter's shoulder.

"Those people have a real sneaky bastard for an attorney," Stoneman said. "They had sworn affidavits, prestigious witnesses, and physical possession of the dog. There was nothing this firm could do but acquiesce."

"So, I am to be thrown from my home for the sake of a dumb animal?" Carter snarled. "Lydia had to have been out of her mind to leave everything to that damn dog!"

"That's just what I needed to hear from you," Stoneman smugly replied.

"What?" Carter asked confused by Stoneman's comment. When he glanced over his shoulder at his attorney the man looked just as confused.

"We need to talk, Mr. Williams, **alone**," Stoneman said with blunt emphasis on the word alone. He didn't need Carter William's attorney butting in with a lot of legal mumbo jumbo.

Sputtering in protest, Carter's attorney tried to dissuade his client from taking Stoneman's suggestion. But Carter recognized the look in Stoneman's eyes; the man was as cold-hearted and greedy as Carter himself. With a wave of his hand Carter dismissed his attorney, ordering him to leave.

"Now that we can speak freely let me outline a plan, I think will be beneficial to both of us," Stoneman said.

"I'm listening. But what about your position here, won't there be a conflict of interest?"

"If you agree with my plan, then I will be resigning my position here. That means there would be no grounds for a case of conflict of interest."

Settling into his chair Carter smiled. "Well then, let me hear this plan."

Several hours later, Carter sailed out past the still fidgeting receptionist. She tried to pretend she didn't see him, keeping her head down, only peeking at him out of the corner of her eye. She noticed. he no longer had a scowl on his face and there was a renewed spring to his step. When he called out a jaunty "Good day" she managed to give him a fleeting smile.

Carter could not have been happier. Stoneman's plan was a good one. Carter figured it would be just a matter of days before he would be home again. Home, counting all his late wife's lovely money.

Chapter Fifty-two

It seemed as if everyone had forgotten about the mysterious death of Lydia Williams. The reporters stopped calling for updates. The District Attorney hadn't dropped by in days. Even the deputies rarely asked about the case anymore. Sheriff King didn't mind since it made his job a whole lot easier. He was a bit of a perfectionist though and liked to take his time scrutinizing every angle in a case without someone looking over his shoulder. This morning he was reviewing all the witness statements taken when the boat had first docked back at the marina. There was a niggling little kernel of doubt lingering in the back of his mind. Something he had missed. An insignificant little something which might just prove to be the missing piece of the puzzle.

Two hours later the words on the pages were beginning to blur. He needed a break. Grabbing his hat, he headed for the door yelling to the dispatcher that he was going out to see Bosco and Isis. He couldn't believe it, but he kind of missed those two kooks. It would be good to see them again.

*****

Turning onto Pennyroyal Road Sheriff King was pulled up short by a line of rag tag vehicles inching down the narrow street. He knew they could only be headed one place, the former Williams estate. *Wonder what trouble those two are concocting now,* he thought.

Following along behind the string of cars it took Sheriff King close to twenty minutes to make it from the corner to the entrance gate of the house's main drive. He let out a hoot of laughter when he saw Bosco Blue standing at the front entrance. The man was wearing an old white pith helmet and holding a bright red bullhorn in his hand. They were a nice contrast to the orange and yellow tie-dyed shirt and electric blue shorts that he was wearing. King inched his vehicle forward ducking low behind the steering wheel, waiting for Bosco to notice the squad car creeping up on him. He didn't have long to wait.

"Hey, man, this is private property oinker," Bosco's voice loudly boomed out across the line of cars.

Chuckling, Sheriff King turned on his flashers while inching closer.

"We got us a whole bunch of lawyers, dude, so just back up and go away," Bosco yelled.

Sitting up to pop his head out of the cruiser's window, Sheriff King bellowed back at Bosco. "You old reprobate, I ought to arrest you for wearing that outfit."

"Hey, Sheriff King, man is it good to see you," Bosco thundered through the bullhorn. "Isis is gonna be on cloud nine when she finds out you're here."

King eased his squad car off onto the shoulder of the road. As he was climbing out, he was almost bowled over by Bosco. The man threw a bear hug on him strong enough to choke an ox. King hugged back, slightly red-faced by the blatant show of affection. He tried his best to return the complicated handshake Bosco laid on him.

"What's going on here?" he asked, following Bosco back up the drive. "You folks throwing some kind of shindig?"

"No, it's moving day," Bosco grinned. "This place is like some feudal castle. It's huge! We decided to invite some of the folks from the commune to share the place with us."

"Just how big is it?"

"I don't know, man, something like 25, 26 acres of land, a lake, a greenhouse and a tennis court. Plus, there's a main house big enough to hold about a dozen families." Bosco shook his head still unable to believe the place now belonged to his wife. "Oh, and get this - it came with servants, dude."

"Servants," King snorted. "You've got to be kidding."

"No joke. There's this head servant butler dude named Darryl or Dillweed or something like that. He's real uptight. Keeps calling Isis Madame, it's driving her crazy. Then there are about thirty more folks who I'm not real sure what they do. We gave them their freedom. Told um all to go get a real life. All except that Dill dude - he like wanted to stay and take care of us. Said even if we stopped paying him, he couldn't just up and leave. He kept mumbling stuff about 'the butler's oath'."

Rounding the bend in the drive the two men stopped for a moment to gaze at the enormous house that dominated the landscape. A steady stream of people scurried up and down the main stairs carrying an assortment of bags, suitcases, and boxes through the open front doors.

Bosco chuckled at the glazed look that had come over Sheriff King's face.   "Told ya the place was a whopper."

"Whoa, I can see why Carter was pissed to lose it," King said. "It must be worth a couple of million."

"Sheriff King!" the delighted voice of Isis Winters floated down from the top of the stairs.

Soon King was being subjected to more hugs. Just when he had managed to squirm out of Isis' grasp, he heard another squeal. It was Janie Grayson, followed by her husband Jimmie. Janie raced down the steps grabbing Sheriff King in yet another bear hug. Not used to such demonstrative welcomes King blushed all the way to the tips of his ears.

Settled in the huge kitchen at the back of the house, Sheriff King sipped coffee from a delicate blue flowered cup. It took Isis a few minutes to roust several members of the commune from the room so they could talk in private.

"What brings you by, Sheriff?" Isis finally asked, sinking down in the chair beside him.

"Oh, just wanted to see how you all were doing." He

glanced around at the smiling faces of Janie, Jimmy, Bosco, and Isis.

"Have you learned anything more about what happened that night on the boat?" Janie said nervously stirring sugar into her cup.

"No, I sure haven't. My gut tells me there's only one person with a reason to have wanted that lady dead. I just can't seem to find anything substantial to legally nail that suspicion down."

"That slimy weasel Carter," Bosco and Jimmy grumbled in unison.

"I've been going back over all the statements from everyone on board that night. Someone told me something that's stuck in the back of my mind. It didn't seem important at the time, but now it's nagging away at me." Sheriff King glanced around the table, hoping someone would say something that would drag the elusive thought into the light of day.

"Maybe if we rehashed everything you might remember what it is," Isis suggested. "Let me put on a fresh pot of coffee then we can all pool our recollections of that night, see if anything stands out."

Over the next four hours the group went back over the entire fateful trip aboard *The Last Hurrah*. They sketched out the boat, noting where everyone had been before the storm hit. They picked apart the food fight between Lydia and Isis. They mulled over the merits of one of the crew having been the culprit. They even discussed the possibility of someone sneaking onto the boat. Still, Sheriff King could not pick out any new clues or directions to take the investigation. When he suggested they stop for the day Isis invited him to stay for the evening meal. Before he could answer, Jimmy told him they were grilling T-bone steaks. They had found a whole case of them in a basement freezer. King smiled and told them that was an offer he couldn't refuse.

While the guys trooped off to fire up the huge gas grill on one of the back patios, Isis and Janie started tossing together the ingredients for a salad. Four other women appeared in the kitchen, pitching in to make loaves of garlic bread, a plate of raw veggies with spinach dip, and several cakes for dessert. It didn't take long before the meal was ready. Bosco used his bullhorn to bellow out a "come and git it" that echoed across the lawn. People started flowing towards the house from all over the grounds.

A mismatched assortment of tables and chairs had been set up on the edge of the lawn to serve as the dining room. Folks popped up, grabbed a plate, and got in line for a steak hot off the grill. The air was filled with the smell of charred meat and the sound of laughter.

Looking around at the odd assortment of people sharing the meal, Sheriff King had to smile. All of them were as colorfully dressed as Bosco Blue. They ranged in age from newborn babes to an old fellow with a foot long white beard who looked to be at least a hundred. Everyone shared in the chores, the meal, and the lively conversation. It was kind of like being at a family reunion.

"Did they get your steak grilled right?" Isis inquired, taking a seat beside King her plate piled high with salad and veggies.

"Sure did Ms. Isis," King mumbled through a bite of hot buttery garlic bread.

"Didn't you want any of the browned onion and fresh mushroom topping for your steak?" Isis asked.

Before King could answer a man in a gray, striped, three-piece suit strode stiffly out of the back door carrying TooFoo. He took the tiny animal over to the edge of the grass setting him gently down next to a rose bush. TooFoo gave a happy yip and ran over to the closest tree, lifted his leg, and let go a hissing yellow stream.

Sheriff King stared at the tiny dog. With a loud gasp he leaped to his almost over-turning the table.

"Oh, my God! That's it, that's it," he yelled, dancing around pointing at a startled TooFoo and his handler. Everyone thought he was upset by the sight of the animal whizzing so close to their dining area. Isis had to admit it was rude of Doyle to let TooFoo down so close to the food. *I'll have to try and talk to the man*, she softly sighed, dreading the task. She still hadn't gotten used to having a servant. And from the frozen frown on Doyle's face, she knew he hadn't gotten used to them either.

Before she could speak up to apologize about TooFoo's toilet habits, Sheriff King pulled her from her chair and swung her around in a circle. "I know how and when Carter poisoned his wife!"

For a moment no one said a word then Sheriff King was bombarded with so many questions he felt a bit dizzy.

"Whoa, simmer down everybody. I can't answer that many questions at once," he bellowed over the din.

A sudden piercing whistle brought all the shouting to a halt. Bosco stood on a chair, bullhorn in hand, grinning like a baboon. "Now that I have your attention, let's hear what Sheriff King has to say. Go ahead, Chief, let 'er rip."

Steeling himself for another outburst King replied, "Afraid I can't go into detail right now. Don't want to jeopardize the investigation. Isis, I need to talk with you, Bosco, Janie, and Jimmy – alone."

Shushing the rumblings that began to rise from the others gathered on the patio, Isis grabbed Sheriff King's arm directing him back inside the house. She tugged him down a marbled hall to a small sitting room. Once the others were inside, she closed and locked the door.

"Okay, Sheriff, spill it," Bosco demanded.

"The first mate saw him get off the boat," King said, his face split by a dazzling smile.

"Saw who get off the boat?" Jimmy asked.

"It was in the first mate's statement and in the ship's log," King said his face lit with a dazzling smile.

"What?" the others cried in unison.

"Carter got off the boat that night, before the storm," King told them. "He made a big deal out of having to take his wife's dog over on the beach to do its duty. He took so long the first mate got worried and almost went to look for him."

"But Carter never got off the boat for TooFoo to do his duty," Janie blushed. "The crew always had to hose off the decks because Carter let TooFoo go wherever he wanted."

"Exactly," Sheriff King crowed. "He never got off the boat before that night for any reason."

"That means he had an opportunity to pick the death cap mushrooms," Isis said a deep frown creasing her brow. She sank back in her chair, shaking her head, looking just as forlorn as before Sheriff King's statement. "It doesn't prove he picked them, or that he knew they were poisonous, or that he used them to kill his wife."

"You're right, Isis, it's not solid proof," King sighed. "But there's something else. He was seen in the kitchen later that night after the meal and before the storm."

"Still doesn't mean he did it," Isis calmly reiterated.

"Gees, Louise, Babe, who's side are you on?" Bosco complained.

"If Sheriff King has no eyewitness who saw Carter pick the death cap mushrooms or chop them up and put them in with my good mushrooms, then there is still no proof," Isis sighed.

"Man, that blows," Jimmy snorted. "We know Carter did it."

"Well, then I guess unless he confesses it looks like he'll get away with it," King sighed. He knew Isis was right but still he had hoped there was a way to prove Carter had poisoned his wife. Shaking his head, shrugging his shoulders, he said, "The one good thing - since he was stupid enough to give you that dog, he isn't going to profit from Lydia's death. That has to be really sticking in his craw."

"Don't give up hope, Sheriff," Isis gently smiled, "Good karma will out in the end."

Chapter Fifty-three

Stoneman was being extremely cautious in his dealings with Carter Williams; he couldn't afford to have their plan backfire. If it did, he would not only be out of a job at Caldwell & Caldwell, but he might even get disbarred or face criminal action. That was why he had chosen to meet Carter at a little out of the way coffee house two towns over. No one knew him there and probably no one would recognize Carter either. Sipping a double mocha skim milk latte, Stoneman reviewed his plan. It seemed fool proof.

Carter was not amused by the early hour or Stoneman's choice of meeting place, but he had few options left. If this plan didn't work, then he would truly have lost everything. Just as he pulled into a parking spot outside the Java Joint Coffee Bar his cell phone began chirping.

"You've reached Carter Williams," he answered.

"Good morning, Mr. Williams, this is Sheriff King."

"Ah, Sheriff, it's been a while," Carter sniffed. "Did you need something?"

"Just wanted to update you on the progress of your wife's case."

Carter felt a lump rise in his throat. "Progress? Wha- wha- what progress?"

"A review of the witness statements has given us some new avenues of investigation," King smugly said.

"What does that mean?"

"Just that we have some things to check into that could help solve the mystery of your wife's death."

"Things? Things? What things?" Carter spluttered.

"Well, I'm afraid I can't go into detail. Wouldn't want to let the cat out of the bag too soon you know - spook off the murderer," King cheerily affirmed.

"So why did you call me? Do you think I know something?" Carter screamed into the phone.

"No, no, Mr. Williams, I just wanted to let you know that I will leave no stone unturned in this investigation. I will find out who poisoned your wife. That's a promise, sir." King listened closely to Carter's response. He was thrilled to hear a note of panic in the man's voice. "You have a real lovely day now, Mr. Williams," he added jovially. He hoped for just the opposite; that Carter Williams had a terrible day worrying about what they had found out about his wife's death.

When Carter finally stumbled inside the coffee house, collapsing in the chair across from him, Stoneman thought the man looked positively ill. His hands were visibly shaking, his face so pale it looked almost translucent. Stoneman could see a large vein in Carter's forehead pulsing angrily.

"You look like hell, Carter."

"That annoying Sheriff just called me hinting that he had found new information about Lydia's death." Carter darted a quick glance over his shoulder as if expecting Sheriff King to be sneaking up behind him.

"What did he say? What information does he have?"

"How the hell should I know? Do you think he laid out the evidence in my lap, you idiot?"

"Whoa, don't jump down my throat, Carter. I'm on your side, remember," Stoneman snapped back. "Get some decaf and a donut for Christ's sake, maybe you just need to eat something."

Stoneman signaled for a server ordering for Carter when the man just sat staring at the woman. Once they had their orders, Stoneman quickly got down to business.

"I called a friend from law school whose specialty is wills and trusts. He had some great insights. He thinks we could win back at least the house for you if we handle things right."

"Just the house," Carter bitterly snorted. "Well, at least I wouldn't be out on the street. What do we need to do?"

"First of all is there anyone you can think of who would be

willing to stand up in court on your behalf? Either as a character witness or with information about the role you played in the household."

"I suppose some of our old friends from the Country Club might."

"These have to be people who knew both you and Lydia, and have sterling reputations," Stoneman cautioned.

Carter sat sipping his coffee for a long time before answering. "There's Margaret Chessman. She and Lydia were doubles partners for years. Her father owns several small banks in the area, and she is president of one of them. She and I always got along famously. I'm sure she would remember several incidents concerning the construction and decorating of the house. She could confirm the fact that Lydia asked my advice on the design."

"That's not a bad idea," Stoneman mused. "If she can convince the jury that the home was a joint project between you and Lydia it might help sway them in your favor."

"Oh! There's Lydia's personal assistant, Doyle, whom I hand-picked to manage the household. Lydia was always telling everyone what a jewel he was and how I had chosen him just for her. She said she would be lost without him," Carter smugly smiled. "Doesn't that show she not only trusted my judgment but that we worked together to take care of the home?"

"That is brilliant!" Stoneman gushed. "That's just the kind of thing we need. The more people we can get to say that the building and care of the estate was a joint project between you and your wife, the better. We need to show the jury that certain expectations of ownership would normally be assumed by anyone in your situation. Therefore, the property should be yours."

The two spent the rest of the morning drawing up a list of potential witnesses. Stoneman was a bit dismayed by the brevity of the list. He told Carter to think about it a bit more and call him back if he thought of anyone they could add. Before they left, he also outlined his strategy for using the press to help sway support for the return of Carter's home. They needed to make Carter look pathetic, grieving, and lost. They also needed to show his willingness to compromise. He would be more than willing to let the hippie couple keep the dog and the bulk of the estate - he just wanted his home back. What they didn't need to know was that Carter would be selling the estate and all its contents as soon as he got his hands on it. The cars, furnishings, clothing, artwork, and even the plants in the greenhouse would all go to the highest bidder. Stoneman figured his share of the sale would be at least two million. Not a bad haul for one lawsuit.

Chapter Fifty-four

Janie and Jimmy were stunned when Isis asked if they would be interested in moving to the estate. Isis told them they could pick a spot anywhere on the 27 acres and build their own home. Until it was completed, they could stay at the big house in one of the suites. It was a real tempting offer. The apartment they lived in was cramped and a bit dingy.

"Don't you have too many people crammed in here already?" Jimmy laughed.

"About half of these folks are just here to get things set up. We're going to have a gigantic yard sale and sell off most of the stuff in the house. I swear those Williams people had the worst taste in furnishings. However, everything looks expensive, so maybe we'll be able to sell most of it for a decent price."

Janie gave Jimmy 'the look' which meant she wanted to discuss the offer in private before they gave Isis an answer. He knew better than to dismiss that look. He'd done it one time, to his everlasting regret. He didn't relish sleeping on the sofa again for another two weeks.

"Let us have a day or two to think it over."

"Sure, you do that," Isis grinned at him. She'd seen Janie give him 'the look.'

"Ahem," the servant named Doyle coughed, halting their conversation. He'd popped his head silently out of the kitchen doorway like some errant spirit. None of them had heard him approach. Whenever he popped in like that it spooked the hell out of Bosco. He swore the man wasn't human, but some alien transplant or government spy.

"Madame, there is an attorney here to see you, a Mr. Stoneman. Shall I show him to the drawing room?" Doyle asked, his face set in its usual frown. Janie and Jimmy burst into laughter, which only made Doyle's expression deepen.

Isis took a moment to glare at them before answering. "Just bring him on back here, Doyle." *I wonder what he wants*, she mused.

"Probably here with some scheme up his sleeve to earn more of those billable hours them attorneys are so fond of," Bosco snorted. "Why didn't you just have Daryl throw him out?"

"Bosco don't be rude," Isis admonished. "He might say something we can relay to Sheriff King."

Stoneman came walking in behind Doyle with a broad smile on his handsome face. He gushed on and on about how nice it was to see them all again. He asked after their health, and that of TooFoo. He commented on the hustle and bustle going on around the place.

"So, tell us why you're really here," Bosco snorted, interrupting the man's cheesy tirade.

"Yes, I suppose laying the cards on the table would be best," Stoneman replied. "I'm here on behalf of my client, Carter Williams."

"What does that conniving weasel want now?" Jimmy snapped.

"Yeah, how come you're working for that slime bucket? Thought you were associated with the dead woman's firm," Bosco added with a scowl.

"Please, please let's not start off on the wrong foot," Stoneman soothed. "I'm here on what I'd guess you could call a mission of mercy. If you would just hear me out."

"Spill it," Bosco growled.

"This ought to be good" Jimmy muttered.

Stoneman changed his expression to one of deep sadness. "My client is desperate. Not only is he still reeling from the death of his wife, but he has been left homeless and destitute," Stoneman stated letting out a long sigh. "He is hoping that an appeal to your sense of morality will lead to an amicable solution to his problem and yours."

"Our problem? What problem would that be?" Isis asked.

"Why the hefty inheritance taxes of course. And then there's the fallout from all the bad publicity to deal with as well,"

Stoneman stated taking in the startled faces staring back at him.

"We already have a plan for paying the taxes," Bosco said. "Guess you can run along now." He made shooing motions with his hands as he pointed to the door.

"Wait! What bad publicity?" Isis asked.

"Ah, well, this is a bit awkward," Stoneman mumbled. "One of the local papers has taken it upon themselves to champion the return of Carter's home. I'm afraid they aren't the most reputable company. They're doing it without the permission of my client, of course, but it could still prove to be unbelievably bad publicity for you and the commune."

"Son of a bitch!" Bosco roared. "You lawyers are all the same, just blood sucking weasels. Get the hell out of our home before I really lose my temper and do something we'll both regret."

Stoneman looked around at the others and quickly realized he had lost this round. Better to leave on a friendly note. "Sorry you folks feel that way," he sighed. Moving towards the door he added, "I'll just leave and give you time to think things over. Maybe you'll be inclined to listen to my client's more than equitable proposal once you have time to discuss the matter. I'll leave a copy of it with you to read. Call me if you have any questions." Gathering up his briefcase and files, Stoneman laid a folder on the table before disappearing out the side door.

"Do you believe that shit?" Jimmy snorted.

"They're up to something sneaky. We need to get a hold of Jay Woods and have him review this proposal of theirs," Isis murmured, flipping through the multi-page document.

"What about the yard sale?" Janie asked. "Should we wait or go ahead with it?"

"Since we need money for the inheritance taxes we go ahead," Isis declared. "The ad will be in tomorrow's paper, so it's too late to cancel it even if we wanted to."

Chapter Fifty-five

The next morning brought big surprises for all of those involved in the Lydia Williams case. The local gossip rag devoted their front page to the story of Carter Williams, garishly detailing the death of his wife, they glossed over the missing heir but tore into Isis and Bosco's reputations. They reported that "The grieving widower's home has been stolen out from under him by a nefarious pair of gold-diggers." Bosco and Isis, reading the article over their morning coffee, had a good chuckle. Anyone with half a brain would consider the source, taking the story with a grain of salt.

On the other hand, the small but colorful ad in the hometown paper for the "Yard Sale of the Century" had Carter Williams screaming with rage. He was on the phone to Stoneman before he even had one sip of coffee.

Over at the County building Sheriff King carefully read both papers. *This could be the catalyst we need to get this case rolling again*, he smiled. He figured Jay Woods was already on top of things for Isis and Bosco, so he wasn't too worried about them. However, he figured Carter's attorney was more than likely scrambling to cover his ass, hold onto his lucrative client, and stop the sale by any means possible. Juggling all those balls would put the man off his usual sharp game. *This could be just the right time to pay him a visit,* King mused. Whistling cheerily, he strode out to his cruiser looking forward to the confrontation ahead. He just loved putting the squeeze on bad guys.

*****

Pulling up in front of Caldwell & Caldwell's legal offices Sheriff King took a moment to call back to the station. He informed the dispatcher on duty that if Bosco, Isis, or Jay Woods called to patch them through at once. Grabbing up his very official looking black leather binder and taking a moment to pluck his gun from the glovebox, securely tucking it in his shoulder holster, Sheriff King headed into the building.

"Is that Stoneman fellow here, I'd like a word with him," King announced to the pretty young woman behind the front desk.

The woman looked flustered for a moment then said, "I'm sorry, Sheriff, but he isn't in the building right now. Could one of the senior partners be of assistance?"

King figured what the heck; one lawyer was about as good as another. "Sure, whichever one is available would be fine." He took a seat across the room on one of the soft leather chairs.

Moments later a tall, impeccably groomed older man appeared in the doorway. He stopped to hold a hushed conversation with the receptionist before turning to stare over at King.

Shooting his cuffs, the man strode over to where the sheriff sat slouched in his chair.

"Good morning, Sheriff King, what brings you by our offices?" the man asked, extending his hand for King to shake.

"And you would be…" King inquired, deliberately ignoring the man's outstretched hand.

"I am Richard Caldwell, senior partner of this firm," the man sniffed, his hand dropping back to his side. "What can I do for you? I'm a busy man."

"I was looking for that young fella that works for you, Stoneman. He and I and his client need to have a conversation," King said.

"And which client would that be?" Caldwell impatiently huffed. "We don't take criminal cases."

"Carter Williams," King replied.

With a haughty glare Caldwell informed the Sheriff that they did not represent Carter Williams. He also made it clear that they no longer represented the estate of the late Lydia Williams either. "We have washed our hands of the whole distasteful situation; sorry we can no longer be of any assistance to you, Sheriff."

"Well, now, ain't that strange," Sheriff King muttered,

rifling through his binder as if looking for a document. Glancing back up at Richard Caldwell he frowned. "Carter and Stoneman were just in touch with Isis Winters and Bosco Blue about the ownership of the estate's heir. Stoneman appeared to be representing Mr. Williams."

"That is news to me," Caldwell retorted. "As far as it concerns this firm, we do not represent Carter Williams. We therefore have no knowledge of any lawsuit in which he may or may not be involved. I am afraid there is nothing more I can say about the matter. Now if you will excuse me, I have clients waiting. Good day Sheriff."

Richard Caldwell was seething as he strode back to his office. That idiot Stoneman could ruin them if he was actually representing Carter Williams. Paging his brother, he paced his office formulating a plan of action. When Michael entered, Richard briefly outlined the situation. Michael readily agreed with Richard's idea for heading off any possible bad publicity for their firm. Stoneman would be fired, retroactively of course, with a significant enough severance package to insure both his silence and his cooperation. The press would be discreetly notified of Stoneman's exit from the firm, and their subsequent total lack of involvement with one Carter Williams.

Chapter Fifty-six

Sheriff King took his time driving over to the south side roach trap motel where Carter Williams was supposedly staying. Though still registered there the manager told King that Carter was seldom around. Questioning the staff King discovered that Carter was staying at a four-star hotel up town. They said he showed up now and then for meetings with several other people. Further questioning elicited no additional details about the meetings. As Sheriff King headed back to his squad car he decided to stop off for an early lunch before paying Carter a visit at his new uptown digs.

Just down the block from Carter's new hotel King spotted an old-fashioned diner. He quickly discovered that the only thing 'old fashioned' about the place was the décor. The menu was filled with yuppie gourmet fare, and the prices were just this side of ridiculous. Ordering the cheapest thing on the menu, Tomato Soup Florentine with a grilled cheddar cheese sandwich with organic tomato slices for $16. 95, he sat back in the booth to people watch until his food arrived. This was becoming one of the trendier spots in town, so those who thought they were somebody liked to be seen strolling the area. A steady parade of elegantly clad ladies flowed past the diner's oversized windows. There were also dozens of generic looking men in dark business suits, cell phones glued to their ears, laptop cases banging on their hips. Everyone was scurrying by in a dizzying rush. It gave King a headache just watching them. *"Looks like an army of ants on the march,"* he muttered.

His server barely managed a smile when she delivered his meal. The bowl of tomato soup had something that looked like seaweed floating around in it, and the sandwich had more bread than cheese, but at least it was hot. Taking his first bite of the thick sandwich, he glanced back out the window just in time to spot Carter Williams go sailing by.

"Hey, Williams!" a voice bellowed behind Carter. Jerking his head around, Carter spotted Sheriff King standing in the doorway of the Red Spot Diner, waving his hands, and shouting Carter's name. Grumbling under his breath about *"stupid people not deserving to live"* Carter retraced his steps back to the doorway of the diner.

"Really, Sheriff, your lack of manners is an embarrassment," Carter snapped.

"Just thought we could have a friendly conversation over a cup of coffee, Mr. Williams" Sheriff King smiled. "I tried your motel, but no one could remember seeing you there in a while. And they told me you were staying on this side of town, but still paying for the other room as well. Kind of odd, isn't it?"

"Oh...um... I had to leave there. Too many unsavory people

hanging around," Carter nervously mumbled. He wondered why King was checking on his whereabouts.

"So, which place are you calling home these days?" King asked.

Carter sniffed, raising an eyebrow, trying to edge his way down the sidewalk away from the sheriff. "I really don't think that's any of your concern."

"Just need to know so I can keep you updated on your wife's case," King coldly smiled, the effort not reaching his eyes. "You do want to know how the case is going, don't you?"

"Well, yes, of course I do," Carter snapped.

"So come on in and get a cup of coffee. We have a few things to discuss." Not waiting to see if Carter agreed, King clapped a hand on his shoulder, turning him around, steering him through the diner's door.

The same dour faced server appeared to take Carter's order for a double mocha latte, and Sheriff King's request for the supe-sized mug of regular dark roast along with an apple turnover. Using the old interrogation technique of extended silence, King settled into the far corner of the booth gazing silently across at Carter. King had learned early on in his career that voids demanded to be filled, so giving a suspect the silent treatment usually resulted in them yakking up a storm. This time was no different.

"Are you going to tell me what's happening or not?" Carter irritably snapped, the return of their server delaying King's answer.

Taking three huge bites of his golden-brown turnover, King washed it down with noisy gulps of coffee before he finally answered. "I've been going back over the witness statements from that night on the boat."

When he didn't say anything else, Carter growled, "And?"

"Seems like you took a trip off the boat right before the storm. Any specific reason for that little foray into the woods?"

"In case you've forgotten we had our dog on board. He needed a stroll."

"Well, here's the funny thing about that, you never took him off the boat before that night to do his business. You just let him do his thing on the deck for the crew to clean up. What was so different about that night?"

Sighing in exasperation Carter replied, "Obviously you've never owned a small dog, Sheriff. They tend to be nervous animals. TooFoo sensed the approaching storm; it made him whiny and restless. Lydia suggested a walk to calm him."

"Guess that makes sense. Just figured a rich fella like yourself would have had one of the staff do such a menial chore."

Carter felt his left eye begin to twitch. "My dog walking is the reason for this big meeting? I'm in mourning over the loss of my darling wife and you want to criticize me for walking the dog? Have you no decency? No respect for my feelings at all?"

Sheriff King once again took his time in answering, sipping coffee, wolfing down the last bite of his turnover. "Well, no, Mr.

Williams it's not the only question I had on my mind. I was also wondering why your attorney paid a visit to Isis and Bosco this morning. Thought the question of TooFoo's ownership and inheritance of the estate had been settled."

Carter glared at King, slamming his coffee cup on the table. Standing, he snorted, "What I talk about with my attorney is privileged information. I have nothing more to say to you. And it's obvious you have little of importance to relay to me. I am in mourning, please try to respect that and don't disturb me again!" Shaking with both fear and indignation, Carter managed to find the exit and make his escape.

Sheriff King watched Carter storm off down the street. Then he calmly gathered up the man's cup, placing it in a sealed evidence bag. It should be interesting to check Carter's fingerprints against those found on the bowl of left-over mushrooms in the boat's refrigerator. Or those found on the broken plate from Lydia Williams' last meal. Several prints had yet to be identified and Sheriff King was betting at least some of them were Carter's. Paying the already exorbitant meal charge of $37. 43, he asked the server to include the cost of Carter's mug on his tab. Tucking it under his arm, he whistled all the way back to the station.

Chapter Fifty-seven

The day was turning out to be as close to perfect as one could expect for late fall in the Midwest. Though the temperature was a bit on the cool side the sun was shining brightly adding a touch of warmth to the day. Things were bustling out at the former Williams estate in preparation for the big yard sale. The grounds were alive with dozens upon dozens of people all helping with the tagging and placement of the sale items. The front lawn resembled an ant colony on steroids. Isis was busy directing the flow, set-up, and pricing of everything they hoped to sell. Bosco was busy roping a section of lawn by the front gate for parking. He was a bit miffed that Isis wouldn't let him charge for the privilege. Outside the main gates over a dozen cars sat lined up waiting for the sale to begin. There was barely an hour to go before the official opening of the "Yard Sale of the Century."

With only ten minutes to spare, Isis, dismayed to see a city squad car pull up to the main gate, its lights flashing, quickly headed down to see what sort of problem had sprung up. Bosco raced after her.

"Hey, man, you trying to cut in line for the sale?" Bosco smiled at the young officer approaching the gate. He knew humor could usually keep a dire situation from spilling over into tragedy. Not this time.

"No, sir, I have papers for a Ms. Winters and a Mr. Blue," the young man replied.

Bosco pressed the button to roll back the gate as Isis stepped forward to take the papers. She stood quietly reading them for a moment, before groaning aloud. "Young man, this has to be a mistake."

"No, Ma'am, it isn't. Judge Paulson signed the order this morning."

"What is it, Babe?" Bosco asked, a frown creasing his brow. Isis looked like she was in shock.

"It's an order...a court order. It says we have to stop... to stop...we can't sell... can't sell anything from the estate," Isis stammered. "Oh, Bosco, what are we going to do?"

"It's that damn Carter Williams and his sleaze bag attorney!" Bosco roared. "You just go on back and tell him to buzz off, this place belongs to us, and we'll do what we want with it."

"Afraid I don't know this Williams fellow or anything about who owns what. I'm just following orders, sir."

"We've got every right to do whatever we want with this damn place. So, we'll just be going ahead with the sale," Bosco said.

"Sir, I'm to remain at the front gate here to ensure that you comply with the Judge's order." Ignoring Isis and Bosco's spluttering protests the young man returned to his squad car moving it into a position that blocked the front entry. He climbed out and stepped in front of the vehicle, one hand resting on the gun at his hip. No way was he allowing anyone to get past him and onto the grounds.

"We have to find Jay right away," Isis yelled to Bosco as she ran back up the drive towards the house.

Bosco followed at a slower pace, his mind reeling with visions of the potential problems that could arise if the sale wasn't allowed to take place. Before he was halfway up the drive, he heard a commotion back at the gate. People were yelling at the police officer stationed there, cries of false advertising topping the mêlée. As Bosco watched the stoic efforts of the officer to remain calm, a TV van came screeching down the road, skidding to a halt on the shoulder its bumper mere inches from that of the squad car. Their presence quickly made the situation a whole lot worse. Now that there were cameras aimed at them the crowd of disappointed shoppers became even more vocal. Sighing heavily, Bosco went in search of his bullhorn. It was going to be an awfully long day.

An hour later as Sheriff King arrived at the estate on Pennyroyal Road a mini riot was taking place. One lone city police officer stood forlornly behind the closed gates to the property, ineffectually yelling at the crowd of disgruntled shoppers. A TV reporter was at the head of the mob, her microphone shoved through the gate into the officer's face. She was screaming something about freedom of the press. The crowd was yelling to be let in for the advertised sale. Bosco, also on the other side of the gate, headed a crowd of the commune folks yelling about unfair legal practices, crooked lawyers, and judges on the take. Despite the seriousness of the situation, King couldn't help but laugh. Only Bosco and Isis could create such havoc with a simple thing like a yard sale. Using his 'official voice,' King began pushing his way towards the head of the crowd. As he forced his way towards the front he ran into Jay Woods. An old woman with a large purse was slapping the poor little attorney on the head. King rescued him, assuring the woman that he would punish Woods for trying to slip ahead in line. Holding the attorney in front of him like a shield, King shoved his way through the crowd. Reaching the secured main gates, he waved his badge in the air. The harried looking police officer motioned him forward, hoping he was finally going to get help managing the crowd.

As he stepped towards the gates Sheriff King felt the crowd pressing in behind him. He had to shove people back to keep them from pinning him against the gate. Glaring through the wrought iron bars he yelled, "Officer, what the hell is going on here?"

"Had to serve papers from Judge Paulson shutting down the yard sale," the officer yelled back. "When the gate didn't open up on time these people went nuts. Then the news crew showed up and inflamed the situation even more."

"Why did Judge Paulson order the sale shut down?" King yelled back.

"Something about a lawsuit over ownership of the home

and contents."

"It was that slime ball, weasel eyed, Cro-Magnon idiot Carter Williams who did this," came Bosco's bullhorn enhanced voice bellowing over the angry voices of the crowd.

"Morning, Bosco," Sheriff King yelled back. "I got Woods here with me. Can you safely let us in?"

"I'm not supposed to let anyone onto the grounds, Sheriff," the nervous young police officer yelled, stepping forward with his hands raised.

Sheriff King shook his head and smiled. "Guess I could just leave then and let you handle this situation yourself."

The young police officer looked around at the rapidly increasing crowd, which was getting more hostile with every passing minute. Shaking his head in resignation, he lowered his hands, letting out a deep sigh. "Fine. I'll let you inside but only if you help me get this situation under control, Sheriff.

Squeezing between the squad car and the gate, King held a quick conversation with Bosco, before motioning the young officer closer and whispering in his ear. King then dragged Jay Woods back out through the crowd. King shoved Woods in his squad car then took off down the street. Bosco had told him about a back delivery entrance and the fact that, so far, no one was hip to its location. Circling the entire block, King found the back gate. Isis was there waiting to let them in.

"Oh, we are so glad to see you," she gushed giving King a bear hug. "And you, too, Jay," she added, turning to hug the little attorney.

Extracting himself from Isis's grip Jay said, "I already put a call into Judge Paulson's chambers. I've dealt with him on many occasions and his integrity is above reproach. He must have been given some erroneous information that led him to issue the cessation of sale order."

King clapped a hand on Jay's shoulder. "I have some information that may help. I stopped by Caldwell & Caldwell to talk with that guy Stoneman, and they told he no longer works there. The Caldwell brothers also told me they no longer have anything whatsoever to do with Carter Williams or the estate of his late wife."

"So, Stoneman is acting on his own," Jay mused, a glint of steel in his eyes. "That's definitely interesting news, Sheriff."

Just then Bosco rounded the corner his face split in a huge grin. "Man, this is the most fun I've had in years." The others turned towards him with various looks of disbelief on their faces. "Hey, don't look so bummed. As soon as that news crew gets the word out the crowd will get even bigger."

"And why would you think that's a good thing?" Sheriff King asked.

"More bodies on the lawn, means more money in the sales jar," Bosco chuckled.

"But that judge closed down the sale," Isis reminded him.

"Babe, that's only a temporary inconvenience," Bosco smiled. "Jay will get that order reversed in no time."

"Glad you're so confident of my skills, Bosco," Jay laughed.

"You know, Honeybear, you might just be right," Isis grinned back. "Refusing to allow people in for the sale will keep the crowd agitated, which will keep that news crew filming. It's free publicity. And telling people they can't have something only makes them want it more. All we have to do is sit back and wait for Jay to do his magic." Isis did a little happy dance before adding, "I have time to do up some more goodies for the bake sale booth."

"Way to bring some good vibes, Babe," Bosco grinned. "Nothing smells better than bread baking it will drive the crowd crazy."

Before the group could discuss the current situation any further, Sheriff King's office called trying to patch through a message from the patrol officer at the front gate. Basically, the Dispatcher said the patrolman had screamed for help. More people had shown up, along with two more news crews, plus Carter Williams and his attorney. King heaved a sigh of resignation and headed back to help at the front gate; it was going to be a long day.

Chapter Fifty-eight

Bosco drug Jay Woods off towards the front gate, bending the lawyer's ear with tales of past riots that he had taken part in and their unfortunate outcomes. Isis went off to gather the rest of the folks helping with the sale to apprise them of the latest developments. After that she would be in the kitchen whipping up more goodies to sell.

Back out on Pennyroyal Road Sheriff King had to park three blocks to the west and hike back to the main gate. There had to be at least two hundred people crowded around the entrance, none of them were smiling. The young patrol officer had come out from behind the gate and retreated to the safety of his cruiser's interior. At the head of the crowd the news crews held sway, using the cords and cables from their equipment to hold back the increasingly agitated shoppers. In between the crowd and the squad car stood a weeping Carter Williams, his attorney standing stoically by his side. As Sheriff King got closer, he heard the tail end of Stoneman's impassioned plea on behalf of his client.

"...therefore, we ask you good people to disperse. This poor man has suffered enough indignities since the death of his wife. Please, go back home. Help us resolve this situation amicably. Call Judge Paulson, talk to the press, and call whomever you know who could help this grieving widower get his home back. Carter Williams is more than willing to share his late wife's estate with these cold-hearted people, but they won't even speak with him. He just wants his home returned. He's willing to give up everything else."

Folks at the front of the crowd began to feel a bit sorry for the weeping man standing before them and started trying to move away from the gate. However, the people in the back hadn't been able to hear most of Stoneman's speech. All they wanted was a chance to get inside and scoop up a bargain. When Bosco and Jay Woods appeared the crowd once again began yelling and shoving to get inside. No amount of yelling from the young police officer, or pleas for patience from Bosco on his bull horn could sway the angry mob of shoppers. Sheriff King, realizing that the situation could soon become dangerous if the crowd continued to press forward, pulled his revolver from its holster, firing a shot into one of the oak trees just past the front gate. It immediately got everyone's attention.

"This is your last warning folks - clear out now," King bellowed. Glaring menacingly, he pushed his way through the crowd. The frightened shoppers parted like the red sea.

When Sheriff King finally managed to reach the front of the crowd, he tersely ordered the news people to leave, telling them that their presence was worsening the situation. When they began whining about "freedom of the press," King told them that if they didn't leave, he would have no choice but to arrest them for inciting a riot. Grumbling under their breath they nonetheless beat a hasty retreat to their vans.

Turning to give an equally frosty look to Carter Williams and James Stoneman, Sheriff King pointed to the city patrol vehicle, suggesting they take a seat inside for their own safety. The look on his face brooked no refusal from the two men. Once the news people and Carter were dispensed with the crowd quieted down. They still growled about not being allowed inside, milling about aimlessly, unwilling to return to their cars and lose their place in line.

Just as Sheriff King was going to start threatening them with trespass citations, and call for reinforcements, he heard Isis calling out from behind the gate.   "Sheriff! Sheriff King! I have a solution to the problem. We are offering all these nice folks who showed up a buy one, get one free, rain check certificate. It will be honored on the rescheduled day of the great sale event."

A low buzzing began to drift through the crowd of disgruntled shoppers as word of the offer spread.

"Just ask them to line up, step forward one at a time, and we will hand them a receipt for the exclusive offer," Isis said.

"What if there ain't no sale at all?" an elderly woman at the front of the line called out.

"Then we will honor the receipt at the Sunshine Commune Farmer's market," Isis replied. "Good for any booth there including fresh produce and baked goods."

Borrowing Bosco's bullhorn, Sheriff King informed the entire crowd about the offer. Soon folks were lined up in two orderly rows, stepping up to the gate to accept their slip of paper. Within the hour all the potential shoppers had left the scene. The young patrol officer stiffly thanked Sheriff King for his help, embarrassed by his own failure to control the crowd. Sheriff King assured him it was no problem, that anyone would have needed help dealing with such a large group of unruly people. Isis asked them both to stay for lunch, which the patrol officer declined.

Sheriff King on the other hand said he would love one of her home-cooked meals. "I'll be back in a moment as soon as I fetch my squad car."

Before the young patrol officer left the scene, he freed Carter and his lawyer from the back of his vehicle. The two men scurried off without a backward glance.

*****

Carter and Stoneman stopped in at a small pub on their way back to town to celebrate what they felt was a victory.

"That was just brilliant," Carter crowed. "I swear that one old lady in the front of the crowd was actually weeping."

"Plus, our inside man at that tabloid press will give it just the spin we need," Stoneman smugly agreed. "It was pretty brilliant, if I do say so myself."

"What's our next step?" Carter asked, flipping open his menu to scan the entrees, suddenly feeling ravenous.

"The ball is in their court now. We just sit back and wait for their attorney to make the next move," Stoneman replied. He couldn't help but feel elated, puffing out his chest and smirking at the young waiter who came to take their order. He felt on top of the world.

The two men ordered up the biggest steaks on the menu, plus a bottle of champagne. It had been a great morning as far as they were concerned. The sale had been stopped. The press had shown up. And the public had been eyewitness to the sorrowful weeping of the widowed Carter Williams. The whole thing could not have gone any better as far as Stoneman was concerned. Smiling like an ape with a banana, he barely heard anything his client talked about over lunch. He was too busy daydreaming about the millions he would soon have to afford him the lifestyle he felt he deserved.

Chapter Fifty-nine

Judge Paulson was a bit irritated to see the name Jay Woods added to his morning calendar. The young attorney always represented the oddest people and causes. Paulson had hoped the young man would outgrow that propensity as he was a brilliant litigator. Sighing heavily, he punched the call button on his desk, telling his secretary to show Woods in.

"Good morning, Your Honor," Jay smiled as he strode confidently through the door. He leaned in, shook the judge's hand, and asked about his golf game. Everyone around the courthouse knew Judge Paulson's real passion was playing eighteen holes, not mitigating lawsuits. Unbuttoning his jacket Jay sank down into one of the barrel chairs in front of the Judge's huge mahogany desk. His tiny frame was engulfed by the oversized chair, his feet barely reaching the floor.

"Whose cause are you championing this time, Woods?" Judge Paulson sighed.

"It's not exactly a cause, sir. Clients of mine were served with a Cease-and-Desist Order that you signed. I think you may have been duped, sir," Jay calmly stated.

Judge Paulson gave Woods a look of disbelief before demanding to see the order. Woods quickly handed it to him, sitting back to wait as the Judge perused the papers.

"Yes, I did sign this order. Caldwell & Caldwell raised a number of issues that brought the legality of the late Lydia Williams' will into question. Allowing the sale of any items associated with her estate could have larger repercussions down the road."

Jay frowned. "That's just what I thought, sir. You were given false information."

"That is a serious allegation, young man. Do you have any proof to back it up?"

"Well, first Stoneman no longer works for Caldwell & Caldwell. Secondly, a hearing has already been held to determine ownership of the heir and suitability of guardianship; both matters were resolved in favor of my clients."

"What about the allegations of wrongdoing in Lydia Williams death?" Paulson countered. "A criminal cannot financially benefit from his or her criminal act."

"The Grand Jury determined there was insufficient evidence to hold my client over for trial. Plus, local law enforcement personnel have assured me that they no longer consider my client a suspect in the case."

Judge Paulson's forehead creased into a deep frown. He didn't like being lied to for any reason. "Give me a few moments to verify your information," he rumbled, reaching for the phone on his desk. Jay smiled to himself as he left the room allowing Judge Paulson privacy to make his calls.

When Judge Paulson called Jay back to his office, one look at the man's face had Jay shivering all the way down to his toes. He was glad he wasn't the one who had caused that angry expression.

"I just spoke with Richard Caldwell and Sheriff King," Judge Paulson growled. "My secretary will have the paperwork rescinding the Cease-and-Desist Order ready for you to pick up on your way out. Please apologize on my behalf to your clients." Paulson dismissed Woods with a wave of his hand not bothering to acknowledge Jay's proffered thank you. He was already formulating what he would say to the bar association about the antics of one James Stoneman, soon to be former attorney at law.

On his way out of the Judge's chamber Jay heard Paulson buzz his secretary, telling her to put a call through for him to the State Bar Association. *Sure glad my name's not Stoneman,* Jay thought with a shiver. He'd never heard Judge Paulson sound so angry. Retrieving the Judge's order to rescind the Cease-and-Desist paper from the secretary, Jay scurried off to give Bosco and Isis the good news.

Chapter Sixty

The local news media scurried to update their stories about the mob scene at the Williams estate that morning. When the five o'clock broadcast rolled around the emphasis of their stories dramatically changed. An attorney named Jay Woods had called them to report the rescinding of the stop sale order. He also informed them that his clients had rescheduled the "Yard Sale of the Century" for the following morning, starting at 8:00 A. M. When questioned as to why the order had been changed, Woods was tight lipped, referring them to Judge Paulson's office. Upon contacting Judge Paulson's office, the reporters learned that false statements had been given to secure the initial order. Those allegations were now under investigation. Though the reporters peppered the Judge with questions, he had simply barked "no further comment" and ended the call.

Stoneman was a bit irritated when Carter Williams called him a little after five that evening. The man was such a whining, royal pain in the ass. Stoneman would be glad when the case was over, and he could shed himself of the sniveling snob. Carter was screaming so loudly over the phone, Stoneman missed most of what was said as he had to hold the phone a foot from his ear to keep from going deaf.

"Carter, shut the hell up for a minute and calm down," Stoneman finally bellowed.

"Don't you tell me to shut up, I'm paying through the nose for your services and right now they suck," Carter yelled back. "The Judge is letting those gold diggers go through with selling off my property!"

"What the hell are you talking about?"

"Turn on your freaking TV and see for yourself. You had better come up with a solution quick or I'm not paying you one more damn cent. Hell, I might even sue you for misrepresentation, you idiot!" Carter slammed the phone down cutting off the call. What the hell good was it having a hotshot attorney if he didn't do what you asked of him? Carter was so angry he could barely manage to choke down his before supper martini.

Digging frantically between the sofa cushions to find his TV remote, Stoneman felt a bit queasy. Turning on the plasma screen that hung over his fireplace he raced through the channels looking for a local news station. When he finally found one, he watched in stunned disbelief as a smiling Bosco Blue announced the rescheduling of the sale at the estate. Flipping around until he found another station airing the story, Stoneman watched the report unfold with mounting horror. This time it showed a reporter standing outside the County Courthouse repeating a statement given by Judge Paulson. The statement had Stoneman feeling more than just a bit queasy. He felt the sour taste of bile rising in the back of his throat. *I never should have thrown in with that greedy bastard Carter Williams*, he softly moaned. He was ruined. Judge Paulson would not take his role in the incident lightly. He'd be lucky to escape with just a simple disbarment.

Scrambling to think of a way to save his own hide he decided feeding Carter to the wolves was the only solution. Powering up his laptop, Stoneman went to the on-line Cayman bank account he had set up when this whole incident first started. Though the amount in the account wasn't what he had hoped for it was still enough to allow him to live comfortably. At least it would be if he managed to get somewhere like Mexico or Costa Rica before Judge Paulson caught up with him. Dashing down a triple shot of vodka, he managed to get his nerves under control.

Quickly packing the three large suitcases stowed away in the back of his walk-in closet, Stoneman began formulating his escape. Before calling down to the condo complex's service desk he took a moment to choose several pieces of artwork from his walls. It hurt his heart to have to leave the rest behind, he'd spent so many happy hours choosing them from local galleries. Still, they weren't worth the time it would take to properly pack and ship them somewhere safe. Getting away before his full role in Carter's nefarious plan was discovered seemed a bit more important than moving an art collection. Sighing deeply, he added his two favorite works to his meager pile of possessions by the front door.

Handing the door attendant and the security guy each twenty bucks for helping carry his things down to the parking garage, Stoneman found himself glancing nervously over his shoulder. The men had dealt with him often enough to know that the money he'd given them was paying for more than their baggage handling services. However, even they were a bit surprised when he asked them to put his things into an old panel van rather than his Mercedes sedan. Still, fifty bucks was fifty bucks and rich people were always doing weird stuff. They shrugged their shoulders and followed his directions.

Checking in the glove compartment for the road atlas he kept stashed there, Stoneman plotted out the quickest route to the Mexican border. If he didn't run into any bad weather, or too many road construction delays, he could be there in 48 hours. Taking one last look up at his condo's balcony on the way out of the garage Stoneman uttered one more scathing thought about Carter Williams; *I hope the bastard rots in hell.*

Chapter Sixty-one

Having called both numbers Stoneman listed on his business card at least a half dozen times each, Carter began to get nervous. For what he was paying that oaf of a lawyer he should be able to reach him any time, day or night. Leaving yet another terse message for Stoneman to call him immediately, Carter began pacing the floor of his hotel room. He hadn't slept a wink all night, worried about the loss of even one object from the house he felt was rightfully his. About six A. M. he got a wild idea. Maybe he could make a deal with the hippie freaks himself instead of counting on his lawyer to do it for him. Hell, it was at least worth a try. Calling down for room service to bring him a pot of black coffee, he began mentally outlining his plan. *Those lowlife scum aren't going to take what's mine*, he mumbled as he continued to pace the floor.

Arriving on Pennyroyal Road an hour before the sale was to begin, Carter pulled up to the front gate and began blasting his horn.

Already irritated at having to be buzzed into what he still considered his home, he became further incensed when the blasts were ignored. Though people on the other side of the fence looked up at him, no one came forward to see what he wanted. Cursing under his breath, Carter climbed out and punched the security call button.

"Yes, who is it?" a tinny sounding voice drifted out of the speaker.

"This is Carter Williams; I need to speak with that Bosco fellow."

"Not sure he wants to speak with you, dude."

"Just get him, you buffoon!" Carter roared his patience worn to the breaking point.

Twenty minutes later Carter saw Bosco ambling slowly down the driveway. The man was dressed in his usual appalling fashion, ragged jeans, leather sandals and a loudly dyed t-shirt. The man took his time getting down the drive even though he could obviously see Carter pacing restlessly up and down. *Damn arrogant bastard*, Carter grumbled under his breath.

"What are you doing here?" Bosco sighed stepping up to the gate.

"Mr. Blue, how nice to see you again," Carter oozed. Smiling through gritted teeth, trying to start the conversation off on a pleasant note. "I was hoping to have a word with you and your lovely wife."

"Kind of busy here, man. Plus, I don't think Isis would take too kindly to seeing your face right now," Bosco grinned. "You really pissed her off yesterday. You know, by getting the sale closed down, having a cop parked at our front door, stuff like that."

"Oh, dear, I just knew that idiot of a lawyer was going to mess things up. I told the man all we needed to do was to sit down and have a civil conversation, but he wouldn't listen."

"Right, like you knew nothing about what he was up to. You been trying to hang your wife's murder on my wife, steal TooFoo from us, and keep telling the press we're gold diggers. Nope, nope, nope - don't think letting you in would be a good idea."

"Now see here, sir, I've come to you hat in hand trying to resolve this situation amicably. You could at least listen to what I have to say."

Bosco shrugged. "Guess you'll have to come in like any of the other folks showing up for the sale. We'd be more than happy to sell you a few things." Turning his back on a sputtering Carter, Bosco went whistling back up the drive.

Carter stood there flabbergasted watching Bosco's disappearing back. Yelling and shouting for the man to come back got no response. Carter was still standing there cursing when the first buyers began showing up for the sale.

Realizing who the angry looking man standing at the gate was the bargain hungry shoppers stood as far from Carter as they could get and still keep their places in line. At precisely eight A. M. a young man with waist length blond hair and a scruffy beard strode down and opened the gate. The crowd had swelled to over fifty people by then with more cars pulling up along the street. Opening the gate was like waving a red flag at a bull. The shoppers surged forward at a run, leaving Carter standing dumbfounded in their wake. He knew he'd have no chance of stopping the sale now. His anger boiled over into out and out hatred. Time for a new plan.

Driving around to the delivery entrance, Carter used the set of keys he had squirreled away to slide open the lock and slip inside. Moving through the shadows at the edge of the towering boxwood hedge, he eased up to the side of the garage bays. He could hear voices mixed with the occasional sound of revving engines. slinking closer, he eavesdropped on the conversation. One voice stuck out, Carter remembered having heard it before, it was that young guy named Jimmy something: the one from the ill-fated boat cruise. Carter edged closer, peeking in the bay door. The kid was telling two men in garish cheap suits the attributes of the car collection on display. Carter could hear them haggling over the price of the vehicles. The men were offering about half what the collection was worth. Before Carter could step forward to protest the ridiculously low price, the young man accepted their offer. Slapping the kid on the back the buyers strode off towards the office area of the garage to close the deal. Carter was so angry he could barely breathe. He had spent years, and a small fortune, collecting those cars. Now that dunderhead had sold them for a pittance. He had to put a stop to this nonsense before it went any further. Emboldened by his rage, he stepped out of the shadows into plain sight, heading for the main house.

Rounding the last corner of the expansive gardens, Carter found himself out of both breath and patience. By the time he got to the front lawn, people were walking all over the pristine grass, pawing through tables piled high with his possessions. He could hear their excited voices gushing over the bargain prices. It was just too much to bear. Carter began screaming at the workers and shoppers, calling them thieves. No one paid him any mind, they just kept grabbing up his precious possessions with carefree glee. When he overheard a skinny blond woman in hideous leopard print stretch pants tell her friend she'd gotten a full-length sable coat for only a hundred dollars, Carter went totally berserk. He had bought that coat for Lydia's thirtieth birthday, paying over $75,000. 00 for it at a New York furrier. Shrieking in a voice tight with anger he raced up to the nearest sale table, grabbing the edge and flipping it over. The fragile glass knick-knacks it had displayed were now a rainbow of broken shards glittering on the ground. Nearby shoppers began squawking at the top of their lungs. Ignoring them, Carter raced across the front lawn leaving havoc in his wake. He knocked down shoppers, flipped over tables, and screamed profanities until he was hoarse.

Inside the kitchen, putting the finishing touch on platters of sandwiches for their helpers, Bosco and Isis heard the sounds of the commotion outside and wondered what was happening. Before they could go see what was wrong, they heard Carter burst into the front entrance of the house bellowing their names.

"Show yourselves you slimy, thieving bastards," Carter shrieked as he headed down the main hall. "You are not going to steal from me and get away with it!"

Unnerved by the sound of Carter rampaging towards the kitchen, Isis jumped a foot when the phone on the counter behind her let out a loud ring. She snatched up the receiver as if it were a lifeline. Bosco heard her say, "This is his wife, how may I help you?" The angry frown she threw at him drew his attention away from Carter Williams' tirade.

"So, I guess this is a good news bad news scenario," Isis sighed into the phone as she gave Bosco an exasperated shake of her head. She kept glaring at him as she listened to the caller, finally saying, "Yes, I will tell him. Thank you for calling Doctor."

When Bosco heard the word doctor he cringed. Damn he was in for it now. Stupid doctor's office he'd told them not to call with the test results that he would call them.

"Bosco Blue you are in deep, deep doo-doo," Isis said. Hands on her hips she stepped closer to her husband. "Just when did you plan on telling me about the doctor visit and all those tests?"

"Um...what did they say about the tests?"

Trying to stay angry with Bosco, Isis gave him a savage glare that quickly turned into a grateful smile. The news hadn't been as bad as it could have been. "You have a small ulcer. The polyp they removed was benign. You'll need to be on medication and a strict diet but thank the goddesses there was no cancer." She moved to sweep Bosco into her outstretched arms.

"I'm going to get what's mine if I have to kill every last one of you!"

Bosco and Isis both turned towards the angry words

echoing from the main hall. They had momentarily forgotten about the threat posed by Carter Williams. When Carter came slamming through the kitchen door, Bosco stuck out a foot and tripped him. Carter went sailing across the slick marble floor, crashing into a chair. Before he could get to his feet, Bosco leaped on his back, pinning him down. Thrashing and screaming, Carter tried to throw him off.

"Man, you need to just chill out, dude," Bosco said clinging tightly to the other man's back.

"Chill out! Chill out! You and that cow of a wife have ruined me!" Carter screamed as he tried again to buck Bosco off his back, but the man hung on like he was made of glue.

Isis didn't know whether to laugh or cry watching the two men entangled in the middle of the kitchen floor. Bosco was riding Carter like a wild bronco. Carter, bucking and bouncing like he was demented was screaming profanities and curses. Stepping over to the phone she punched in 911 telling the operator who answered that they needed help to stop an assailant in their home. She gave the address then hung up before the operator could ask any questions.

"Bosco, honey, stop riding Carter he's not a horse," Isis admonished. "Sheriff King is on the way. Can't we just tie the man up until he gets here?"

"Oh, man, sometimes you can be such a drag, babe," Bosco sighed. He was rather enjoying the tussle. When Isis crossed her arms, Bosco gave in; he knew the look on her face meant business. "Get me some rope or something," he muttered before getting to his feet maintaining a firm grip on Carter's right arm, using a foot to pin him to the floor.

Fetching a pair of gold silk cords from the dining room curtains Isis helped Bosco truss Carter up like a holiday turkey. Then he and Isis propped him up in one of the kitchen chairs.

"You better go out and calm everybody down," Isis suggested, shoving Bosco towards the door.

"Maybe I should stay here to protect you," Bosco growled, giving Carter an angry glare.

"Honeybear, he's tied up good and tight. I'll be fine."

Giving Carter a quick jab to the chest, Bosco went off to do his wife's bidding. He knew Isis could hold her own with the little weasel securely tied up.

Chapter Sixty-two

"I'll have you both thrown in jail for this atrocity!" Carter bellowed uselessly kicking his heels.

"Really, Mr. Williams, this situation has gone on long enough. Maybe if you had been nicer to your wife, she wouldn't have cut you out of her will."

"Nicer? Nicer to that stuck up useless excuse for a human being? She used her money to control me. The only thing she loved was that hideous four-legged beast, it wasn't natural. How was I supposed to live the rest of my life like that?"

Isis felt a momentary twinge of empathy for Carter, but it didn't last long. If the man had been that unhappy why not just ask for a divorce?

"If you hadn't stolen that stupid useless mutt, I would still have my home," Carter screamed, trying to kick Isis in the shin.

Backing out of reach, Isis said, "You gave us TooFoo because you didn't want to be bothered with him. You never loved that sweet little animal. I don't think you loved your wife either."

"How could anyone love that self-centered shrew!" Carter shrieked. "I put up with her belittling, sarcastic behavior for years, until I just couldn't take it anymore. Everything had to be her way – everything. It was emasculating."

"Is that why you decided to kill her?"

"Well, I couldn't divorce her, could I. She coerced me into signing a prenup. It was all or nothing – and I wanted it all." Carter smiled a twisted evil grimace that sent shivers down Isis' spine. "You and that idiot husband ruined everything though. The plan was perfect. Perfect. We should have been on that boat alone. It would have been so easy…" Carter's tirade suddenly came to a halt, his eyes gazing off across the room, his brow creasing into a frown. "So easy…should have been so easy." An idea had popped into his head that he needed to give more thought as it might just save him if only…

"I'm curious, why take her on a river cruise? It was obvious she wasn't a boating kind of person." Isis waited for Carter to answer, but he kept staring off into space. "Carter? Carter? Are you listening? I asked why take her on a cruise?"

Swiveling his head around, Carter narrowed his gaze. "Duh! Are you really that stupid? Her death should have been nothing but a simple accident. She would have accidentally fallen overboard. She took so damn many pills and drank so much alcohol no one would have suspected a thing. But nooooo, you and your idiot husband and those stupid kids ruined everything."

Isis stared at him in horror, chilled by his callous words. She managed to control her loathing long enough to ask another question. "How did you know which mushrooms to pick?"

Carter cackled, his smile widening to a toothy grin. "You all forgot about us being in the cabin overhead. Ignore the rich snobs, pretend they don't exist. You talked out on the front deck that day about finding the mushrooms, bragging about your skills in mushroom hunting. You told that silly girl all about seeing the death caps and knowing to avoid them. She asked what they looked like, and you were more than happy to tell her all about them. You know, I had almost given up on my plan to make that trip Lydia's last hurrah. Then I heard you talking on the front deck about those mushrooms. The opportunity was too good to pass up. It was all so easy. A foolproof way to do her in and a ready-made patsy to take the fall." Carter laughed.

"You are a truly evil little man," Isis gasped. "Wait till I tell Sheriff King what you said."

"Oh, really," Carter oozed. "It will be your word against mine. I'm a very convincing liar. Are you?"

Isis stared at the man as if he had just grown horns and a forked tail. Being in the same room with his vileness was wreaking havoc with her usually sunny karma. Shivering, she stepped over to the doorway leading out to the patio praying that Bosco would be back soon. She was going to need a healing ceremony once the day was over. Maybe even a ritual cleansing before she would feel right again. Being in the room with such a soulless, dark evil could bring all sorts of ills her way.

In the distance, she heard a siren drawing closer. Help was on the way. She turned to stare once more at Carter's haughty face, only to be captured like a canary in the eyes of a marauding cat, unable to look away. As she watched, Carter's whole demeanor began to change before her startled eyes. He shrank down in the chair looking small and defenseless. His face paled and huge tears rolled down his cheeks. He began mumbling incoherently, picking at the knees of his pants with restless fingers. Though she knew it had to be an act, Isis had to admit, he looked feeble and not in control of his senses.

When the back door opened, Carter didn't seem to notice, his head drooping so low his chin rested on his chest. His eyes were closed. A line of drool dripped off his chin onto his neatly pleated pants.

Her eyes glancing from Carter to Isis, Janie asked, "Hey, what's wrong with Carter?" She sat the two empty sheet pans she was carrying on the nearest counter. The cinnamon rolls they'd held had been a huge hit selling out in a matter of minutes. "He was just outside turning over tables and running amuck. Is that why you tied him up?"

Isis edged closer to Carter. "He came in here screaming at us making threats, so Bosco jumped him then we hog-tied him and put him in that chair."

Janie moved closer to the hunched over figure stopping close enough to prod his foot with her own. Nothing. She gave him a harder nudge which brought a low moaning sound from Carter. "I think something is wrong with him. Maybe he had a stroke or something."

Still thinking it was just an act Isis stepped over beside Janie. The man looked pale as winter snow. His eyes were closed, drool dripping from his gaping mouth. "He does look a bit ill doesn't he," Isis said. "Maybe we should stretch him out on the floor. I called 911 for help and I can hear a siren headed this way."

The two women moved in to grasp Carter under the arms and behind his knees, gently easing him out of the chair and onto the floor. When they laid him flat, he let out a gargling sound that had them fearing he would choke on his own spit, so they rolled him onto his stomach. His breathing only got worse, he started gasping for air.

"Oh my God!" Janie cried, "he's choking!"

Quickly grabbing a knife from the butcher's block on the counter behind her, Isis stooped down and slit the cords tied around Carter's upper back. When Carter didn't move but continued to gasp for air, she cut through all the cords tied around his body yanking them aside. No sooner did she pull the last cord free then Carter rolled to his side, kicked her in the shins so she stumbled backward, and leaped to his feet. Staggering upright, he grabbed hold of Janie with one hand while yanking a large knife from the butcher's block with the other.

"You stupid cow," Carter crowed pulling Janie tight to his chest placing the knife blade under her chin. "Now you are going to go get a car from the garage and drive it up to the back door." When Isis just stood there gaping at him, he yelled, "NOW!" as he let the tip of the knife prick a tiny hole in Janie's neck.

Backing slowly away Isis said, "Please don't hurt her. I'll get you a car. I'll get you a car." Focusing her eyes on Janie's she added, "Everything is going to be alright I promise."

Chapter Sixty-three

Racing across the back lawn towards the garages Isis prayed to every god, goddess and higher being that she could think of asking them all to keep Janie safe. Yanking the side door of the garage open she dashed inside to find Jimmy sitting behind the wheel of a deep forest green Astin Martin. He looked up at her with a sheepish grin on his face.

"Just daydreaming about owning a fine automobile like this one," he said before the look on Isis's face sent a shiver of dread down his spine. "What's wrong?"

Quickly telling Jimmy about the situation with Carter, Isis tried to keep her voice calm. When she got to the part about Carter holding Janie hostage Jimmy exploded out of the car like a hound dog chasing after a rabbit. Before Isis could stop him, he was out the door headed for the house at a dead run. All she could do was trail along behind him.

Panting from running, something she rarely did at her age, Isis stepped into the kitchen horrified to see that Carter had put another thin slice in Janie's neck. The frightened girl was shaking so hard she could barely stand up. Isis was sure that if Carter hadn't tightened his grip around her chest Janie would have fallen to her knees.

Standing mere inches away Jimmy Grayson looked as if he were carved from stone. Hands clenched in tight fists at his side, eyes narrowed to slits, he was watching Carter like a hawk watches a mouse he's about to pounce on for his lunch.

"You keep back!" Carter snarled pressing the knife blade closer to Janie's throat.

Inching closer Isis held out her hands in a pleading jester. "Please, Carter, don't do something you'll regret. Let her go. Just let her go."

"Did you bring me a car?"

Not sure what to say since she hadn't brought him one Isis kept silent turning her head to stare at Jimmy. She raised her eyebrows as if asking him, "what are we going to do?"

Not moving from his frozen stance Jimmy softly said, "I got this."

Unsure what he meant Isis none the less felt a sense of calm descend over her. She nodded at Jimmy giving him a small smile. "I'm ready when you are."

"What are you two trying to pull," Carter growled. He shifted his grip on Janie's torso pulling her higher against his chest. "I want a car! Go get me a car! NOW!"

Janie felt the knife slice another small cut in her neck. She glanced at her husband tears sliding down her cheeks. She saw him give a quick wink. Not sure what he was going to do but wanting to let him know she was ready for whatever he was planning, she winked back.

Still frozen in place Jimmy let out a long sigh before saying, "Janie, remember the last bend in that rafting trip on the Colorado river?" When he saw his wife give a tiny nod, he added, "on the count of three."

Eyes shifting back and forth from Jimmy to Isis, Carter knew something was going to happen, he just didn't know what. "If you try anything, I swear I'll slit her throat!" His shaking hand had the knife moving back slightly from Janie's neck, but he didn't seem to notice as all of his attention was focused on the other two.

Jimmy smiled and cocked an eyebrow. "One. Two..."

On the word two Janie pulled up her knees, tucked in her chin, and let herself drop forward in Carter's arms so all of her weight was yanking downward. Still waiting for Jimmy to say three, Carter staggered as the girl's falling body suddenly threw him off balance. Not wanting to lose control the situation he pushed her away using both hands to grip the knife. Suddenly free of her weight he staggered backward his butt slamming into the cabinet behind him.

As soon as he saw Janie drop from Carter's arms Jimmy launched himself forward as if his legs were made of coiled springs.

The two men collided just as Isis stepped forward to grab

Janie's arms pulling her from under their feet. Someone stepped on Janie's left leg making her scream in pain, but then she was clear of their tangled feet, pulled upward into Isis's protective embrace.

Struggling to regain control, Carter kicked and shoved at the other man. Younger and stronger, Jimmy held Carter in a full body lock – well almost. Carter realized his right arm was free, and that he still held the butcher knife in that hand. Drawing the arm back as far as the cabinet behind him would allow he plunged it forward sinking it into Jimmy's left side. He felt the rush of something warm on his hand as the arm gripping his body fell away. The kid stumbled backward a look of shock on his face, hand clamped to the bleeding wound in his side. Carter took advantage of the situation giving Jimmy a shove, watching him tumble to the floor at his women's feet. Their horrified screams followed him out the back door.

Still deep in shock from all that had just happened, Janie held her husband's head cradled in her lap softly crooning his name over and over.

"Jimmy. Jimmy. Damn it you open your eyes! Look at me!"

"Honey, he's unconscious," Isis said pressing a fresh kitchen towel to the still bleeding cut in Jimmy's side. "Those sirens are right outside the gate. I can hear them. Help will be here in minutes."

Rocking back and forth Janie began to cry. "Jimmy, you

have to open your eyes. Please!" When his eyes stayed closed Janie felt herself getting angry. Her husband was never one to be coddled. Sitting up straighter she gave him a sharp poke in the chest. "Jimmy Grayson you will not die and leave me to raise this child on my own. Do you hear me?"

"You're pregnant?" Isis gasped.

Janie nodded taking several deep breaths to calm herself. "Yes I am. I was waiting for the right moment to tell Jimmy since I wasn't sure how he would take the news. Things are a bit tight for us right now and having a baby is expensive."

"Oh, honey, there's never a perfect time for having a baby, you just have them, and love them, and things have a way of working themselves out."

Letting out a small laugh, Janie smiled at Isis. "You're right." Giving Jimmy another poke in the chest she raised her voice saying, "Jimmy Grayson you are going to be a father so wake up and get used to the idea!"

Both women were surprised when Jimmy's eyes fluttered open, a dazzling smile lighting up his face.

"I'm gonna be a daddy? Really?"

Janie smiled back nodding yes.

"Yahoo! OUCH! What the hell?"

"Honey, Carter stabbed you."

"He did?

Janie laughed leaning down to rain kisses on her husband's face.

"Hey, stop that," Jimmy groaned, "Wounded man here."

Isis joined in their laughter as all three of them began talking at once about the baby, and everything that had just happened. They all cheered when Raven Night walked in the back door followed by two men from the commune hauling a limp and bloody Carter Williams between them. They quickly tied him to another chair before leaving to direct the ambulance to the back door.

Chapter Sixty-four

Isis heaved a sigh of relief when she heard loud footsteps scrambling down the main hall. Bosco came reeling into the kitchen, Sheriff King close on his heels. One look at Jimmy had the Sheriff calling to direct the ambulance to the back door. King let everyone yammer at him unimpeded until Jimmy and his wife were both taken to the hospital. Once the ambulance left, he shouted for everyone to take a seat so he could talk to them one at a time. Pointing at Isis he suggested she go first.

"Carter confessed to killing his wife," Isis shuddered, sitting encircled in Bosco's arms.

King glanced over at Carter who just sat there staring at his knees, mumbling incoherently, not even acknowledging the presence of the others in the room.

"Babe, what did you do to the guy?" Bosco asked staring at

the obviously distressed Carter. "He's like totally gone, man."

"No, he isn't," Isis angrily snapped. "He's just putting on an act again to get out of being arrested."

"I don't know he looks pretty bad," Sheriff King said. "Folks outside said he was running amuck like a madman."

"I'm telling you, it's all an act," Isis growled in exasperation, "he told me he planned to kill his wife right from the start. That he was going to push her off the boat and make it look like she fell off drunk."

Isis' comments elicited deep groans from Carter as if he were in pain. He began rocking from side-to-side making a low keening noise.

"Carter? Carter, can you hear me?" Sheriff King asked, stepping over to raise the man's head so he could gaze into his eyes. "Stop that whining and talk to me."

Carter only rocked faster almost tipping over the chair. Sheriff King had to put both of his hands on Carter's shoulders to hold him down. He asked Bosco to go outside and tell the deputy by the squad car to call for another ambulance.

Having had enough of Carter Williams' lying, backstabbing schemes, Isis went into action. She stepped up and slapped the crying man soundly across the face. "Knock it off, you rotten little weasel."

Surprised by the attack Sheriff King managed to sputter "what the hell" before Carter went nuts.

"You saw her! You saw that bitch hit me," Carter screamed

lifting his head to glare angrily around the room. His chest heaved as he continued yelling. "Arrest her! Arrest her! Do your job, you stupid oaf."

Isis turned to smile triumphantly at Sheriff King. "Told you he was faking."

"She's lying! She's a greedy lying bitch! I did not kill my wife," Carter continued to shriek, his face turning a deep shade of purple as he struggled wildly against his restraints.

Bosco charged forward ready to assault Carter for calling his wife a bitch. It took all of King's strength to hold him back.

"Calm down, Bosco," King yelled. "The man is tied up he isn't going anywhere."

"Well, he ain't gonna sit there and insult my wife like that, you tell him to shut his mouth, or I'll shut it for him!"

"Calm down, Babe," Isis pleaded. "Let him talk, he's only digging a bigger hole for himself."

Realizing his wife was right, Bosco managed to get his anger under control. "Yeah, don't matter what you say we all know you killed your wife. The Sheriff here is gonna lock you up and throw away the key."

"I did no such thing," Carter roared. "She's lying! It's her word against mine. You can't use any of what was said here today in court, it's hearsay!"

"Is he right?" Isis asked, a note of dismay creeping into her voice.

Before Sheriff King could answer, a loud "Ahem" sounded

from the direction of the closed doors of the butler's pantry. Everyone in the room jumped about a foot in the air.

"Who's in there?" King bellowed. "Show yourself right now."

The swinging doors to the room cracked open revealing the butler, Doyle. He was frowning, struggling to hold onto TooFoo, who was wriggling wildly in his arms. "I was just going to walk the dog," he said.

"Oh, my God! Did you hear him? Did you hear Carter? Oh, please, tell me you heard what he said," Isis anxiously pleaded.

Doyle's frown deepened. He turned to gaze at Sheriff King. "When I came down from the master suite, I heard a terrible ruckus going on here in the kitchen." Shifting TooFoo to his other arm, Doyle continued. "I did not want to intrude on the Mistress's business, so I simply waited in there." He nodded over his shoulder at the butler's pantry.

A huge smile broke out on Sheriff King's face. "You heard the whole argument?"

Doyle didn't answer right away but turned to stare at Isis as if asking her permission to speak.

"Oh, for heaven's sake," Isis sighed. "I am not your mistress. You can think for yourself. Just tell the Sheriff what you heard."

"Very good, Madame," Doyle replied, stooping to put TooFoo down on the floor. "Mr. Williams told Mistress Isis that he picked the mushrooms that were used to poison his wife. He had been planning to drown the poor woman, but then had to change the plan. He was terribly upset about it, but then...things worked out for him...or so he thought." Doyle turned to rake his eyes over Carter, a look of pure loathing contorting his features. "Mistress Lydia did not deserve to be wed to the likes of you. She was a good woman, despite her flaws. You, on the other hand, are a buffoon, sir, and an uncivilized cad."

Carter had been silent throughout Doyle's statement, but now he roared in anger. "LIAR! They paid him to lie for them. Don't believe a word he says, he's lying!"

Sweeping Isis into his arms, Bosco danced a jig. "Woohoo!" he shouted with glee. "I told you that sneaky bastard did it!"

"Yes, he most certainly did. I can testify to that," Doyle calmly stated. He had never liked Carter who'd treated him with disdain, ordering him about to do menial tasks not befitting his station in the household. He was after all the butler not a houseboy. "Mistress Lydia always treated me with respect," Doyle huffed puffing out his chest. "I would be only too happy to appear in court on her behalf."

"Plus, he's guilty of assaulting Janie, stabbing Jimmy, destroying our home here, and oh...lots of other things, lots and lots of other things," Isis added. "He should be put away for the rest of his miserable life."

Carter stopped screeching obscenities long enough to glance up at Sheriff King. He realized he was totally screwed and began bellowing for his lawyer. The expression on his face was priceless. The others dissolved into gales of laughter.

As if wanting to add his opinion to the situation, TooFoo ambled up to where Carter sat trussed up like a prize turkey, lifted his left hind leg, and peed on Carter's shoes.

"Ahhh! Get it away from me!" Carter squealed in horror.

"Guess TooFoo wanted to put in his two cents worth," Bosco chuckled.

"Sheriff, do your duty and remove this trash from our home," Isis smiled, sweeping the yapping little dog up into her arms for a hug.

Sheriff King calmly read Carter his rights while the newly arrived deputy cut him free of the chair, snapping a pair of handcuffs on his wrists. They led the red faced still screaming man out to their squad car, where the press was waiting to capture the moment for posterity.

Epilogue

The murder trial of Carter Williams was a swift one with a guilty verdict rendered in less than an hour. Carter was led from the room screaming that he was being railroaded and wanted a retrial. Jackson Hale, Carter's court appointed attorney, hoped he never had to deal with the man again. Being a defense attorney was never easy but having a client who got up on the witness stand yelling profanities at the judge and jury made the job impossible.

As Bosco and Isis left the courtroom, Isis managed to find a tiny scrap of silver lining in the otherwise dismal situation - Carter Williams would no longer be homeless since he had earned himself a lifelong stay at the Iowa State Penitentiary.

The "Yard Sale of the Century" had been an enormous success bringing in enough money to pay the inheritance taxes for the estate on Pennyroyal Road. The sale of the antique car collection brought in sufficient additional funds to make possible a special purchase - Isis bought *The Last Hurrah* from old man Penderschott. The behemoth houseboat was hauled to the estate where it was permanently docked on the large pond behind the main house. Isis thought it only fitting that the boat no longer be used for river cruising, but instead be a memorial to the woman who had lost her life onboard at the hand of her loathsome husband. The *Hurrah* was now a floating meditation center.

Jimmy and Janie Grayson had accepted Isis and Bosco's offer of ten acres, building a charming small cottage on the far side of the property. Janie taught knitting classes at the main house, while Jimmy ran the mechanic shop. The young couple had never been happier. They were planning on asking Isis and Bosco to be the godparents of their first child.

Isis, along with help from Raven Knight and Jay Woods, established the TooFoo Foundation; a charitable trust dedicated to the rescue of local dogs and cats, plus funding for a free spay and neuter clinic.

The main house of the estate was now an arts and crafts center teaching everything from calligraphy to basket weaving to herbal remedies. A large wrought iron sign posted above the main gates informed everyone that this was the Lydia Williams Arts and Healing Center. Good karma had won out after all.

The End.

ABOUT THE AUTHOR

Winning a Royal Palm Literary Award from the Florida Writers' Association for her debut novel Sour Grapes was all the incentive needed to get this author started on a career writing cozy mystery novels. Living in North Central Florida with her husband and an assortment of feline friends she continues to delight in creating stories that keep her readers smiling long after they've turned the final page.

www.ingramcontent.com/pod-product-compliance
Lightning Source LLC
Chambersburg PA
CBHW071554150726
48000CB00004B/1457